A House by
the Side of
the Road

Also by Jan Gleiter

Lie Down with Dogs

A House by
the Side of
the Road

Jan Gleiter

St. Martin's Press
New York

A THOMAS DUNNE BOOK.
An imprint of St. Martin's Press.

A HOUSE BY THE SIDE OF THE ROAD. Copyright © 1998 by
Jan Gleiter. All rights reserved. Printed in the United States
of America. No part of this book may be used or
reproduced in any manner whatsoever without written
permission except in the case of brief quotations embodied
in critical articles or reviews. For information, address St.
Martin's Press, 175 Fifth Avenue, New York, N.Y. 10010.

Design by Nancy Resnick

Library of Congress Cataloging-in-Publication Data

Gleiter, Jan
    A house by the side of the road/Jan Gleiter.—1st ed.
      p. cm.
    "A Thomas Dunne book."
    ISBN 0-312-18596-0
    I. Title.
    PS3557.L4415H68 1998
    813'.54—dc21   98-10634
                                 CIP

First Edition: June 1998

10 9 8 7 6 5 4 3 2 1

For my children,
Healy, Cooper, and Spenser Thompson,
who are kind and funny and smart,
who can whack heck out of a high, inside pitch,
and who have indescribably enriched my life.

Acknowledgments

It's amazing how much I don't know. Consequently, I am deeply grateful for the gracious help of the following people, who were kind enough to walk me through everything from medical issues to fast cars: Mark Stolar, Laura Lenzi, Dale Shepp, Phil Emmert, Wallace Eldridge, Mike Troccoli, Ed Kirby, and Tony Boshnjaku.

Two Paul Thompsons (only one of whom is my husband), Michael Nowak, Bob Gallman, and Caroline Gleiter were encouraging and hard to please—a good combination. My sister Karin and sister-in-law Kathleen Thompson were, again, of inestimable value.

I'd like to especially acknowledge my dad, Ted Gleiter—a dedicated and knowledgeable beekeeper (and a wonderful guy, though that quality is less relevant here).

Thanks also to my agent, Jane Chelius, for her competence, support, nudging, and cheerfulness, and to my excellent editor, Ruth Cavin.

One

*H*annah Ehrlich watched her young neighbor carefully. "It's all in the fingers, dear," she said. "Just hold the crochet hook like this . . ." She demonstrated. "And ease it through the loop."

Jane Ruschman caught the thread and tentatively drew it back. "Like that?"

"Exactly," said Mrs. Ehrlich, nodding encouragingly. "You just keep going. I think we need more cookies."

She put her hands on the edge of the table and pushed herself up. She had read that a good way to disguise advancing age was to spring to one's feet. "Scootch to the edge of your seat, get your feet under you, gather yourself, and then just *spring* up!" the article cheerfully advised. "You will seem years younger." Well and good, if you could manage it.

She walked across the kitchen. She didn't have too much trouble walking, aside from twinges in her left hip. The arthritis in her wrists and fingers seemed to have been completely cured by the regimen of bee stings she had undergone in the late summer and early fall. Jane had been horrified.

"You're going to *make* those bees sting you?" she'd asked. "Why? Yowtch!"

"Not for fun, my dear," Mrs. Ehrlich had replied. "But bee venom helps your immune system get going. It does wonders for arthritis. Don't watch, child, if it bothers you."

She had used a long tweezers to remove a bee from the jar and placed it on the back of her wrist until it stung her.

Jane stared at the procedure, fascinated. "But doesn't it hurt?"

"Lots of things hurt," said Mrs. Ehrlich. "At least this hurting does some good. You just wait. By October, I'll be stirring up sugar cookies again like nobody's business."

Now it was October, and her prediction had come true. When spring arrived and brought the bees out from their winter hiding places, she would work on her hip. Maybe she'd get to the point where she could start springing to her feet the way the article said. She'd have to find her own supply of bees—she certainly wouldn't ask John Eppler for any more of his—but with the feast her garden provided for them, that shouldn't be difficult.

Just the idea of spring always helped her get through the winter. She would think about the crocuses under the frozen topsoil patiently waiting for the mysterious signal to grow. She would gaze out at the wren houses and imagine the energetic little birds darting in and out as soon as the weather warmed. This next spring would be even more exciting than usual, revealing as it would the flowers from the special bulbs she had planted.

The older she got, the more she realized that life was to be lived each and every day. She had good insurance, even the outrageously expensive home-care insurance that she'd kept up the payments on over the years for fear of being shuttled into a nursing home. She had cash in the bank and plenty of investments in reliable stocks, passed down from her husband's parents to him, and from him to her. Regrettably, there were no children or grandchildren, but at least that meant there was no reason not to indulge herself in the things that gave her pleasure. So spending a sizable amount of money on the new narcissus had been a perfectly pragmatic decision. They would be beautiful, and thinking about them would make the times that weren't so pleasant easier to bear.

She arranged cookies on the china plate. It wasn't one of her best. Those, like her best silver, she had carefully stored in the attic. Since she had stopped entertaining, except for having Jane or Teddy or Christine over for cookies and tea, she saw no reason to expose her precious china to the risk of her clumsiness. The silver wouldn't break, but it was easy to transport and far too valuable to lose to a burglar. One gleamingly ornate spoon she kept in her bedside table, for the liquid medicine she occasionally took when she had a cough.

Luckily, she didn't have a cough now, though her arrhythmia had been acting up, her heart startling her with sudden and irregular thumps and skips. She wondered how much of it was caused by worry. Probably all of it, and it would go away when she had confronted the situation she needed to confront and dealt with it. It was foolish to take her health for granted. It was foolish to take anything for granted.

She glanced at the child working industriously at the table, her dark gold hair falling forward, her hands busy. She was growing up and looking more and more like her mother. She would be confident like her mother, and cheerful and sensitive. She already was.

"How does this look?" asked Jane, holding up a crooked chain.

Mrs. Ehrlich put down the plate of cookies and refilled the two teacups. "Very good," she lied. "Let me show you how to turn your work and start back with the second row."

She moved her chair to sit closer to the child but was interrupted by a meow at the back door. "There's Charlie," she said, taking the few steps to the door and pulling it open. A muscularly compact black cat walked in and rubbed against her legs as she shut and locked the door.

"I'm locking the door," she said.

"What?" said Jane.

"Nothing, dear," said Mrs. Ehrlich. "I just said, 'I'm locking the door.'"

"Why?" said Jane.

"You'll know when you're eighty-five," said Mrs. Ehrlich, seating herself at the table and guiding Jane's hands to turn the chain of stitches. "When you're my age, you'll find that just as soon as you're all settled in your nice cozy bed, and the chill is gone from the sheets, you realize you don't remember if you locked the door when you let the cat in. You'll know you let the cat in, because he'll be curled up in his spot next to you, but you won't know if you locked the door. You'll be pretty sure you did and just hate the thought of getting up and putting on your slippers and going to check, but you won't be *sure,* and since you're not sure, you'll have to do it. So, eventually, you figure out that if you take all those habitual actions and comment on them when you do them, you'll make them memorable. 'I'm turning off the oven' is a good one. 'I'm locking the door' is another. There are *lots* of them."

Jane put down her crocheting, took a cookie, and grinned at her neighbor. "Or you could just reach for the phone and call me up, and I'd put on my jacket and come over and check."

Mrs. Ehrlich laughed. "You would, too," she said, "because you're the perfect neighbor."

Jane looked slyly at her from the corners of her eyes. "And if we're gone on vacation or something, you could call Angie Morrison," she suggested, unsuccessfully trying not to giggle.

Hannah Ehrlich, struck by the vision of Angie, in the skimpiest possible negligee, racing down the road in her purple sports car to help out a neighbor, laughed again.

"Oh, dear," she said. "We shouldn't be unkind. If we got to

4

know her better, maybe we'd find out that she's really a very nice person."

Jane shook her head. "I don't think so."

Children are funny creatures, thought Hannah Ehrlich, regarding the girl, who was hard at work again on the gradually lengthening strip of tight loops. There wasn't a bit of a chance that getting to know Angie better would reveal any niceness at all, of any kind, and Jane somehow knew it. What if Angie were the only neighbor on this long road? What a thought.

"I wonder," said Jane, looking up at her neighbor, "if Mrs. Marriott knows Angie very well."

"Angie's not Louise's type of person, is she? Poor Louise. I doubt that she knows Angie at all."

"When you've visited her at the nursing home, did you ever tell her about Angie?"

"Well, no, child. What would be the point? I'm sure Louise would have rented her house to a more sedate lady . . ."

Jane frowned slightly.

". . . a more proper lady, if she'd known. But Angie doesn't do any damage to the place, so far as I know. And Louise will never be living in that house again, anyway. She doesn't need more worries than she already has."

Hannah had not been close to Louise Marriott, but she had enjoyed having another elderly woman nearby. Well, at least she had the Ruschmans; she had Jane. And she felt blessed in that. Not every trusted person turned out to be worthy. Her heart lurched, again, at the prospect of the conversation she was going to have to initiate.

"What's the matter?" asked Jane, looking up, startled and concerned.

"Nothing, dear, why?"

"You sighed. A really big sigh," said the child. "Do you feel all right?"

"I feel just fine," said Mrs. Ehrlich. But she didn't feel fine at all.

$\mathcal{T}wo$

$\mathcal{A}$ngie Morrison slid one long, slim leg over the sill, bent to avoid hitting her pretty head on the window frame she was holding up with one hand, and maneuvered herself into the room. It had been a simple matter to unlock the window the day before. Everything was working perfectly. The ground was firm and dry—no snow even though it was January—and would leave no sign of the crate she had stood on to raise the window and slip inside.

All she had to do now was to find the right place to leave what she needed to leave. Near the couch, but not where it would be discovered if the couch was unfolded into a bed, which Angie was sure it would be.

It hurt her to have to take these steps. People who loved each other should trust each other. She wanted nothing more than a reason to trust. Instead, she had ample reason not to.

She took a deep breath and let it out slowly. Just being in a room where he spent so much time made her feel fluttery. Every woman in town wanted him; she could see it in their eyes. She felt their desire throbbing in the air around them, heard the breathiness it brought to their voices when they spoke to him. But she was the one who had him, and, if they had known, they would have hated her for it. She wanted—oh, how she wanted—to let them know. She didn't care if they hated her. She didn't care at all.

Instead, she had to settle for stolen time, completely insufficient and unsatisfying. Seeing him so infrequently, only in secret, was like never being able to adjust to the temperature of deep, cold water. It was always a leap from the dock. Every moment a new leap, a leap without a history, the first leap, again and again.

When she first arrived, she had dated every available man in town, and several who were not supposed to be available at all. She'd enjoyed their pathetic efforts to impress her, to please her, to intrigue her. But no one had succeeded for quite some time. And then she had met him.

Being in this room, his room with his things, was painful. How could he be so cavalier about her? He loved her; she was sure of it. She had seen the look in his eyes when he watched her move across a room to greet him. She had felt his hands on her skin. Yes, he loved her. Yet, for some reason, he was moving away from her emotionally, and she suspected it had to do with the woman who would be visiting him today.

She had heard the husky, purring voice on the answering machine before he had a chance to turn it off. He had responded to her suspicion with a laugh. "Don't be ridiculous," he'd said, encircling her with one arm. "That's my cousin, Debra. She's coming to stay with me, just for a night. Didn't I tell you?"

Angie had pulled away, fear clutching at her. No, he hadn't mentioned it. She wouldn't have believed him if he had; she surely didn't believe him now. One look at him, at his wary eyes, convinced her it would be wiser to pretend to a faith she suddenly did not feel.

If the woman was his cousin, if their relationship was as innocent as he pretended, she would know soon enough. If not . . . well, she'd have time to think about what to do.

They would be here soon, if this was where they were coming. Angie was sure this was where they were coming. She didn't want to waste any of the precious two hours of tape, so she would wait to turn on the machine until she daren't delay leaving any longer.

She found the perfect place to put the small recorder. He would never see it. He would certainly never hear it. It was expensively silent even while its spools were turning, to give her the proof she needed, the proof she would soon have, about whether he was who he pretended to be or whether he would have to change.

She had to know, so she could figure out how to change him.

Two days later, listening to what had been recorded, Angie felt sick. She had thought she was prepared, that the depth of her doubt had made her ready for its confirmation. She had been wrong. Twenty minutes into the tape, she slammed the "off" switch savagely and paced her bedroom, kicking discarded clothing out of the way, her eyes furious. She picked up the machine to hurl it against the wall and then stopped, driven to know it all, to put herself through whatever she needed to endure in order to know it all.

She poured a glass of bourbon, fortification against the pain. Within a short time, she was very glad she had been so brave. She had suffered, but she had also discovered how to make sure she'd never suffer again.

Three

*A*ngie didn't notice the clean smell of the April night that came through her open window. She rarely noticed anything so subtle, besides she was busy looking at herself in the bedroom mirror with satisfaction as she ran a brush through her shining hair. Her reflection in her tight jeans was worth the discomfort they caused. She hooked her thumbs in her belt and tipped one hip, her cropped shirt revealing a few inches of smooth midriff and the top of her flat stomach above the large, solid silver buckle of her belt. She looked . . . what would be the right word? Delicious.

She smiled, narrowing her eyes at her image, and then glanced at the photograph on the dresser. The man in the picture gazed back, caught forever in a moment, a not atypical moment, of self-assurance. Other than the photograph, the dresser top was bare. Most of her personal belongings, and a few that supposedly went with the house, had been packed into cartons and carried away, that afternoon, by the movers. Unfortunately, other than a few old prints that she'd taken for their frames, the house hadn't contained much beyond her own possessions that was worth moving.

When she had first learned that her landlady had inconveniently died and, worse, that the new owner intended to live in the house, Angie had been furious. Later, as she thought about the situation, she realized how well it suited her purposes. Tonight, those purposes were much on her mind. She picked up the photograph and stood holding it. He would never give her what she wanted, what she needed, while he was living in Harrison. He needed a fresh start as much as she did, and the sudden requirement that she move would provide it for both of them. She had been clever enough to take advantage of the situation and plan a move, not of several miles, but of several hundred.

"You," she said, addressing the picture, "are going to have a very pleasant time tonight."

She put the photograph away in the dresser. He didn't know she had it; undoubtedly he thought it was still in the drawer where she had discovered it. She'd had no qualms about taking it, but if he knew she had, he would take it back. And then, at least for the present, she wouldn't be able to lie in bed at night with the feeling that he was in the room.

She went into the bathroom, took a small bottle of cologne from her makeup bag, and sprayed the scent into the air, stepping into it. Just a hint of lilies of the valley clinging to her hair, to her clothes. He liked just a hint. She wouldn't miss the bathroom with its immovable window and inadequate shower. She would, however, miss the huge, claw-footed bathtub, which was, as well she knew, big enough for two.

Her bare feet moved silently across the old, dark green rug of the living room and then the worn maple floor of the kitchen as she went to pour a drink into one of the two glasses she'd left in the cupboard. She swirled the bourbon briefly and downed it, needing to steel herself for the first glimpse of him, knowing the effect it would have on her. She had to be calm tonight because tonight she would tell him that he was moving with her, not in the six months or so that he had promised, but soon. Within the next few weeks. Before the end of April.

All through the winter and early spring, she'd enjoyed her secret power and his ignorance of the fact that she had it. It had made her casual, and that had stopped the easing away he had started late last fall. She'd intrigued him again, and she hadn't needed to use her knowledge. But now it was time. Just this morning, he'd denied that he had ever set a specific date to join her in Boston. It would be better, he'd said, for him to stay here for the rest of the spring and the summer. There were people who depended on him, he said, and a lot of work he had to finish. Besides, breaking the news of their involvement would require delicacy, and time.

No, he wasn't staying for the summer, and she would let him know about that tonight. At first, she wouldn't mention it. She would just slide her hand up his arm to grip the muscles of his shoulder, bury her face in his neck, and let her sweet-smelling hair fall over his face. Then, later, she would let him know about their future and what it would be like.

A key turned in the lock of the kitchen door. He had walked over, as usual, so there would be no sign of his presence. She arranged herself on the couch, assuming a languor she did not feel, and picked up a book so when he walked in she could let it drop and stretch like a cat—a beautiful, soft, purring cat.

When she stretched again, an hour later, it was without planning it. She snuggled closer to the man next to her and draped one arm across his chest, admiring the gold of her skin. The man lifted her arm and got out of bed, sliding into his jeans.

"Where are you going?" she asked sleepily, patting the sheet next to her. "Come back."

"I'd like to," he said, smiling down at her. "Can't. I gotta get home."

She sat up and leaned over the side of the bed to reach her clothes on the floor. "You promised you'd stay," she said, as calmly as she could. She concentrated on keeping her voice neutral. He hated anything that sounded like a whine. "After I move, it may be weeks until you've finished what you have to do and can join me."

"Look, Angie . . ." He hesitated. The pretense had gone on too long, but he had dreaded the scene she would make. Still, it wouldn't be a public scene. One here in this lonely house, no one would hear her scream at him, accuse him. And much as she might want to upset him by talking about their affair all over town, she wouldn't, because she would never admit to being dumped.

He sat down on the side of the bed and looked sadly at her. "I told you. I have to stay for the summer. We'll see how soon in the fall I can come."

She'd give him one chance. "You can't stay, darling. You can't. I love you too much. I can't spend five or six months without you. I need you. You can't leave me."

He made his voice light. "Actually, Angie, you're leaving *me.*"

The dismissiveness in his tone frightened her. How could he fail to see what was so obvious? They were perfect for each other. He used to know that. He would see it again as time passed.

"You know perfectly well I'm not leaving you," she said softly. "I'm moving. I'm moving to allow the person who inherited this piece of trash to live in it, which she seems in one damn hurry to do. You know I'd never leave you." She put a hand against the side of his face. "Don't say we won't be having a life together, because it's just not true."

"I'm afraid it is," he said, relieved to have the delayed conversation underway. If she wouldn't let him spare her, that was her choice. "Look, I'm sorry it didn't work out. But, if you must know, I'm tired of this whole thing. I can't stand being clutched at. It's time to go our own ways."

Angie stared at him. Her chest felt hollow. "Are you crazy? You will *never* find anyone who is as right for you as I am!"

He laughed. "Oh, Angie, Angie. Look at us! We don't exactly go together, do we? It was fun but it's over. It's just over, all right?"

She stood up and slapped him across the face. "No," she said, breathing hard and looking down at him. "It's not all right. And it's not happening, either. This is what you planned all along, isn't it?" Her voice, never her best quality, was harsh. "That's why you thought Boston was such a good idea. Well, I'm warning you, it's not happening. Do you hear me?"

He looked at her stonily, the left side of his face showing the mark of her hand. "I hear you," he said. "I'm just ignoring you."

She took in a breath that hissed between her teeth. He was her world; he knew it. He had to know it. If she lost him . . . But she couldn't. She wouldn't.

"That's not smart," she said. "I know what you did."

His brow furrowed. "What are you talking about? What do you mean, what I did?"

She just nodded and regarded him, then started pulling on her clothes. She smiled. "I know. I know. I know all about you and your 'cousin.' If she's your cousin, darling, you all must come from someplace where the branches on the family tree get a bit tangled."

He reached out one hand and gripped her by the belt, his knuckles biting into her smooth skin. He pulled her toward him and down until she was on her knees between his. He leaned closer, looking directly into her eyes. His voice was soft. "So she's not my cousin. So she and I enjoyed each other. So what? Who cares, besides you?"

He let go of her and put his hand against her chest, pushing her away. She laughed, keeping herself from falling backward by bracing herself with her arms.

"No," she said, "the fact that you're a cheat may not be all that big a secret. Maybe nobody except me would much care about that. But the other things you and she did together, now *that* would be more interesting."

He stared at her, disbelieving and horrified, and she giggled. "I need a drink," she said, getting up and striding toward the kitchen. She felt her hair swinging behind her, her heels against the floor. She felt strong and alive. "Want one?"

When he came into the room, she was standing with her back to the kitchen window, sipping from a tumbler. He poured bourbon into the other glass on the countertop and took a long swallow.

"You're crazy," he said, shrugging with assumed dispassion. "I don't really care what you think or what you say. I've got a good reputation in this town. What've you got? Six months' worth of speeding tickets. So, go on, talk. Talk to anybody."

He spoke quietly. His eyes, watching her, were cool. But he saw everything he had worked for crumbling. *How much did she know?*

"Oh, I will. If you make me," she replied. "I don't want you to make me. I want us to go on happily together. Forever." She hitched herself up onto the edge of the counter and crossed her feet, took another sip from her glass. "You and she have been involved in something interesting. Everyone in town will find it fascinating; I know I did."

She put one heel up on the countertop and hooked her arm around her leg. She reached out her other foot, pointed her toes, and rubbed them against his thigh.

He realized with horror that she was flirting with him. "I don't know what you think you know," he said coldly, moving beyond her reach. "But if you're planning to spread something you hope will damage my reputation, no one will believe you." He lifted the bottle by its neck and tipped it to pour more bourbon into his glass.

She looked surprised. "Did you think I was just planning to *gossip*? Oh, no, darling! I've got proof! Right here."

It frightened him, and fear made him angry. "There *is* no proof, you dumb bitch," he said.

She threw her glass. The movement was so unexpected that

the tumbler struck him directly in the chest before hitting the floor and rolling away. It was a heavy glass, and Angie was a strong young woman. The intensity of the pain shocked him. He took two steps forward and swung his right arm. She started to raise her hand, to turn away, to scream, but the bottle he was still holding caught her on the side of her head. She crumpled onto the countertop and lay motionless, then started a slow slide to the floor.

The bottle dropped from his fingers and rolled heavily away. He staggered toward the sink, overwhelmed with nausea. When his stomach stopped heaving, he knelt beside the woman. There was a widening pool of blood under her head. He pushed her silky hair aside and put two fingers against her neck. Her pulse was faint and irregular.

He stood, swaying, and looked at her. Her skull was fractured, that was evident. He went into the living room and lifted the receiver of the phone, which responded with a dial tone. She hadn't canceled the phone service; he could call for help. No one would be able to recognize his voice if he whispered.

No. He replaced the receiver. If she survived, he might be able to make her understand that the whole thing was a horrible accident. But if she died, there would be an investigation. A careful investigation. Before he called anyone, he had to wipe away any prints he'd left—on the bottle, his glass, the faucet. That wouldn't be enough. He had touched things in her room, in the bathroom, the handle of the door . . .

It was while he was scrubbing frantically at the bourbon bottle that he remembered what she'd said. She had proof. She couldn't. What proof could there be? Photographs would prove nothing. A diary or notes would be awkward, but not proof. What could she have meant?

Damn his rage! That hadn't been him, that violent man. He wasn't an animal. He was a calm, reasonable person and intelligent enough to stay out of trouble. If she had been telling the truth—she couldn't have been telling the truth—but, if she had been telling the truth, she had something. What? Maybe she'd sent it on to Boston. No, probably not, or why would she have said, "Right here." In the house?

What proof? There couldn't be. But if there was, it meant he couldn't risk having the house unavailable to him. It could not be sealed off with yellow tape, could not be searched by anyone but him.

He went through the rooms methodically, wiping the surface of anything he might have touched. That required little thought, so he concentrated on what he would need to do. He had no time. The new owner was arriving almost immediately. He had tonight, he knew. Did he have tomorrow night? He couldn't count on it.

He had to be both thorough and efficient, which meant he needed a plan. It took some time, but he worked it out while he listened to the quiet of the night and waited for Angie to die.

Four

Sunlight was bouncing off the hood of the car and the narrow road it traveled. Meg Kessinger drove with her left elbow resting on the open window. She made small contented noises from time to time, breathing in the soft Pennsylvania air with its mingled faint scents of freshly turned earth and growing things. Around one of the curves ahead, the house would lie off to the right—her great-aunt's house for many, many years. Her own house now.

She drove slowly, gazing to the right and left at farms and fields and trees and the occasional house set well back from the road, sometimes stone or brick, usually tidy white frame with a generous porch. She had passed through Harrison, the closest source of grocery stores, druggists, and a library, ten minutes before, delighting in its air of settled stability and the huge park that seemed to take up a good sixth of the town. She knew the weeks to come would contain hours of anxiety about her decision to leave Chicago, but at the moment she felt only euphoria. Her most treasured possessions filled the trunk and backseat. The rest should arrive tomorrow morning, if the movers were as good as their word.

Just beyond a pretty little house with a huge tree in the front yard, from which hung a swing, a hand-lettered sign caught her eye: DAFFODILS—500 yards." The sign, attached to a stake at the edge of the road, was a new one, unbattered by wind or rain, so the chances were it was accurate. Meg looked eagerly down the road, slowing more as a small roadside table came into view. Another sign was taped to its edge: "DAFFODILS—Picked Today." The table held only a small metal box and a stack of newspapers, but next to it stood a washtub filled with flowers. Behind the table, which was shaded by a cluster of tall trees, sat a girl in a lawn chair, reading a book and scratching her ankle.

Meg eased onto the shoulder and braked, and the girl looked up from her book and smiled shyly. She was about twelve, with shoulder-length tawny hair and thick bangs above wide hazel eyes. There were grass stains on the knees of her jeans. Presumably, she could verify the "Picked Today" claim.

Meg got out of the car and gestured toward the washtub. "They're beautiful," she said. "How much are they?"

"Seventy-five cents a bunch," the girl replied. "There's a dozen in a bunch. Or three bunches for two dollars."

Meg looked at the flowers. She wanted every single one of them. "I'll take six bunches," she said. She dug into a back pocket and extracted a crumpled five-dollar bill. "Keep the change," she said. When the child hesitated, she went on, "Consider it a bribe to be nice to your new neighbor. I'm moving in down the road."

The girl took six dripping bunches of daffodils out of the tub and wrapped them loosely in newspaper. She handed them to Meg and declined the proffered bill. "Housewarming," she said.

"Oh, but you worked to pick them!" said Meg, dismayed. "Please let me pay you."

"Mom would have a fit," said the girl. "You can buy some tomorrow or next week, if you want. But not today."

"In that case," said Meg, "I'd like six more. Today." The second she spoke, she regretted it. She did not know this child and, therefore, this child did not know her. It was unfair to tease a stranger, especially one so young. But the girl's laughter was immediate.

"I'm *so* sorry," she replied, motioning toward the scarcely diminished tub. "There aren't any left."

Aha, thought Meg with relief, laughing. "I'm Meg Kessinger," she said. "I'm moving into a house down that way." She gestured toward the east. "The one that used to belong to Louise Marriott. She was my great-aunt."

The child nodded. "You'll be right next door. Mrs. Marriott's house is the next one. I remember her from a long time ago, and my mom used to visit her in the nursing home. There was another lady living there for a while, but a moving truck came on Friday, and yesterday her car was gone."

"Yes," said Meg. "A renter. Aunt Louise left her house to me, and I decided to move in, so the renter moved out. Do you have a name?"

"Gosh, I'm sorry! I'm Jane. We're the Ruschmans. There's me and Mom and Dad and Teddy. He's seven."

"And you're . . . thirteen?" It was wiser, thought Meg, to err toward older. The opposite of dealing with adults.

"Twelve," said Jane. She looked at Meg curiously. "Are you, like, a Boy Scout leader or something, Ms. Kessinger?"

Meg glanced down at her dark green shirt with the embroidered "Boy Scouts of America" above the right pocket in red. "No, I just like the shirt."

"So do I," replied Jane, settling back into her chair and picking up her book. "I'll tell Mom we've got a new neighbor. She'll be glad."

A dog came bounding down the driveway, barking an excited greeting, and Meg stooped to welcome him. "Hey, good-looking," she said, ruffling his ears as he pushed his head against her and wriggled happily. He was a large, burly, well-shaped dog, a young Labrador with a cream-colored coat. He jumped against Meg, knocking her onto the ground and licking her face.

Jane got up. "Get off, Harding!" she said, tugging at his collar and yanking him away.

"It's okay," said Meg, getting to her feet. "He didn't mean any harm, and none was done. What a gorgeous guy! Harding?"

"Uh-huh. Actually Warren G. Harding, but Mom's the only one who ever uses his whole name, and she only does when she's mad. She's the one who named him. She says he's handsome and sociable but has no reliable moral center."

"Well," said Meg. "He's young . . ."

"Just barely a year," said Jane. She patted him affectionately. "Do you think he might *get* a moral center?"

The dog whined, rising onto his back feet and hopping in place as he lunged against the restraint.

"Sure," said Meg. "Give him time."

She raised her free hand in farewell and placed the flowers carefully on the passenger seat. Pulling back onto the road, she drove around the curve. "Right next door" proved to be about a quarter of a mile away. As the house came into view, she pulled onto the shoulder again and stopped to look at it from a distance.

It was old and shabby, but the graceful proportions shown in the photographs Meg had received were even more evident to her now. It was a low house with a wide front porch and a huge, unkempt lawn and had been painted, seemingly many years ago, a shade of yellow that had faded under the onslaughts of sun and rain to a dim, unattractive hue. Rosebushes grew in abandon against the walls and the picket fence that stretched, with noticeable gaps, from the house almost to the road, across the front of the property, and then back again.

The roses, sturdy and tangled, were just beginning to get leaves. It would be a while before they bloomed; no telling what colors they would reveal as spring turned to summer. Tulip foliage had emerged near the house, and the earliest flowers were beginning in pink and white and yellow. There was a driveway on the left side of the house. From it, by following a flagstone path, one could arrive at the front porch. A second door, on the side, presumably to the kitchen, had only a stoop.

Meg sighed with satisfaction. She knew the property needed work, large amounts of work. First she would have to fix the fence so the puppy she planned to get would be safe from traffic. The house sat back a good distance, but cars moved swiftly on country roads.

Pulling into the driveway, she stopped again to look more closely at the fence. The posts looked all right; the problem seemed to be simply one of missing pickets. If so, repairs would be easy. The house itself would probably present more difficult challenges, but this she did not mind. Her anxiety about moving to a house seen only in photographs had been based on the worry that, in real life, it wouldn't be a house she felt anything for. That was not going to be the situation.

There would be furniture inside—furniture she had been warned she wouldn't want—but the Salvation Army truck was scheduled for the next morning to haul away whatever she rejected. With any luck, it would arrive before the moving truck came with her possessions.

She eased the car down the driveway, which curved around the back of the house, and stopped. There was no door in the back except for cellar doors slanting up from the ground and held shut with a padlock through their handles, so she walked back around to the side. She gazed at the cracked cement of the kitchen stoop, seeing herself seated there in a faded cotton housedress, a crockery bowl in her lap, snapping the ends off green beans with competent efficiency. She smiled at the vision, in which her sturdy frame had attenuated and her skin had a delicate blush from the sun. No, five feet three was, at thirty, as tall as she would ever be, and it was no more likely that she would become as slender as her vision was than that she would begin to wear housedresses. A crockery bowl would be simple to get, however, and the beans were just a matter of digging up some piece of this suddenly acquired forty acres and recalling what she'd once known about planting vegetables.

She couldn't decide whether to get out her key and go in the house or walk across the meadow and through the wooded section at the back of the property to find the creek. She knew there was a creek. Michael Mulcahy, the lawyer who handled her great-aunt's will, had described the land in detail when she'd called him after receiving his letter, one from her great-aunt, and the photographs.

"It has live water," he had said on the phone, and she had needed to ask what that was. "Sorry," he said. "A creek, as opposed to a lake or pond. It's your back boundary."

"Rock bottom or mud?"

"Rock," he replied. "Your property is generally level, but you're close to the mountains."

A rock-bottom creek! Her hesitations fell away. "So it babbles?"

"I guess." His voice betrayed perplexity. "It curves up from the south to border your land. I only saw it the once, when Louise was making her will sometime back, and I wanted to know what all was involved in the real property part of her estate. Is babbling important?"

"To me," sighed Meg. "Don't sell it. I want it."

The lawyer was silent a moment. "You mean you want to come see it."

"No, I want it. I can't afford to come see it. I don't have the time or the money. My landlord is selling the building I live in, and the new owners want my apartment, so I've been looking. I have to be out in five weeks. I will be. I'll move to my new house. Send me directions and a key."

"Don't you have a job?"

"It's portable."

"Look," he said, "I wouldn't advise this. You may regret it. If you want the place, it's yours. Of course. But there are people who'd buy it, people who want the land. You could sell the place and buy something in Chicago. You don't have to move here to benefit from this inheritance."

Meg's decision seemed not to fit with this lawyer's plan. "Yeah, well, I can sell it next month if I hate it," she said. "And I'll know better what price to ask." That was as pointed as she felt justified in being without having even met the man, but she wondered if he was one of the people who'd be willing to buy.

She thought for a few days that she was undoubtedly insane and then decided she didn't care. She concentrated on the positives. She could plant flowers, get a dog, hear crickets. She could take her cartons and cartons and cartons of books out of storage and have room for them. She could live someplace she wouldn't have to leave until she wanted to, if she wanted to. She could never run into Jim again. All because of a great-aunt she had barely known, a woman who had paid one visit to her family and sat for hours helping seven-year-old Meg expand her list of names for horses.

Meg's mother had dreaded the visit, and there was a pervasive tension in their small apartment as she cleaned and waxed and polished. It had made no sense to Meg. If an aunt was visiting, surely it was an occasion for joy. Recently widowed, Great-Aunt Louise was on her first trip away from Pennsylvania, visiting each of her relations in one extended burst of familial devotion, which, Meg's mother told her later, was out of character. Still, she had been kind to Meg and endlessly agreeable to the task no one else had time for.

Together, they had brought Meg's list to two hundred names. Meg still remembered her feeling of triumph looking at the loose-leaf pages covered with handwriting. Some of her great-aunt's suggestions were mysterious, but they had the right sound. She could hear the announcer calling them out as the horses pranced, manes tossing, to the gates to start the race. Years later, she found the list in a box of books and games and smiled at "Standard Deviation." It still seemed a good name.

After that, there had been Christmas cards. The ones to Meg's parents contained brief notes, but Meg always received her own, with longer messages and much more interesting news. "The doe I call 'Lucky' had twins this year, one much bigger than the other. Oddly, it was the smaller one who was more bold. Mama sometimes had a hard time keeping him hidden."

Every year, Meg carefully chose a card to send—the only card she did send. She made sure it had a religious picture rather than Santa Claus and tried to write her own news in the correct Zaner-Bloser style. Aunt Louise had strong feelings about penmanship. In answer to her great-aunt's request, these cards had always enclosed the most recent school picture.

That, as far as Meg had ever known, had been the extent of it. The news that she had inherited the bulk of her great-aunt's estate—her house—had been a shock. Most of the photographs Michael Mulcahy sent he had taken himself. All exterior shots and taken in the wintertime, they had given her only the vaguest idea of what the property was like. The other photographs had been a complete set, carefully organized and framed together, of Meg from third grade through twelfth.

Now that she was actually at the house, she felt a qualm about the all-important creek. What if it turned out to be just a gash in the land, a deep and sluggish ribbon of wetness or a patchy trickle? She took a deep breath and set off across the meadow. The grass and assorted plants that grew there were turning green, but it was not yet the knee-high expanse it showed every sign of becoming. Before she even got to the woods she heard a sound, a gentle murmur that hurried her steps.

The path continued to the edge of the woods and then, less obviously, through it. Maples, oaks, and hickories dominated, but mountain laurel and honeysuckle shrubs had taken hold at the edge. Walking through the trees was a simple matter, although the dimness and utter quiet, save for the gentle noise of running water, made Meg feel suddenly vulnerable.

Near the creek, a few pale purple hepatica, with their distinctive dark green foliage, were growing. The water ran swiftly but it was shallow, accounting for the noise it made. She could have crossed its twenty-foot width without wetting her feet, simply by jumping from rock to rock. Instead, she sighed with satisfaction and turned back to find out just how bad the inside of the house was. It could be pretty bad without making her regret her decision, given the creek.

As she walked back through the trees, a rustle to her left pulled her gaze in that direction. She would need to get used to the small sounds of rabbits and squirrels. But the shape that suddenly separated itself from the trees was neither a rabbit nor a squirrel. It was a dog, an ugly, mud-brown dog that stood silently, watching her with a baleful look, and then turned and loped away.

Meg whistled. The dog gave no sign of having heard.

Her key turned smoothly in what was evidently a brand-new lock. She let the screen door slam behind her and set her purse down on the closest cabinet. She was standing, as she had expected to be, in the kitchen. There was a wide old sink under a window that looked out onto the side yard and wooden cabinets—once glossy white, now the color of French vanilla ice cream—lined two walls. Plain glass-fronted cabinets bordered the window above the sink. A huge stove had a griddle between the left and right burners and two ovens side by side, and there was a refrigerator with a rounded top, which was humming faintly. Everything except the linoleum floor looked as if it had been there since the 1930s. The floor was individual black and white tiles in a checkerboard pattern—pretty, but, to fit the feel of the room, it should have been one unbroken piece.

At right angles to the door to the yard was a large pantry with a wall of shelves on each side and a built-in cabinet at the back. The shelves were empty. Meg had hoped to find a canning jar or two or, perhaps, a bucket somewhere. Failing that, she put the rubber plug in the bottom of the sink, turned on the water, and went outside to get the daffodils. She propped them up inside the sink.

She opened her purse and took out the letter that had been such a surprise. The envelope bore her name in beautiful, swirling handwriting. Inside, there was a single piece of paper, covered in the same elegant hand.

Dear Meg,

I am leaving you my house. If you don't want it, if your life in Chicago is a happy one, put it up for sale and do whatever you like with the money. I didn't tell you I was leaving it to you because I didn't know if I could or if I'd have to sell it. It has all depended on whether my savings or my time ran out first. Since you're reading this, it looks like my time did. You probably wonder why I left it to you, so I'll try to explain.

As you might know, since Lawrence died, I've had my books and the church and the house. I haven't had close friends, though I got on all right with my neighbors. Your mother and I were not fond of each other. I guess I grate on most people. Heaven knows they grate on me. Anyway, after Lawrence died, I thought I should visit the family I had but wasn't looking forward to it.

When I arrived at your house, your mother fretted and dithered, your father shut himself up in the bedroom, and you took my hand, sat me down, snuggled up, and said, "You got any good names for horses?" You were foolish enough not to realize that I was an unsociable, difficult old woman. You looked just like my sister Henrietta (Bee, we called her) when she was seven, small for your age and dark. (And, as the years have passed, you haven't lost the resemblance.) You acted like her too. She was one of the few people I ever cared for. I didn't like her husband (your grandfather), so she and I parted ways, and then she died. Your mother reminded me of my brother-in-law. You reminded me of Bee.

To get to the point, you're the only relative I have any real fondness for. That, I'm sure, says more about me than it does about my family, but it's true nonetheless. So, now you have a house if you want it. It's a poor old thing, but I was contented in it. If you actually come to live in it, there are two things you need to know. You have to get the attic door shut just right, or it swings open. If the young brunette at Sanderson's Variety waits on you, count your change.

Your Aunt Louise

Meg read the letter twice, refolded it carefully, and stood looking out the window above the sink. Across the driveway and, again, near the kitchen door, spirea grew. In another few weeks she would be able to stand here, doing dishes or washing vegetables, and look out at gracefully arched branches and crowded clusters of bloom.

"How did you know, Aunt Louise?" she asked quietly. "How did you *know?*"

A car was coming down the driveway. It stopped near the path to the front door. Craning her neck to see at the awkward angle, Meg watched a man get out of the car and walk around it to the flagstone path. She went through the dining room and into the living room to open the door, but as she reached for the knob, a key turned in the lock, and the door swung open.

"Hello, Mr. Mulcahy," said Meg, jumping back to avoid a broken nose.

The man stared at her. "Ms. Kessinger?"

"Yes," said Meg. "Whom did you expect?" She looked curiously at the visitor. He wasn't much over six feet, but his broad shoulders made him seem larger than he was. He had wavy brown hair, cut short, and brown eyes. An attractive man, despite his startled look. He was wearing a thick pullover shirt and corduroy trousers.

"Nobody," he answered. "I surely didn't expect you, at least not yet. I thought you were getting here tomorrow morning."

"Well, that's what I thought, too," said Meg. "But I left earlier than I'd planned. You *are* Michael Mulcahy, aren't you?"

"Forgive me. Yes," he replied. "Please, call me Mike. I wanted to make sure the men had come and ripped out the old carpeting like you asked, and that nothing dreadful had happened. Like the roof falling in." He grimaced.

"Which is due to happen?"

"Don't ask me," he said. "But I wouldn't be surprised. I'd get the place inspected if I were you."

"For?"

He grinned at her. "Imminent collapse?"

"Come on," said Meg, walking toward the kitchen. "Come look at this. I know, you've seen it before, but look again."

She stood in the center of the kitchen and gestured. "Have you ever seen a more perfect room?"

"Well, the floor's nice. Nicer than it used to be."

"The floor is not nice. It's okay but it's not *nice*. It's everything else that's nice. It just needs a big table and some curtains on the window. And a coffeepot. It definitely needs a coffeepot."

"And a new stove, and a refrigerator that will freeze ice, and a dishwasher, and a microwave . . ."

Meg suppressed the desire to tell him he was crazy. If the kitchen were his, he'd ruin it. She didn't want to admit that the idea of a refrigerator that wouldn't freeze ice had given her pause. "I'd love to offer you some coffee, believe me. But I can't."

He waved a hand. "I've got to be going, but you've got my number if there's anything I can help you with, right?"

"Yes. The phone, however, isn't connected. But the guy's coming the day after tomorrow."

"Okeydoke," he said. "If you need representation at a court appearance, give me enough warning to get my suit pressed. If you just need a can opener, come over to the house. We're almost neighbors."

He handed her the key ring he was still holding. "Here are the other keys. Like I said on the phone, I got both locks changed for you."

"We're neighbors?"

"Indeed. You have the Ruschmans to the west, and I'm the house past theirs." He gestured over his shoulder. "Thataway. Well, I gotta run. Lost my secretary, and I've got piles of stuff to type at my blazing twelve words a minute."

Meg looked down at the keys in her hand. "Is there another one? A small one for the lock on the cellar doors?"

He shook his head. "Sorry."

Oh, well, thought Meg. Bolt cutters will make short work of it, if I ever put a washer down there and hang a clothesline in the backyard.

When Mike was halfway to his car, she called after him. "Hey! Do you have a dog? A smallish brown dog?"

He stopped and turned, a concerned look on his face. "She's not mine," he said. "She's been around a few weeks. She's one strange, spooky dog. Did she bother you?"

"No. I just saw her in the woods."

"Stay away from her. She was hanging around one day by my place, and I tried to see if she was wearing a collar under that matted hair. She nearly took my thumb off."

"Maybe," Meg said under her breath, "she knew you were a lawyer."

Five

As Michael Mulcahy's car turned out of the drive, another pulled in. It was a well-rusted station wagon, and it stopped by the kitchen door. A tall woman got out. She looked to be in her early forties, but the thick blond hair caught into a ponytail high on her head was not as incongruous as it might have seemed on another woman of a similar age. She was wearing faded jeans and a football jersey, and her smile was wide and friendly.

"Hey, neighbor," she said to Meg, who was standing in the doorway and holding the screen door open with her shoulder. "Jane said you'd arrived, so I brought coffee and sandwiches in case you need them." She reached into the car and dragged out a basket. "Want some lunch?"

Meg, whose coffeemaker was in the moving truck, nodded vigorously. "Yes, yes, yes!" she said. "Mostly I want coffee, but I've never turned down lunch." She stood out of the way to let her visitor in.

"I'm Christine Ruschman," said the woman. "You must be Meg Kessinger." She set down the basket and motioned toward the daffodils in the sink. "I brought some jars. Janie told me about the flowers, and I thought you might need something to put them in."

"While I was drifting off to sleep in the Motel Six last night, I said a prayer," replied Meg. "It went like this: 'Dear Lord, Please let me like the house and give me a neighbor who anticipates my every need.' I never had a prayer answered so fast. Except one time when I asked for a highway patrolman to ignore me, and he did. Your daughter is a darling."

Christine poured from a large thermos into two mugs and handed one to Meg. "Cream? Sugar? No? Yes, she is, isn't she? So, you do like the house?"

Meg smiled blissfully. "Coffee! I don't know for sure, haven't seen much of it."

"But the kitchen?" Christine sighed. "The world's greatest kitchen? I'm so jealous of this kitchen, I could spit."

Meg looked around. "I love the kitchen. But how were you brave enough to say that? What if my burning desire was to rip out all this stuff and put in sleek, Euromodern cabinets and track lighting? Wouldn't I be scared to tell you?"

Christine leaned against the counter, grinning. "I could stand to deal with you if you wanted to ruin this kitchen but not if you both wanted to ruin this kitchen and were scared to admit it. See, it was a self-correcting situation. Why waste time?"

"Okay," said Meg. She took a deep breath and said with a pretense of great nervousness, "I like Charles Dickens, Bach, barbershop quartets, and lilacs. I hate houses that are painted orange, and I will not live down the road from an orange house and have to look at it every time I drive to town. If you paint any part of your pretty white house orange, I will have to move. Or, if I've gotten attached to this place, sneak over at night and change it back."

"Hmm . . ." said Christine, hitching herself onto the countertop. "All right. *I* like Angela Thirkell novels, Chopin, and peonies. Big, blowzy peonies. If you put in one of those little black coachmen statues standing by the front walk holding a lantern,

I will come over while you're at the movies and smash it with a hammer."

Meg nodded. "This is going to work."

Christine lifted her mug in agreement. "You bet." She slid down from the counter. "Let's see the house."

"If you like the kitchen, you're going to like this," said Meg, gesturing through the doorway into the dining room. "It's got a, whatever-you-call-it, linoleum rug."

"It does!" said her visitor. "I never saw it. Louise had carpeting everywhere."

She stooped and ran a hand over the floor, which was covered to within a foot of the walls by a sheet of pale green linoleum, interspersed and bordered with a floral design in blues, pinks, and darker green. "It's not even in bad shape, probably because of the carpeting. It must be, what, sixty years old?"

Meg shrugged. "I don't know. It's sure as heck not recent. Let's keep going. Maybe there's a Murphy bed somewhere."

There wasn't. But the downstairs had, besides the dining and living rooms, two nicely proportioned bedrooms and a long, narrow bathroom with a wide, shallow medicine cabinet built in above the sink and what must have been the original cherry wainscoting. Several of the hexagonal mosaic tiles on the floor had disappeared, and the window was frozen in place. When the two women, shoving together, managed to raise it, it fell back down again with a crash. The stairs to the smaller second story were behind a door in the hallway. They creaked, and tattered paper in a pattern of immense camellias clung, in torn sections, to the walls. At the top of the stairs was a large attic. The air was stale and the several windows were smeared and dirty, but enough sunlight came in to produce shafts of dancing dust motes. Some boxes and cartons, presumably abandoned by a previous tenant, were stacked near the steps.

"Storage space!" said Meg.

They went back down the stairs and Meg closed the door at the bottom. It immediately swung open again a few inches. She shut it more firmly and turned the knob, which seemed to take care of the problem. Nearby was the door to the basement. She pulled it open and located a light switch on the stairway wall. Christine had to duck her head for the first few steps. The cellar was cramped, with a low ceiling and a huge heating system that took up most of the area. The walls were not straight up and down but curved like the walls of a cave. There were stacks of old newspapers, and piles of broken and unappealing household items. It smelled, however, exactly as Meg thought an old basement should.

"Well," said Christine, looking around. "At least that's not a coal furnace, which I halfway expected."

"It's immense," said Meg, "and a little scary. I hope it works."

They went back up to the first floor and looked at the items that had allowed the house to be rented as "furnished."

"Not exactly a treasure trove, is it?" said Meg. "Everything's so beat up."

"Except the floors. The carpet did a good job of protecting the floors; they're beautiful."

They were. They glowed softly, in contrast to the abused furniture.

"I'll keep the couch," said Meg, indicating a pleasant old sofa in the living room, "and the dresser in the front bedroom, and the dining room table and chairs. They're beat up, but sturdy. The rest'll go to the Salvation Army tomorrow. Unless you want any of it?"

Christine shook her head. "Too many years of tenants who didn't care what they spilled. Anyway, we've got too much stuff already. Let's have lunch."

The two women sat on the kitchen stoop and ate ham sandwiches. "So that's Aunt Louise's house," said Meg. "Doesn't tell me much about her. I didn't know her very well and hoped it would."

"It doesn't tell you much because her books are gone. She had more than four thousand books. She took every last one to the nursing home, which now has a substantial library." Christine grinned. "If she had *A Beginner's Guide to Home Repair,* she shoulda left it for the tenants."

"We wrote letters, that was all," said Meg. "And not often. My mother was scared of her, I think."

"Don't conclude your mother was unjustified. The lady wasn't exactly affable. I admired her 'If you don't like it, screw you' attitude, but that's because I intend to adopt the same one the day I reach sixty-five."

She leaned against the wall of the house, stretched out her legs, and pointed to a toolshed beyond which the driveway began its curve to the back. "You could take one of the dressers you don't want and put it in there to hold nails and screwdrivers and sandpaper. You're going to be needing nails and screwdrivers and sandpaper. And pliers and saws and a really, *really* big garbage can."

"I know." Meg sighed happily. "But that big old claw-footed tub must be seven feet long, and the shrub outside the front bedroom is honeysuckle. The smelly kind, I hope."

"If it's not, you can plant one. And you'll have roses. But the tulips must be surviving on a pension—and none of the tenants planted anything. If you want to see a gorgeous yard, go look at Mike Mulcahy's garden on the other side of us. Not much to see yet, but it's something."

"Michael Mulcahy's place?" asked Meg. "How can a lawyer have enough time to keep a fabulous garden? And why does he have a swing? This sandwich is *good.*"

Christine pushed the basket closer to Meg. "Have another. He didn't plant the garden. He inherited the place, complete with swing, from Mrs. Ehrlich last fall. I guess this is the year for inheriting property. He gets his aunt's house; you get your great-aunt's. I don't know if he'll have a clue how to take care of the garden, but I hope he figures it out. She worked like crazy on it. Lots of old flowers you hardly ever see, with names like Kiss Me over the Garden Gate."

"It sounds wonderful," said Meg, unwrapping a second sandwich.

"It is. But, like I said, at least you'll have roses." Christine poured more coffee into Meg's empty mug. "There's a white climber that grows right up the side of the porch. You need some of those big, comfy metal lawn chairs to put out there, the ones that give a little when you lean back, you know, so you can just sit on the porch until incipient starvation forces you into action."

"Or, sporadically, when I decide to try to make a living."

Christine sighed. "Yeah, there's that. What do you do?"

"I are a editor," said Meg. "Well, more of a writer. Freelance. Educational material. Mostly reading and language-arts stuff . . . vocabulary worksheets, spelling masters, whatever. You?"

"Substitute teach when we're at the point of boiling Nikes for supper. My husband's a contractor. Sometimes things are busy—right now, they're busy—and sometimes they're not. When they're not, I slap a steely look on my face and turn into the dreaded *Mrs. Ruschman,* every kid's worst nightmare. Then I stomp around and pull rank." She grinned wickedly. "I love pulling rank."

She fished a pair of half-glasses out of the purse next to her and put them on, lowering her chin enough to look sternly over the top.

"You'd scare *me,*" said Meg. "I'm feeling a little trembly already."

When Christine had driven away, after extracting a promise to come to supper, Meg separated the daffodils into three jars. It made her happy just to look at them, to lean over and breathe in their scent, and distributing them on the countertops took the edge off the loneliness of the house.

She ate that night with the Ruschmans—a chicken casserole and peaches. The peaches had to be home-canned; they had flavor. After greeting her with wild enthusiasm, Warren G. Harding lay silently under the table.

"If you feed the dog from the table, I will put on my glasses and give you the look," said Christine. "There is only one bad or disgusting habit he does not have. He does not *yet*"—she looked pointedly at her children—"beg at the table."

Christine's husband, who had been introduced as Dan, was big and broad-shouldered and had hazel eyes like his daughter. The children, Jane and the solemn but friendly Teddy, were making an obvious effort to remember their manners.

Meg found herself witness to what was, evidently, an ongoing debate.

"If nobody says they'll coach by the end of the week, we won't have a team," said Jane, pushing minced pieces of celery from the casserole to one side of her plate. "You know, Dad, I can't improve if I can't play."

Dan set his iced tea down with a thunk. "I can't do it, Janie. I could make it to most of the games, but a coach has to run practices. Lots of practices. I can't. I would if I could. I can't, and I'm getting really tired of talking about it."

Christine rolled her eyes at Meg. "Baseball," she said.

"You play baseball, Jane?" asked Meg.

"I *used* to," the child replied. "But a team can't get in the league without a coach, and our coach from last year moved, and my parents have *other* things to do."

Christine sighed. "I don't know enough! Your dad knows enough, but he doesn't have time. I might, I *might* have time, but I don't *know* enough."

"I do," said Meg.

Everyone looked at her.

"You play baseball?" asked Teddy.

"Don't look so surprised," said Meg. "I'm short but what they call sturdy. Come on, Christine, it'll be fun. We'll do it together. You do what you can do, and I'll do the rest."

"We're talking about thirteen kids," said Christine warningly. "Three or four are decent players; a couple are good; the rest are klutzes. The practice season starts in a few days, and the games at the beginning of May. Are you even sure you're staying?"

"With a creek three hundred yards from the house and a climbing rose on the porch?" She scooped up a peach slice and tipped it into her mouth. "And a neighbor who cans peaches? Are you kidding? And I love baseball. And I can stand a small percentage of the children I meet. And we'll kick *butt.*"

Jane looked at her mother. "Mom?"

Christine looked at Meg, who clasped her hands in an attitude of intense supplication. "All right," she sighed. "I'll call the league commissioner tomorrow and find out when we can get the field." She aimed a forefinger at Jane. "You call the kids. You call the kids every time they have to be called. All season. Deal?"

"Deal!" said Jane. She and Meg slapped hands across the table.

"Well, you all work out the details," said Dan, pushing back his chair. "I've got to get the rest of the floor down in the Bensons' addition. I'll be back late."

"Again?" asked Christine, looking stricken. "But, honey . . . again?"

"I know. Sorry. There just isn't anything I can do except do it." He smiled at Meg. "It's been a pleasure meeting you. I hope we'll see you often."

After dinner, Christine and Meg sat in the living room with coffee while Jane and Teddy washed the dishes. A small black cat jumped onto the couch and pushed his head against Meg's hand.

"That's Charlie," said Christine. "Just give him a shove if he's annoying."

The cat rumbled contentedly as Meg scratched him. "You

lean toward burly pets, don't you?" she asked. "Warren G. is a major hunk of dog and this fellow looks like he's on kitty steroids."

"Ain't none of us dainty," replied Christine. "But maybe Mrs. Ehrlich had him lifting weights; I don't know. We kind of inherited him when she died."

"The lady with the great garden?"

"Uh-huh. She had one of the most detailed wills in the history of the county. 'And to Christine Ruschman, my neighbor to the east, I leave all of my kitchen and table linens, both those in the top drawer in the pantry and those in the large oak trunk with the flat top in the attic,' but it made no mention of Charlie."

"So that's where you came by your tablecloth. I wondered. Those old flowered ones from the thirties are getting hard to find."

Christine nodded. "Tell me about it. I am now, however, happily awash in them."

Meg regarded the cat, who had been overtaken by the need to remove some invisible impurity from his haunch. He sat splay-legged, bracing himself while twisting around to clean it off. "He's really a chunk."

"He was still a tom when he came meowing to Hannah's back door, so that's probably why he's such a muscle-bound guy."

"Well, she ruined his night life," said Meg, "I'm glad to see."

"It was probably a relief to him," replied Christine, an odd look passing briefly over her face. "Hey, girl, just where do you get off roping me into co-managing a baseball team? I can't believe your nerve. I've got nothing else to do?"

"Aw, don't be a poot," said Meg. "You've got all that experience as the dreaded Mrs. Ruschman just going to waste. I'll need somebody to scare the kids and keep order, so I can concentrate on being the one they like. Besides, Jane needs to play. It's one of the most important things she can do. What's she going to say ten years from now? 'My mother never had time for me, so I couldn't do any of the things I really liked. But I didn't care, because our house was *so clean!*'?"

Christine laughed. "I said I'd do it. But I intend to hold it against you."

"I'll bear up," said Meg. "She wants to play. And I want to coach. So if you don't like it, tough. Anybody married to the man you're married to needs to feel some pain. It's only fair. Does he have any idea how good-looking he is?"

Christine smiled. "I don't know. I wonder sometimes. He is cute, isn't he?"

"Oh, yeah," said Meg. "He's that."

Meg parked outside the kitchen door. She wished she'd thought to leave a light on inside. When it got dark in the country, it got very dark. Tomorrow, the house would be filled with her own possessions, her own kitchen table and chairs and bed and heaps of boxes. It would feel more familiar, more like home. Tonight, it was still someone else's house. She opened the hatchback of the car, pushed the fire extinguisher and a carton of books out of the way, picked up a box of sheets and blankets, and unlocked the kitchen door.

She had already stored her toothbrush, toothpaste, shampoo, and a few makeup items in the medicine cabinet. She opened the mirrored door, admiring the cherry wainscoting— the same as on the walls—that had been used to make the cabinet. Earlier in the day, putting things on its shallow, wide shelves, she had noticed the small slot in the back for used razor blades. Now, brushing her teeth, she gazed at it, wondering how many worn, dulled blades had tumbled down into the space between the studs and lay rusting inside the wall.

Something was odd. She was sure she had put the bottle of vitamin tablets on the bottom shelf, because she had moved it to look more closely at the slot, realizing what it was. The bottle was now on the second shelf.

She stared at the other objects, arranged so neatly, far more neatly than they would remain after she had filled the cabinet with the normal jumble of items that, like gas, would expand to fill the available space. The few things she had placed there were still there. Why wouldn't they be? She must be wrong about where she'd put the vitamins. There was no reason for anyone to come into her house, empty her medicine cabinet, and replace the objects. She was just being silly, spooked by the silence and the house's unlived-in feeling.

She shut the cabinet door firmly and went to bed.

Six

The Salvation Army truck arrived as the coffee in Christine's old spare coffeepot finished percolating. The workers cheerfully carried out load after load of dismal furniture and ugly, heavy curtains. At ten o'clock, the moving truck drove up. By noon, known objects had made the house comforting, despite the stacks of unpacked cartons.

The sound of barking in the early afternoon drew her out into the backyard. Two dogs were racing toward the trees, Warren G. Harding hot in pursuit of the ugly brown dog. Even with his longer legs, he stood no chance of overtaking her, but she whirled and came toward him, and they met in a tumbling pile of cream and brown.

Meg took off running, unwilling to let nature take its course. They separated, the bigger dog with his front legs on the ground, his rear end high, and his tail up. He made a short bounding motion at the other dog, who stood panting and then gave in to the invitation and romped around him. Meg slowed to a walk, glad that no one had witnessed her misunderstanding.

"Harding!" she called, and then whistled. "Hey, Harding!"

He ran eagerly to meet her, jumping up to pat at her with large paws.

"Who's your friend with the mean eyes?" she asked, pushing him down and bending to scratch his neck with both hands.

The other dog hadn't moved. She stood at a distance, watching Meg intently. Her chest was broad, her legs wide-set. Her ears were forward, and her tail stood out horizontally behind her.

"Come on, girl," said Meg, patting her leg. "You're interested, I can tell. Let's get along with each other."

The dog still didn't move. She barked once in a peremptory fashion, and Harding loped off to rejoin her.

Meg walked back to the house, reminded of wanting her own dog. She'd grown up with dogs, and it seemed unnatural to live without one, but Chicago landlords were, most often, unsympathetic. Hers surely had been. She wanted . . . not a scruffy, bad-tempered dog. Not an ugly little dog. A clown, perhaps, like the Airedale she'd liked so much in Chicago. Or a bold and beautiful Kuvasz. Or . . . She wanted to begin the search, but she needed to fix the fence before she could start looking. And she couldn't start on that until she'd made some headway with unpacking.

She set up her tape player, chose *Peter and the Wolf* for its energetic passages, and worked steadily. By evening, she was exhausted, but the house seemed much more like home.

She took a mug of coffee and went out onto the porch to lean against the railing and look out over the yard and the meadow beyond. Twilight tinged the grass with silver where the land rolled away in the distance. A faint, sweet-smelling breeze moved the leaves on the apple trees just past the fence. This, she thought, was given to me to love.

The next morning, she pulled on a sweatshirt and went out to count the missing pickets. A fog lay heavily over the broad valley, thick enough so she could barely see the road. A car passed, ghostly in the mist.

By the time she had finished breakfast, the fog had begun to burn off, and by eleven o'clock it was gone. There were twenty-three pickets she would have to replace, and about forty others that needed to be fastened more securely. She wrenched a loose one free to use as a sample and went into the house to look through the Yellow Pages that the telephone installer had left earlier in the morning, when he connected her to the world. She called Christine.

"Is Meyers Lumber and Hardware right in town?" she asked.

"Turn left at the second light. It's out a little ways, a half mile maybe. You get your phone in?"

"No, I drove six miles into town to call you from a booth. Yes, I got my phone in." She gave Christine the number. "Want some coffee?"

"If you're going to Meyers, stop here on the way. I just made some *and* some cookies, which are the best things you ever tasted. I'll see you in a few minutes."

A half hour later, with a canister full of cookies beside her on the seat, Meg drove the rest of the way into town and found the lumberyard. A tall, rangy man got out of a red pickup truck next to her in the parking lot and passed her to hold the door open, nodding pleasantly as she went in ahead of him. He looked, in his flannel shirt and faded jeans, as if he belonged in Wyoming, but there was no drawl in his voice when he spoke to her as she stood surveying the hammers.

"Can't make up your mind?" he asked. His voice was deep and friendly.

"I know I want a claw hammer," she said. "But I don't know how heavy."

"Well, if you're framing a house, you probably need about twenty-four ounces. If you want something more all-purpose, sixteen ought to do."

43

Meg indicated the picket she'd rested against the shelves. "I've got to fix my fence."

"I have this one," the man said, selecting a hammer with a rubber coating on the handle. "I like the balance, and it's not too heavy to use for long periods." He held it out. "But your hands are small. See what you think."

Meg gripped the handle. "No, it's fine. Feels good. Thanks. I'm assuming they can cut pickets from stock here."

"Oh, sure," he said. "They can match that one easy." He pointed to a neighboring aisle. "Rust-proof nails are over there and paint's two aisles down."

"Thanks," she said again.

"Anytime."

Meg watched him walk away, wishing she were more skilled at flirting and hoping that her quick glance at his ringless left hand had not been apparent. It took a while to get the pickets she needed, and by the time she moved her car to load them in the back, the pickup truck was gone.

The deceased citizens of Harrison who had been lucky enough to be Lutheran took their eternal rest in a particularly lovely cemetery. Behind the old stone church with its steeple and heavy wooden doors, a groundskeeper was busy mowing, but Meg was no more bothered by the noise than were the other people there. It was a pleasing hum behind her thoughts as she sat in the sunshine and looked at the inscription on her great-aunt's headstone. "He that keepeth thee will not slumber."

"Behold, he that keepeth Israel shall neither slumber nor sleep," murmured Meg, wishing she had known her aunt better, wishing she had visited. "You knew me much better than I knew you," she said, running her hand across the rose-gray stone.

As she neared her house, Meg decided to keep driving, wondering who or what lay just beyond her own property. On her right, there was a large house that appeared to be empty. The road dipped slightly, rose again, then curved. Beyond the curve there was a small pale green house on her left. She pulled into the driveway and parked behind an old black sedan, which indicated that someone was at home.

There was no answer to her knock. She stood, hesitating, on the front porch and then returned to her car. As she opened the door, a man who looked to be in his late sixties came around the side of the house and waved. He was wearing a faded plaid shirt, stained corduroy trousers, and a shapeless blue hat.

"Thought I heard a car come up the drive," he said. "I was collecting some pollen in the back."

"Hi," said Meg. "I didn't mean to interrupt you; I just wanted to introduce myself. I've moved into Louise Marriott's house—she was my great-aunt. I'm Meg Kessinger."

"John Eppler," said the man, approaching with a hand extended. "Come on in and sit a minute." His handshake was strong.

"Oh, but you're in the middle of something."

He gestured dismissively. "Pollen can wait," he said. "How often do you get a new neighbor? I was going to sit down a minute anyway."

He pushed the unlocked front door open, took off his hat, wiped his shoes carefully on a hemp doormat, and preceded Meg into the house. His hair was snow-white, and he was a striking-looking man.

"Come on to the kitchen," he said, passing through a cheerful living room with furniture in chintz slipcovers and a low table bearing jars of honey in various sizes, each with a neatly printed price label on the top. He walked energetically, his back poker-straight. "Have a cup of coffee."

Meg followed him through the dining room, where a parakeet startled her by fluttering overhead to land on a curtain rod, into a large, bright kitchen. Mr. Eppler took a delicate flowered china mug with a thin gold rim out of a cupboard, filled it with coffee, and put it on the enameled kitchen table. Refilling a thick yellow mug proclaiming that today was the first day of the rest of his life, he asked if Meg wanted milk or sugar.

"No, nothing, thanks," said Meg, pulling out a chair and sitting. "Company gets the pretty cup?"

He opened the cupboard door and indicated five mugs that matched Meg's crammed onto a shelf next to an assortment of considerably less lovely ones.

"Got plenty of 'em," he said, "but I don't see the point in using such fancy ones. My daughter, Ginny, she's trying to get me to throw out the others. She lives in Philadelphia now, brought these out last fall. When she left, I found eleven perfectly good ones in the trash." He chuckled. "Can you imagine that? She just threw 'em away."

Meg didn't have any trouble imagining it but thought it wiser to be noncommittal. "Mmm . . ." she said. She sipped strong coffee and looked out the kitchen window at a row of stacked white boxes about thirty yards from the house. "You're a beekeeper, I take it. This a good area for bees?"

"Near perfect," he replied, sitting down across from her. "Plenty of alfalfa around, and clover in the meadows. I've got vitex shrubs in the back to keep 'em happy in July, when the tulip poplars are through. You ever need honey or pollen or bees, you just come see me. The county calls me when somebody needs a hive removed from an attic or gets panicky over a swarm, so I got no shortage of bees."

"Good to know," said Meg.

"I was sorry to hear about Louise," he said, shaking his head resignedly. "Not surprised, mind. She must have been, what? Past ninety, I guess. We've had our share of passings along this road." He shook his head. "Hannah Ehrlich last fall, then Louise. My bees took care of Hannah's arthritis; couldn't do too much about her heart."

46

Meg looked questioningly at him. "Took care of her arthritis?"

He put down his mug and held up both hands. "Before I started keeping bees, my hands had gotten so bad, I could hardly hold a spoon." He flexed his fingers. "See that? Bee-venom therapy. Beekeepers rarely suffer from arthritis."

"Bee stings?"

He nodded. "Most people figure they'd rather have arthritis. Phobias, you know. But Hannah, she said sure, let's try it. Worked, too." He nodded again, this time sadly, and looked out the window. His mouth twisted. "Sure do miss Hannah Ehrlich. Knew her for thirty-five years."

"I'm sorry," said Meg.

The man turned his gaze back to her. "Course, it's too bad about your great-aunt, too. She was in the home so long, we kind of lost touch. But she was a fine woman. A fine woman." He took a swallow of coffee. "She loved that place of hers, that's for sure. Too bad she had to leave it."

"I love it, too," said Meg. "Already."

"Good," said Mr. Eppler. "Place like that shouldn't be rented out. Just goes downhill. But Louise wouldn't sell it. Been plenty of people interested." He frowned. "Mike Mulcahy tried to make her sell, thinking lawyers know better what's good for people than people do themselves. But she wouldn't let it go. She got rid of her nice furniture and all that, but not the house. I imagine you've got your work cut out."

"That I do," said Meg. She cupped the pretty mug in her hands, feeling warmth on her palms. "It's a bit run-down."

"Louise tended to save her money," said her neighbor, nodding. "And what she spent, she spent on books. Then, when she went into the home, she wasn't near careful enough about who she rented to. I'd think the hot-rod kid didn't help the place any."

"Who?" asked Meg.

He looked disgusted. "Bit of nonsense who lived there before you. She'd barrel down this road in her fancy sports car like she thought she was at Indy. Nearly run me down the morning she left while I was coming home from the hives I keep across the way. Didn't see me in the fog, I guess. A morning a lot like this one—we get fogs like that every so often. Oh, she was a pretty thing, all blond hair and big eyes. Kept to herself. But I never saw her doing a lick at Louise's place. And she drove too doggone fast."

Meg unloaded her purchases, dumping them onto the grass near the driveway, and unlocked the kitchen door. She went through the house and into her bedroom to change into older jeans before spending the afternoon kneeling on the grass.

She sat down on the edge of the bed to unlace her shoes, facing the squat, ugly dresser she had kept to put in the toolshed but hadn't yet moved. The bottom drawer was not quite flush with the ones above it. She stood up and shoved at it, but it wouldn't fit in place. Turning, she kicked it with the bottom of her foot. No use. When she pulled on the drawer above, it moved smoothly, almost loosely, in its tracks.

She yanked the loose drawer all the way out and set it on the floor, then removed the bottom one. They looked to be exactly the same size, but they probably weren't. Reversing them solved the problem. Both drawers closed all the way.

She sat down again and pushed off her shoes, glancing out the window at the honeysuckle and the side yard. It was a beautiful afternoon. It was pleasant to live here, not to worry about shutting and locking the windows when you left the house just because the screens could be slid out of their tracks by an eight-year-old. Except on the chilliest nights, she could leave the window open a good foot all the time.

She looked at the dresser more carefully. No, she told herself. Don't be stupid. If anyone had come in, he would have done more than remove the drawers from a dresser and accidentally reverse them while putting them back. Besides, why would anyone want to remove the drawers from a dresser?

Still, she got up and went into her study. The computer, the only valuable thing she owned, was just as she'd left it, her desk seemingly untouched.

I guess being alone can make your mind do funny things, she thought. But she found she was shivering, although the room was warm.

By late afternoon, the missing pickets had been replaced and the loose ones reattached. The tedium of the work had been relieved by a game of catch with Jane. Still, it had been too many hours of bending and wrenching and pounding nails. Meg straightened and sighed, a dull ache tensing the muscles in her lower back. She looked around. When the fence was painted, it would look good.

A red pickup came along the road, crossed into the wrong lane, and stopped on the shoulder. The driver rolled his window all the way down and leaned out, lifting a Pittsburgh Pirates cap as he did so.

"Looks like the new hammer worked pretty well," he said.

"Sure did," replied Meg. She was unreasonably pleased to see him again.

"So this is your place? There used to be another woman living here."

"She moved," said Meg. "It's mine now, fence and all."

"Well, welcome, neighbor." He smiled. "My name's Jack Deutsch. Like a Hollander, but spelled e-u-t-s-c-h. I'm about a mile down this road." He pointed ahead of him. "On the other side."

Meg shifted the hammer to her left hand and held out her right across the fence. Jack stretched out of the cab to shake it.

"Meg Kessinger," said Meg, "I'm glad to meet you." She

wished she weren't still wearing her Boy Scout shirt which, by now, was looking rather disreputable, and that she had on a better pair of jeans. "I just moved in a couple of days ago."

"Met the Ruschmans?" he asked. "Next place down?"

"Yes," she said. "All four of them."

"You couldn't have better neighbors. The people in the next house on your side"—he pointed over his shoulder back down the road—"don't live here much of the year. But if you need something Christine doesn't have, feel free to bang on my door. My name's on the mailbox by the road."

"Thanks," said Meg, confident that thinking of something Christine didn't have was a challenge she was equal to. "And I've met John Eppler and Michael Mulcahy, who is, I guess, kind of across the road from you."

"I'm a little further," said Jack. Meg got the impression he'd been tempted to add "not further enough." "Anyway," he went on, "if you run out of nails or need a heat gun . . ."

Meg laughed. "I'll definitely be needing a heat gun, though there are places where I may just opt for a sledgehammer."

"Got that, too," he said, grinning. He settled his cap more firmly, pulling it down over sandy hair. His eyes were blue, and they crinkled at the corners when he smiled.

Meg watched the truck until it disappeared around the curve, then turned toward the house. On the far side of the driveway, the ugly brown dog stood watching her.

"The yard looks better, doesn't it?" asked Meg. "It's going to have a puppy in it soon, and you'd better be nice to him. Or her."

The dog's tail relaxed toward the ground.

"See, you're getting used to me," said Meg. "I don't see any reason for us not to be civil to each other." She walked up the steps to the front door.

When she came outside again after dinner, coffee cup in hand, the dog was still there. She was lying under a maple tree near the driveway but sat up as Meg emerged.

"I've got some cookies," said Meg in a singsong voice, putting a small plate down on the porch and then walking slowly toward the gate at the side of the yard.

The dog didn't move as Meg opened the gate, turned back, and sat down on the steps.

"They're really good cookies, from Christine's house," she said conversationally. "Harding didn't get any. He wanted some awfully badly, but he didn't get even a bite. Unless Teddy gave him some. I suspect Teddy gives him anything he wants. Do you know Teddy?"

The dog did not reply, but she was standing now and had moved closer.

"Oh, don't be silly. You must. He lives right over there." She pointed toward the west. "If you wanted just a little bite, I could spare it."

She broke off a corner of cookie, stood up, and tossed it lightly. It landed a few feet on the other side of the gate. The dog took several steps, sniffed at the offering, and then took it delicately.

"There's more," said Meg, looking out toward the road. "But I think it's terribly rude to expect to be served. If you want to share, you should come close enough so I wouldn't have to get up."

She ought not to feed someone else's dog. Some people felt strongly about such things. Tough. The dog was watching her hungrily. She tossed half a cookie onto the grass about six feet away.

"You can have that if you want," she said quietly but in a cheerful tone. "I'm paying hardly any attention to the fact that you're even here. You can tell, because I'm not looking at you. I don't really care if you want it or not. But it's really, really good."

She turned her back on the dog and started to whistle *Eine kleine Nachtmusik*. The dog walked into the yard and ate the cookie, then sat down calmly and looked at Meg.

"You like Mozart?" asked Meg, glancing toward the dog and then away. "Good for you. Some dogs don't like anything but country and western. I'm glad to see you have broader tastes, since it appears we're neighbors."

The dog didn't move.

"All right," said Meg. "One more. But then you have to go home to your own house. Your person, or your people, may be worried. Feel free to come back anytime."

She held out a whole cookie, gazing off to the dog's left. The dog stood up and stretched and then walked slowly forward. She stopped and reached for the food, taking it gingerly from Meg's hand.

"So, good night," said Meg. She stood up. The dog backed away slightly, holding the cookie in her teeth. Meg went into the house.

She was propped up in bed reading when Christine called. It was the first time the phone had rung.

"We've got our choice. We can be the Atlanta Braves or the Houston Astros. Do you care, Coach? I do."

"No, I don't care. Why do you?"

"Okay, then we're the Astros. Because the Astros, for some reason, have gray pants and the Braves have white, that's why."

"Ah. I'm surprised you didn't have to fight for the uniform then."

"Are you kidding? All the other coaches are *men*. Like they've ever washed the pants? Ha!"

Christine had a list of the times the diamond was available, and they worked out a practice schedule.

"Do you make a habit of calling people at ten forty-five?" asked Meg. "Don't you have to get up and milk the cows or something?"

"Oh, yeah," laughed Christine. "That's why we moved to the country. So we could have *cows* and get up at four-thirty. There are plenty of cows along this road, but not a one of them belongs to us. I *like* cows. I just don't like their schedule. I wouldn't have called so late if I'd realized it was. I've been reading a sewing magazine and didn't notice the time. I was engrossed." She paused. "It was a real seam-ripper."

Meg laughed. "Wrench yourself away; there's work to do. Make me a list of the team members while you're burning the midnight oil. And note the positions they played last year—if they played last year—along with whatever you know about them. Bring it over tomorrow and have lunch."

"I can tell you're good at delegating," said Christine. "I don't like that in a person."

"Can I hang up now?"

"In a minute. Did you hear about the break-in?"

The disconcerted feeling that had plagued Meg during the early afternoon came back. "What break-in? Where?"

Christine chuckled. "Would you believe someone broke into the Salvation Army store?"

"What *for?*"

"That's the big mystery. What for, exactly! Probably kids on a dare or something. Nothing was even taken, so far as anyone knows."

"How bizarre."

"Tell me about it. But excitement is hard to come by in this town. Anyone with a taste for it is driven to odd activities."

The numbers on the clock by Meg's bed said 2:22 when she woke up. She lay, blinking at it, wondering what had awakened her. Then she knew. A dog was barking near the house, a throaty, challenging bark.

Meg tensed. She was glad she had taken two nails and driven them into the window jamb. It still opened easily, but no more than five inches, so she could leave it open at night without feeling unprotected. The other windows in the house were shut and locked; she had taken care of that before getting to bed. Dogs bark, she told herself. They just do, at almost anything.

The barking stopped. Meg lay in bed, staring upward at nothing and listening to complete silence. I should, she thought, have thrown rocks instead of cookies. She went back to sleep. In the morning, the dog was still there, lying on the mat outside the front door.

Seven

*T*he phone rang while Meg was painting the fence. She raced inside, the screen door slamming behind her.

"Mike Mulcahy," said the caller. "How's it going?"

"Slowly," replied Meg. "But I like the place; I really do. I've got the fence repaired. I was painting it when you called."

"Oops. Sorry to interrupt. Don't you have to, like, find paying work?"

"You offering?"

He laughed. "If you can type, spell *deposition,* and repress hostile glares at people you figure are guilty as hell, sure. Why not? Like I said, I lost my secretary. And since it's your fault, you kinda owe me."

"What do you mean, my fault?"

"The woman who lived in your house, Angie Morrison, was my secretary. She rented month-to-month, and when I told her you were taking the place, she decided to leave town."

"Oh, please!" said Meg. "It's my fault there's no rental property in this burg?"

"There is, actually. I don't think she left because she'd have to move. I think she wanted a more exciting life. However, if I can get some leverage by making you feel guilty, why not try?"

"Charming," said Meg. "And lawyers wonder why they have such bad reputations. But no, I'm not looking for paying work. Scratch that. I'm usually looking for paying work, but I brought my job with me—writing vocabulary worksheets for middle-school kids. My next deadline's a few days off, though, so I'm taking a little time to settle."

"How about taking a little time to have dinner? You need to get a sense of the elegant night life this town has to offer."

Meg hesitated, feeling unprepared. "I don't know . . . I've got so much to do."

"You have to eat."

"Yeah, but . . ."

"We'll make it quick. The Main Street Cafe has great onion burgers. You can show up in paint-spattered overalls, and nobody will even blink."

"Okay," said Meg. "I'll meet you there. What time?"

"Six-thirty," said Mike. "Eat lunch early. The portions are large."

Christine rode up on a bicycle at noon and admired the fence.

"It's going to take me the rest of my adult life to paint it," said Meg. "And it's hopelessly boring. Any chance Jane likes to paint? Pays better than baby-sitting."

"She might," said Christine. "She likes doing almost anything. And she likes you. Anyone who invites her over to play catch rates pretty high with her. And she's saving money to buy stock, so she'd probably like a job."

"Saving money to buy stock?"

"Mrs. Ehrlich left her a few shares along with her sterling silver, and Janie's decided to become a force on Wall Street, which I don't discourage, being as how I'll need somebody to support me in my old age."

"Stock and sterling silver . . ." said Meg. "If her house is the

56

"I'm having dinner with him tonight," said Meg. "I guess I'd better not tell Jane."

Christine gave her an appraising look. "I thought we were going to figure out clever ways to throw you and Jack into the same social circles, and here you are with your dance card filling up."

"Oh, yeah," said Meg. "Just call me Belle."

When Christine had ridden away, the dog moved closer to the porch. Meg looked up from reading through the team notes and saw her watching. The dog's chin dripped water and her paws were wet.

"Been down to the creek, I see, which probably accounts for your peaceful demeanor," said Meg. "It has that effect. Why have you decided to hang out here? Somebody was nice to you, back when you were a puppy, right? A smallish woman with short dark hair, I bet. You got socialized and you learned about people, and now you're reluctant to give up on the entire human race."

The dog lay down, stretching her head out on her paws, and sighed.

"You're too proud to ask, but you're hungry, aren't you?" asked Meg. "I really stepped in it, didn't I?"

She went into the kitchen, scrambled some eggs and made toast, which she crumbled on top. She carried the plate outside, put it down on the grass, and sat cross-legged a few feet away.

"No, I didn't lace it with arsenic," she said as the dog sniffed from a distance. "Anyone with sense would have, but I didn't. If you want it, come get it. Come on, girl."

The dog got up and walked over to the food, sniffed again carefully, and ate. Her left ear drooped more than her right.

"You are truly hideous," said Meg. "Not that looks are everything, but . . . You'll never be a pinup, but if somebody got the burrs and stickers off you and trimmed you up? And you could work on that mean look in your eyes. It's *not* attractive."

The dog finished licking the plate and looked at Meg. She gave one short bark.

"You're welcome," said Meg.

During the afternoon, the temperature fell. Even with a sweatshirt on, Meg was chilled. Her back had started to hurt again from bending over, and she decided to unpack some more cartons in the kitchen.

She had scrubbed out the cabinets while the movers worked on Monday but hadn't needed to clean the outsides, which were spotless. She knew she should paint the insides before she unpacked, but she was tired of searching through boxes for a saucepan or colander. After a few hours the dishes, glasses, and flatware had all been stored away.

There were only a few cartons left. The top shelves were much too high for her to reach from the floor. They would do, however, for the large casserole dishes she rarely used. She stood on the countertop to put the selected objects on the top shelf and, sliding the last casserole into place, knelt to get down again, holding on to the cupboard. Her head brushed against her arm, dislodging an earring, which bounced on the countertop and disappeared.

She got down on the floor and searched. The earring was a tiny ruby, and she didn't want to lose it. She put the side of her face against the floor and examined its surface, but nothing small and gold and red revealed itself. She stood up. Where had it gone? She looked at the countertop again. There was the slightest gap where it met the wall. The countertop had no backsplash; it merely ended in a chrome strip. She moved her head closer to the wall. There was just enough room for something very small to have fallen through.

Meg sighed, then opened the base cabinet and looked inside. It did not appear to be attached to the wall. The original cabinets had probably been ripped out to upgrade the plumbing or to rewire. The replacements were free-standing. She would have to remove the strip of quarter round that edged the floor where it met the kickboard, but she could replace that if she ruined it. It looked new, and had been painted more recently than the walls. She couldn't replace the earring, and this pair was her favorite.

She managed to pry the quarter round away without breaking it. Then, gingerly, she wrestled the cabinet outward and up over the edge of the linoleum. When she had managed to get the cabinet out enough to tip it, she slid a blanket underneath and gradually tugged it out sufficiently to get behind it.

The earring was lying next to a small dried puddle. There were several drip marks on the wall from whatever had run down in rivulets and pooled on the floor. She recovered the earring and put it carefully on the windowsill, then got a bucket and a scrub brush and started to work. The drips were easy to remove, although they left faint stains on the paint. On the floor, the dried liquid had mixed with several years' worth of dust and crumbs. Cleaning it up would not be pleasant, but neither would it be particularly difficult.

She ignored the ache in her back and started scrubbing the entire area that moving the cabinet had made available. Dipping the scrub brush into the soapy water, she noticed that, under the suds, the water had taken on a pinkish hue. The drips, she guessed, were blood. Someone had carved a rib roast on the countertop without paying enough attention.

As she cleaned, she noticed the grain of the narrow boards that formed the floor. They were maple. Not oak, but well worth sanding and refinishing someday. She'd always wanted a wooden kitchen floor. She could just pull up the tiles—pretty easily if they were self-stick, which they seemed new enough to be. It would be a shame to waste a perfectly nice, well-laid floor, but though the black and white squares were attractive, they weren't wood.

Maybe someday. In the meantime, she had more pressing work. She made sure the floor was dry, carefully pushed the cabinet back in place, renailed the quarter round, emptied the last carton that was standing on the kitchen table, and looked at her watch. There was just time to take a bath and put on clean clothes, which seemed necessary, regardless of Mike's assurances about the cafe's forgiving attitude.

"I'll give you this much," said Meg. "You were right about the onion burgers."

Hers was just the way she liked it, crisped around the edges. The bun had been grilled in butter. Mike, who had ordered the same thing, nodded. "You will find I am rarely wrong."

"About anything?" asked Meg.

"Very nearly," he said.

Meg pushed her cleaned plate away and sighed happily.

"I like a woman with a good appetite," Mike said.

"I like a man who likes a good woman with a good appetite. I worked one up today."

"You don't look it. Hardworking girls don't look so pert."

"Hardworking girls with blow-dryers do," said Meg. "Even when they have to plug them into ancient sockets and risk blowing fuses."

Mike tapped one finger against his forehead. "I'd grasped a certain failure to conform to code," he said. "I tried to tell you."

"You'd also concluded that I'd be better off staying in Chicago and selling the place, sight unseen. Proof that you can be wrong, rare as it may be. But not about dinner. Thanks. And thanks for having the kitchen cleaned so well."

"Just following orders," he said, "which required me to hire a crew and pay for it from the estate. I'm surprised they did a good job. Somebody who could really clean, no, who *would* really clean, could make a fortune in this town."

"Well, to tell the truth, they didn't do a particularly good job except in the kitchen," said Meg. "Even in there, inside and behind things needed work. But I'm grateful for what got done.

You get sick of cleaning the place you're moving out of so you can move into another place and clean it too. One or the other, sure, but it never seems to work that way."

"It did for me," said Mike. "When I moved into Aunt Hannah's place, there wasn't so much as a cat hair anywhere."

"Which reminds me," said Meg. "Why didn't you take Charlie, so he could stay where he was used to?"

"You mean the cat? Jane wanted him. She would barely speak to me, but she made that much clear."

Meg remembered what Christine had said. She did her best to appear innocent. "Why wouldn't Jane speak to you?"

Mike looked puzzled. "Beats me. She was just hostile, in that stony, adolescent way. Lots of ill-concealed, angry glances. You've seen the swing in my front yard?"

Meg nodded. The ropes that supported the plank seat were at least thirty feet long.

"Aunt Hannah called it 'Janie's swing.' She put it up when Jane was three, and Jane loved it—right up until the day my aunt died. I told her to use it, just like she always had. She hasn't sat on it since." He gave his head a half-shake and looked away. "She asked me once if it was normal for an heir—that's exactly how she put it, 'an heir'—to also be the lawyer who wrote the will. The question was more than a little pointed."

"Is it? Normal, that is?"

"No. It's legal—at least in Pennsylvania it is—if the lawyer is closely related to the person, but around here I don't think it would be looked on kindly. You have any idea how conservative this little piece of heaven you've landed in is? Lawyers watch their step, along with anyone else whose livelihood depends on respectability. Besides, if I'd drawn up her will, I would have done a better job. She didn't use a lawyer, but it was witnessed and binding. I was just the executor. I tried explaining that to Jane. As far as she was concerned, being the executor was just as bad."

He put his thumb to his temple and rubbed the middle of his brow with his forefinger, looking suddenly tired. "I don't know what she's got on her mind. It's hard to tell with kids."

Meg regretted questioning him. It wasn't any of her business, and it was a rotten way to repay him for dinner. She changed the subject.

"Christine and I are going to coach Jane's baseball team," she said. "Christine claims it won't be easy."

Mike brightened. "Neither easy nor, in the end, fruitful," he remarked.

"Meaning?"

"Meaning that the team I coach will undoubtedly hand your kids their teeth on a platter."

"Wanna make a bet, Mr. Smug?" asked Meg.

"You haven't even seen your kids practice yet," he said.

"Doesn't matter. Wanna make a bet? Or are you a great, big, clucking chicken?"

He looked at her, his brown eyes amused, and ran a hand through his crisp hair. "It just doesn't seem chivalrous," he said. "But you ask for it, you get it. What do you want to bet on? First game between our teams or league standings at the end of the season?"

Meg was no fool. She'd been through Christine's notes. "League standings," she said. "And bet something that matters. Not cash."

"Okay," he said. "How about the loser must, with great sincerity, tell the winner, 'You're a better coach and a finer human being than I am or could ever be'?"

"Oh, please!" said Meg. "You're a lawyer. You're used to saying things you don't mean with an appearance of astounding frankness. But I'd have to practice for hours in front of a mirror and, even then, it would nearly kill me to choke out the words. Forget it. It's like a Rockefeller and a panhandler making a hundred-dollar bet."

"Then you decide," he said. Meg noticed he did not argue her assumption. "But before the season starts. Dessert?"

"As a bet?"

"No, now. I want dessert. Do you? Or are you a great, big, clucking chicken?"

She was very full. She ate dessert. It was lemon meringue pie, and it was good. On the way home, she stopped at a grocery store and bought dog food.

Eight

$\mathcal{G}$et down on the ball, Bobby!" yelled Meg. She peeled off her batting glove and stuck it in a back pocket of her cutoffs, then walked out and stopped in front of the second baseman. She waved the other fielders to join them.

"You all need to hear this again," she said. "You get a grounder, get in front of it. I want your mitt touching the ground with your body behind it, knees bent, weight on your toes. Then you come up however much you need to."

She borrowed Bobby's mitt and demonstrated, the muscles in her thighs tightening as her body rose, her hands moving up and back, into her stomach. "Your other hand goes up like this, behind the mitt. If you judge the bounce wrong, your body's there to block the ball. Let's try some more."

She glanced around the group. "Let's divide up into two groups. Half of you can take grounders, and the other half can go out into right field and bunt."

"Who's going to pitch to us?" asked Suzanne. She was a skinny little girl who could beat any of the others around the bases. If she could bunt reliably, thought Meg, she'd have a .600 batting average, easy.

"Coach Ruschman," said Meg. "Pitching is one of the many things that Coach Ruschman does with brilliance."

She assigned her group to positions and started working, loving the feel of the bat in her hands, even just hitting infield practice, enjoying the *crack* it made on contact. She used a wooden bat just to hear it make that sound instead of a *whang*.

"Quit dogging it, Jason!" she yelled at the third baseman. "You play like you practice!"

After twenty minutes, she called her group in. "Better," she said, smiling and leaning on her bat. "But at least half of you had your weight on your heels until you saw the ball coming. There's no way a fielder can move as quickly as necessary if he—" She glanced at Jane. "When I say *he*, I mean 'he or she,' and it's grammatically correct, so don't give me that look—if he has to shift his weight to his toes. It's like dancing."

The children looked blank. "Never mind. Just take my word for it. Keep your weight on the balls of your feet." She lifted her heels from the ground several times. "If you can do that, your weight's on the balls of your feet."

She looked around at dusty, attentive faces. "Then, on every pitch, you say to yourself, 'Hit it to me. Hit it to *me*. Hit it to *me*, to *me*, to ME.' I don't care if it's the truth or a lie. Say it. You'll field twice as well and, I guarantee, there's no way you can keep your weight on your heels while you're saying, 'Hit it to *me*.' Okay, go switch with the other kids."

It was warm for April, and exertion had made her feel damp. She pulled her T-shirt out of her cutoffs and wiped her face with it. A voice from behind the backstop said, "Cute tummy."

Meg looked up, embarrassed. Jack Deutsch was grinning at her, an impressive camera dangling by a strap from his hand.

"I thought the batter was unusually good for a twelve-year-old," he said. "Then I got closer and realized she was the coach. I liked your speech."

Meg eyed him. "So it sounds stupid. It works."

"No, I mean I liked your speech. You're a great coach. I've been watching for a while. The league may be in for a surprise."

Meg picked up a ball, tossed it into the air, and caught it. He made her want to have something to do with her hands. "You know about the league? Why? You freelance as the sports photographer for the local paper?"

"I watch games when I can," he said. He lifted the camera. "No, I take pictures, but not of baseball. You should come see them sometime."

It seemed a splendid idea to Meg. She would have liked to continue the conversation, but the bunters had arrived, each pleading to be assigned to shortstop. Jack lifted a hand.

"Get back to work, Coach," he said. "Let's have breakfast tomorrow. You make coffee; I'll bring the rest."

"Okay," said Meg. "*Not* before seven-thirty."

"Yes, ma'am," he replied. "But not much later."

She went through the same routine with the new group, trying to concentrate on the task at hand. Did he really think she had a cute tummy?

Meg liked the way Christine drove, confidently maneuvering the big car. They had driven to the park together from Christine's house.

"When does your team start practice, Teddy?" asked Meg, twisting around to look at him and Jane in the backseat.

"Tomorrow," he said.

"It sure was nice of you to help out with our practice."

Teddy had taken the throws in from the field while she hit. He shrugged. "I like it. And it was fun to listen to you."

"Whoa!" said Christine. "High praise." She gestured toward the back of the car. "What I want to know is, who died and made me equipment manager?"

"Do you or do you not have an immense, boatlike station wagon?" asked Meg. "Do I or do I not have an itsy hatchback?

I'd have to attach a trailer to haul two huge duffel bags full of shin protectors, batting helmets, and bases."

Christine pulled into her driveway and stopped next to Meg's car. "Come on in and have some iced tea while I start supper," she said. "The kids have homework to do . . ." She raised her voice as Jane and Teddy scrambled out of the car: ". . . which they will be *starting on immediately,* so we can talk."

Warren G. Harding had gamboled around the children and now ran up to knock Meg against the car as she got out.

"Off, Harding!" said Christine sternly and the big dog dropped his forefeet to the ground. He barked joyously.

"Progress!" said Meg. "He obeyed a command!"

"I know," said Christine. "It's staggering. For a while, he thought his name was Bad Dog." She touched his head as she went by. "You doof," she said affectionately.

The big kitchen was airy and pleasant. Meg helped herself to iced tea, poured a glass for Christine, and sat down on a sturdy, cream-colored chair at the table. Christine washed her hands and dried them on a towel with a beautifully stitched border hanging from a peg next to the sink.

"I have a towel like that," said Meg. "I've never dared use it."

Christine shrugged. "I guess I could frame them, but it makes me happy to use them. We don't go on cruises; we have casseroles for supper much too often; the phone bill isn't always paid on time. But every night we all rest our heads on one-hundred-percent cotton percale pillowcases with beautiful embroidery and crocheted edges. And I use these towels. All thanks to Hannah Ehrlich."

"I like your kitchen," said Meg. "I like your whole house."

"The benefit of being married to a contractor," said Christine, picking up a potato and beginning to peel it, "is cheap labor. My kitchen isn't as classic as yours; it doesn't look like you entered it from a time machine, like yours does."

"Well, no," said Meg. "It does contain the ubiquitous microwave . . ."

"Which, despite my love of huck-toweling kitchen linens, is not something I am willing to live without," replied Christine. "What do you think of the quiet rural life? Doesn't Harrison seem *slow* compared to Chicago? Are you bored to death?"

"No," said Meg truthfully. "I'm not. It's . . . *too* quiet sometimes. At night. But it's incredibly beautiful here. There are things I like a lot and other things . . . It's funny what you miss, you know?"

"I know. What do you miss?"

"Well, let's see. I'll bet Harrison doesn't pay a lot of attention to when the new Beaujolais arrives, and that'll be hard on me."

"Come *on*. What do you miss? I mean, besides your friends."

Meg thought about it. How could she explain how she'd felt hearing the shouts and laughter of adolescent boys playing basketball in the alley behind her apartment, seeing Asian children and black children and Hispanic children clambering over the equipment in the tiny city playground on the corner, watching middle-aged men playing bocce in the park while conversing in a language completely unknown to her?

"There's not a lot of diversity here," she said.

Christine slid the rubber band off her ponytail and shook her head, her hair falling down around her shoulders. "Tell me about it," she said. "No. Diversity is not our strong suit. You have to go all the way to New Hope to find that."

"Maybe I'll import some city kids," said Meg. "Build a dormitory out in back. Put up a hoop. Is Dan at work?" She upended her glass to slide an ice cube into her mouth and crunched it.

"Aiiii!" said Christine. "Stop! You're giving me the willies. Yes, he's at work. Or so he says." She gathered a handful of potato peels from the sink and threw them into the plastic bucket she kept for compost. The action was more violent than it needed to be.

"Where else would he be?" Meg didn't want to pry but was curious.

"He wouldn't be anywhere else." Christine sighed. She stood, gazing down into the sink. "I'm just being silly. He works all the time, when there's work. He's a good, solid, responsible, funny, wonderful man. But, damn! He's been acting so weird. He's gone all the time lately, and when he's home, we never talk. If he is around in the evening, he dozes off on the couch and then stumbles up to bed, and no matter how fast I get up there after him, he's sound asleep." She paused. "Or pretends to be."

She dropped a quartered potato into a pot and turned, leaning against the sink and looking at Meg. "You know what I miss? I miss sitting up in bed reading my book while he's reading his. I miss those minutes just before drifting off when I can rub the top of my foot against the bottom of his without worrying that I'll wake him up, because he isn't asleep yet either."

She looked past Meg to the clock on the wall and then turned and selected another potato. "Why am I telling you this?" she said. "We barely even know each other."

"Oh, pooh," said Meg. "We've been friends for, what? Almost a week? People have gotten married after knowing each other less time than that."

"Stupid people," said Christine. "But you're right. There are some people you can know for decades and not feel you have a clue about, and then there are others . . ." She used the peeler efficiently. "Along with a lack of diversity, one problem with the bucolic life is loneliness. After Hannah died and before you moved in, well, there just wasn't a woman around here except me. I don't know how pioneer ladies survived."

"I know you didn't ask for advice . . ." said Meg.

"Go right ahead."

"Follow him. Call up where he's supposed to be working. Go through his wallet. Look at the charge-card bills. Does he have a cell phone? Look at that bill."

Christine turned and fixed Meg with a disbelieving look. "Are you serious? I love him. I trust him."

"Yeah, you love him. No, you don't trust him. Not completely, or you wouldn't be worried. Why be worried? It takes too much out of a person to worry. Has he ever, uh, worried you before?"

"Not like this," said Christine slowly. She picked up her iced tea from the countertop and sat down across the table from Meg. "He's really private. Even after fifteen years, there's a lot about him I don't know, that he seems not to want me to know. He had a rotten childhood. I know that. He barely speaks to his parents. But he won't tell me much about it. And he has a brother I've never even met who, I think, has been in jail."

"You *think*?"

"Uh-huh. Odd, isn't it? Dan got a letter from him once, years ago. I wouldn't even have known about it, but I found it in a desk drawer at his office in town while I was looking for some deposit slips. I asked him about it. 'His name is Alan. He lives in Houston. He got in some trouble and I need to send him a thousand dollars,' he said."

She got up to put the pot on the stove and turned on a burner. "We didn't have a thousand dollars to spare. Had to borrow it. I wouldn't have minded—I mean, I'd find *ten* thousand dollars for my sister if she needed it—but he wouldn't even tell me what the trouble was. We had a major fight. It's the only big fight we ever had. He kept saying, 'You don't understand,' and I kept saying, 'That's right, but I'd like to.' I was furious."

"Old ties," said Meg. "They can get you."

"Yeah. Well, it's not his brother I'm concerned about now. It's that secretive side of my otherwise perfect husband. If he's upset about something, I want to know what."

"Maybe he really is just working too hard." Meg badly wanted to believe that. She didn't like the tightness she heard in her friend's voice.

Driving home, she passed Dan's dark blue truck as he came around the curve. He smiled and raised a hand. She waved back.

"Talk to your wife," she said grimly. She wished he could have heard her.

Sara's voice mail promised a return call, and it came as Meg was finishing dinner.

"If you'd stay home once in a while, you wouldn't have to pay for as many long-distance calls," said Meg.

Sara, her closest friend in Chicago, was full of questions.

"The house? I love it," said Meg in response. Her phone made the clicking noise that meant she had another call, which she ignored. "It's kind of a wreck, but I love it. It's got slanty cellar doors, can you believe it? And rosebushes. And a honeysuckle. And a huge pantry. And an attic with room to store things." The signal came again. "And everything smells good."

"Don't you want to get that call?" asked Sara.

"No," said Meg. "I've been waiting too long to talk to you."

"I won't go anywhere," said Sara. "It's probably the MacArthur Genius-Grant people."

"Gosh, you're right. I keep forgetting they're due to call. Hang on." She pressed the switch hook, but no one replied to her hello. She retrieved Sara.

"They gave up," she said. "I'll just have to keep struggling. But, like I said, this ain't a bad place to struggle."

"We've been hoping you'd hate it and come home again. Everybody misses you, and we're pining."

"I doubt that *everybody's* pining," said Meg dryly.

"Everybody who deserves you is pining."

"So come see me. I have a nice new friend named Christine you'd really like, and the town is cute and clean, and the cafe has homemade pie, and I miss you too."

They chatted for a few minutes until Sara's date arrived. She promised to call back soon, and Meg was smiling as she eased into a bathtub full of hot water. She leaned back and sighed contentedly and then felt her heart leap in her chest when the dog began barking furiously right outside the window.

Her sudden fright, and embarrassment at the intensity of it, made her angry. "Be *quiet!*" she yelled. What was the dog's problem? She wasn't the type to burst into excited yaps when she detected an interesting scent. Unlike Harding, when she gave chase, she did so silently.

Whatever had occasioned this uproar was undoubtedly harmless, but the heat and depth of the water had lost their ability to soothe, and Meg scrubbed hastily, eager to finish and dress and feel less vulnerable.

She was seated in front of the computer, halfway through a vocabulary exercise, when she remembered the call-waiting tone. Her fingers stopped moving across the keyboard. She sat back and took a deep breath. No, that was ridiculous. The caller had been Christine, or Mike, or perhaps Jack calling to cancel breakfast, and whoever it was would call back.

But by the time she went to bed, no one had called back.

The alarm woke her at six forty-five. She felt groggy and confused. With birds singing cheerfully outside, she lay still, trying to remember why she'd set the alarm. She'd started to slide back into slumber when she remembered and sat up, smiling happily.

Pulling on a chenille robe, she went into the bathroom to stand in front of the mirror. Her dark eyes looked puffy and surely, she thought, her hair could have more *shape*. Start some coffee, first. Coffee would make everything else that needed doing seem possible.

An hour later she was reasonably pleased. Clean, faded blue jeans and a rough, white, pullover shirt were the correct degree of presentable, she thought. Icy water had taken away the puffiness around her eyes, and shampoo and the blow-dryer had worked their magic. Her glossy dark hair curved away from her face. Daily labor on the fence had given her a faint sunburn that showed on her cheeks, her forearms, and under the V-neck of her shirt.

The dog barked in the front yard and, a moment later, a horn honked twice. Meg went out onto the porch. Jack's red pickup sat in the driveway, the window on the passenger's side rolled down.

"You want to save me from this ravening beast?" he asked, leaning toward the window from the driver's seat. "I thought I'd ignore her and just stride on up to the door with my normal, testosterone-charged *savoir faire,* but she's having none of it. 'Nice doggie, nice doggie' didn't impress her."

"Good grief," said Meg. "I guess you're the first visitor besides Christine since Canine Contentious decided she lives here. She keeps her distance from Christine, but she's never challenged her. I'm sorry!"

She wasn't sure how to handle the situation. She didn't yet have a secure enough relationship with the dog to train her. She wasn't sure if the pecking order had been clearly established. Still, the dog had submitted to being petted and, gradually, had come to request it. She stayed in Meg's general vicinity whenever she was outdoors and had spent one whole evening in the house, listening with a polite pretense of interest while Meg read aloud the worksheets she thought particularly witty.

"Just a minute," said Meg. "Stay there."

She went into the bedroom and took the sash out of her bathrobe, then went down the porch steps to the flagstone walk that led to the driveway and approached the truck. The dog was standing stiff-legged in the open gate, her tail raised and bristled, her nose wrinkled. She was emitting a low growl. Meg squatted and looked her blandly in the face.

"Enough!" she said, firmly but with no anger. The dog's eyes moved from the truck to Meg. She closed her mouth and stopped growling.

"Good girl," said Meg, reaching out a hand and putting it on the dog's head. She looped the sash around her neck, tied it, and stood up. "Heel," she said, tugging lightly at the sash.

The dog, moving reluctantly, walked with Meg onto the grass.

"Go on in," said Meg, and Jack swung down from the truck, lifted out a brown paper bag, and disappeared into the house. The dog watched him intently, growling softly, and, when Meg untied the sash, ran up onto the porch to scratch at the door.

"I feel like an idiot," said Meg, having left the dog, discontented, outside and joined Jack in the kitchen. "It never even occurred to me that she'd hold her ground. She tends to avoid people, unless, like Mike, they grab at her."

"Sounds like Mike," he replied. "Grabby."

Meg looked at him. He waved a hand. "Tell you later, when I know you better. Listen, no dog worth its salt lets a stranger walk right into a yard. You should be proud of her, not embarrassed. What's her name?"

"It keeps changing," she said. "Today 'Scrappy' seems good. You like dogs?"

He nodded. "All except the tiny little yippy ones. Even them, I don't mind; I just don't think they're dogs, really. That one, however, is a *dog,* regardless of the peccaries among her ancestors."

Meg laughed. "I'll admit, she leaves something to be desired in the beauty department. And, come to think of it, the fragrance department . . . But she's making progress in the 'Don't come near me or I'll chew on your face' department."

"I hope she continues that progress," said Jack. "I will woo her assiduously, but there have been times when my charm has taken years to work."

"But eventually it does, right?"

He winked at her. "You bet." He started taking things out of the paper bag—a large covered bowl of strawberries, a plate of ham sliced paper-thin, and a box that, when opened, revealed huge golden muffins.

"Yum!" said Meg. "Blueberry muffins! Where did those come from?"

78

"Long and arduous toil," he replied. "First I milked the cow, churned some butter, gathered eggs—"

"Did you, at least, really make them?"

"No. They're from the bakery. But they're still warm, so pour some coffee, ma'am, and let's eat."

It would be hard, thought Meg—looking at him as he leaned back, coffee cup in hand, long legs stretched out under the table—to imagine a more pleasant way to start the day. He was wearing a blue work shirt with buttons in the shape of rabbits. In the pocket was an envelope.

"I like your shirt," said Meg. "I didn't know they made work shirts with bunnies on them."

"The market for this style is small," he said. "Apparently, many men think buttons in whimsical shapes give the wrong impression about their masculinity. I've just written to my niece, suggesting she set a new fashion trend in the third grade by spending her allowance in the notions section of the dime store and following my example." He patted his pocket.

"You write letters?" asked Meg. "I don't know anyone besides my parents who still writes letters. Don't you have a phone?"

"Don't you know what phone calls cost?" He smiled at her. "It's amazing to me that people blow money that way. My niece and nephew don't think a thing about it. My phone'll ring and it's Jeffrey, long-distance, with his latest uproarious joke. I love it, of course, but it doesn't make any sense to me. I thought schools still taught kids how to write."

"Not really," said Meg.

When he arose to carry his plate to the sink, she held up a hand.

"Stop. You've done enough. I'll clean up. You can drop by sometime and pick up your dishes. Or I'll bring them over."

"Great," he said. "The guys tease me when I show up with dishpan hands. But before I get going, I noticed a dip in your dining room ceiling. You got a leak in the attic?"

Meg lifted her shoulders. "I don't think so, but I don't *know.*" She walked into the dining room and stood peering up at the ceiling. The dip was barely noticeable. "It looks all right to me."

"Show me the attic stairs," he said. "I'll just go up and check it out."

Meg found it odd that she enjoyed his good-tempered bossiness. She had bridled and, more often than not, flat-out balked when Jim had told her what to do. Jack, however, had no arrogance in his voice, just an easy confidence that they were of like minds.

The door at the foot of the stairs was ajar. She pulled it open all the way and climbed the creaking steps with him. He paced off a distance from one wall and pushed a foot against the floor.

"What?" she asked.

"I think you're all right," he said, looking up at the rafters. "But I'd like to check again sometime right after a rain." He smiled at her and indicated his foot as he pressed it downward again. "This isn't a thorough analysis."

Meg pointed around the room at small metal boxes that stuck up through the planks that formed the floor. "What are those? Those things the pipes lead to?"

"Junction boxes," he said. "For wiring. The wires are in the pipes." He glanced at her. "You know, junctions. Where things come together."

"The wires are in the pipes? Doesn't wiring go through conduit?"

He laughed at her. "Get used to living in an old house, babe," he said. "Conduit hadn't been invented when this work was done." He looked critically around the room. "I'm not sure if the cotton gin had been. You know, the boxes should be covered, especially in a house this old. Want me to get an electrician to come by?"

Meg shook her head. "Not right now," she said, trying to think about her dwindling checking account, trying not to think about his casual and probably meaningless familiarity. "Soon, though, if it's important."

He looked around again. "It is. Just don't store stacks of magazines up here in the meantime."

"Heck, no," said Meg. "What would I use for an end table?"

"Right," he said. "Let's go feed leftover ham to The Beast."

Meg had to admire him. Not many people would have been willing to make an effort to become friends with such an unappealing animal. She had, of course, but the dog hadn't been aggressive to her. Jack squatted and held out a hand. The dog regarded him suspiciously.

"Don't glare at her," said Meg.

"That's not a glare. That's me not showing fear."

"Oh," said Meg. "Well, shift your gaze."

"I think I see a friendship blooming," she said as Jack stood, wiping his hand on his hip. "You are a brave soul."

"Who has to get crackin'," he said. "I promised to get the Delaneys' living room sanded by noon. God willing and the creek don't rise, I will. But barely."

He opened the passenger's door of his pickup and lifted out a beautifully made wren house. "Housewarming," he said. "It just needs a post in a shady spot."

"It's wonderful!" said Meg. "Deutsch colonial, is it? But do wrens actually care if their homes are sanded and stained?"

"Maybe not yet. But good taste is largely a matter of exposure to beautiful things. Next year, they'll be back, educated by their experience and unwilling to live in anything but the best." He pitched his deep voice high. " 'No, Seymour, I won't even consider this . . . this *slum* after that lovely place we had last year! You just keep flying, mister!' "

Meg was still grinning as he maneuvered the truck around in the driveway and waved good-bye. When she turned to go into the house, she nearly tripped over the dog and realized for the first time that the animal hadn't left her side.

"Now what are you so clingy for all of a sudden?" she asked.

Nine

$\mathcal{J}$ane dipped a brush into white paint, smoothed it on the rim of the can, and stroked it against the fence.

"Fresh paint looks so clean," she said.

"It sure does," said Meg. "And you're doing that very nicely, but I'm worried about your sweater."

"I won't make a mess."

"That's what they all say," said Meg. "It's virtually impossible to paint anything, even a birdhouse, without making some sort of mess. You've already got paint on your hair."

"I do?"

"Yup. So let me get you an old sweatshirt. That's too nice a sweater to ruin."

When Meg came back out with a sweatshirt, Jane stood up and shrugged carefully out of her cardigan. "It's my favorite sweater. I wear it all the time."

Meg could see why. It was hand-knit, made of a thick yarn in periwinkle blue. The color was good with the child's burnished hair. "It's beautiful. Did your mom make it?"

"No. She sews things, but she can't knit or crochet. Mrs. Ehrlich made it for me." Jane pulled the sweatshirt on and, when her head had emerged, continued as she worked her arms into the sleeves. "She was teaching me to crochet. She'd already taught me to embroider. I can do all kinds of embroidery stitches. I embroidered a toaster cover for her that looked like a little house with a door and windows and flower boxes on the windowsills."

She picked up her brush and started working again, with Meg painting alongside. "You miss her, don't you," said Meg.

Jane sighed. "A lot."

They worked for a while in silence. Then Jane spoke quietly. "Did you ever notice that if somebody old dies, people just say, 'Oh, dear, that's too bad.' If somebody young dies, they say, 'No! How awful! What did she die of?' "

"But that's just because it's more shocking when a young person dies, don't you think?" asked Meg.

"*I* think it's shocking when anybody dies who shouldn't have," said Jane. She turned an accusing eye on Meg. "Did you ever ask what she died of?"

Meg was taken aback. "No, I don't think I did," she said. "I guess I just assumed it was . . . you know, because her heart stopped."

"Well, *every*body's heart stops when they die," said Jane. "That's *not* very specific."

"No," said Meg. "You're right. I'm sorry. I didn't think about it carefully. What *did* she die of?"

Jane moved down several pickets, taking her paint can with her. "She had a jumpy heart. She said her medicine made it all right. So she must not have taken her medicine, and that's what she died of. I feel mad about it all the time, but I shouldn't have been mad at you. You didn't even know her."

"It takes a while after someone dies to stop being mad about it," said Meg. "Sometimes it takes a long time."

"But I'm not just mad she died," said Jane. "I'm mad because nobody was watching out to make sure it didn't happen. All she had to do was take her medicine, and she didn't. And so she died, and now one of the people who should have been more careful of her is living in her house and another one is using her best silver and lots of them have her stocks. It isn't fair."

"But you're the one who got her silver, and you *were* watching out for her."

"Somebody else got her *best* silver," said Jane. "Probably somebody who should've been helping her not forget. She had lots of beautiful things, you know, so greedy people might have been happy she died instead of being careful that she wouldn't. And *somebody* got a whole house."

"Michael Mulcahy couldn't drive a forty-mile round trip every morning and every evening just to make sure his aunt took her medicine, could he?" asked Meg in what she hoped was a mild and reasonable tone. "And he doesn't seem the type who'd rejoice over someone's death."

Jane kept painting. "He could pick up a telephone, couldn't he?" She was not giving in, and Meg had to admit she had a point.

"But there's no reason to think she *didn't* take her medicine, honey," she said. "Medicine isn't magic; it won't keep a person alive forever." She glanced at the girl and found her looking seriously back, the brush dangling, momentarily ignored, from her hand.

"I think she forgot," said Jane. "She was worried about something, really worried, and maybe she was thinking about that instead of her medicine. She started forgetting a lot, so much that she had to have tricks to help her remember things. She even forgot her favorite silver box."

"Her favorite silver box?"

Jane sat back on the grass and stretched out her legs, then resumed her crouched position and went back to work. "She was telling me about how fancy some people's houses used to be and the things they used to use, like napkin rings and little trays to put calling cards on and fancy bottles for ink. And rich ladies had jewel caskets. That's what they were called, *caskets*. Weird, huh?"

"But it's a different meaning," said Meg. "Just a small box for something valuable."

"I know. I said, 'Were those for buried treasure?' And she told me what you said. She still had some that her husband inherited. Her favorite was a silver one his mother got on her twelfth birthday, and she sent me up to the attic to get it. But when I brought it down, she just kept looking at it and looking, and she said it wasn't the way she remembered. It made her really unhappy to forget. She had to go lie down and couldn't help me study for the spelling test."

"Then maybe she did forget her medicine," said Meg. "But it still doesn't seem fair to blame people who may not even have realized her memory had gotten so bad."

The girl was silent for a few moments, then spoke again. "Mom says it was just 'her time.' Maybe it was. But it was too soon."

It always is, thought Meg. When you love somebody.

"How come your mom says that Harding has no reliable moral center?" she asked, when enough silence had passed to rob the change in topics of abruptness.

"He steals things," said Jane, giggling. "He's really good at it."

Meg carefully removed a small tuft of dog hair that had blown onto the wet paint and wiped her fingers on the grass. "Like what?"

"He opens the refrigerator, for one thing," said Jane. "I mean, he used to. Didn't you ever wonder why Mom puts a big clamp on the refrigerator doors when she leaves the house if he's indoors?"

"I guess I never saw her leave the house when he was indoors," said Meg. "He opens the *refrigerator?*"

"Yeah. And he eats everything he can stuff into himself and hides everything else." Jane moved down another picket. "One time he ate a pound of raw hamburger, a loaf of whole-wheat bread, half a roast chicken, a package of cream cheese, and the rest of the eggs. He ate the eggs in the living room. On the rug. Mom was *really* mad."

"I'll bet!" said Meg.

"And then we found a tub of margarine in the hall closet in Teddy's gym bag under his cleats and a bag of salad in Dad's fishing net in the basement and a package of hot dogs in the trash can in the bathroom. And one time, he came with me to Mrs. Ehrlich's and he went in the kitchen while we were in the living room and he ate a whole plate of cookies off the table *and* her evening pills. I didn't take him there anymore."

Meg noticed that Jane's eyes were bright with laughter. She could talk about Mrs. Ehrlich without necessarily descending into angry misery.

"Does the clamp work?" asked Meg.

"Oh, sure," said Jane. "When we remember to put it on."

Jane had gone home for supper, and Meg was pressing plastic wrap around the brushes when Mike pulled into the driveway. The dog, who had been lying on the porch, got up and ran toward the fence, barking.

"Ah, we meet again," said Mike, moving his hands off the top of the pickets and putting them in his pockets. He was wearing pleated trousers and a soft, cream-colored shirt with a banded collar. Meg thought he looked yummy.

"Those down by you are dry," she said. "But don't touch anything much farther along."

John Eppler's car passed, going toward his house, and Meg lifted a hand in greeting, but the man's eyes remained fixed on the road, and no wave was returned. That's odd, she thought.

Mike indicated the dog. "I don't know why she hates me," he said.

"She probably doesn't," replied Meg. "But she doesn't seem to have much use for men. And you did try to grab her. For all she knows, you're a vivisectionist."

86

"That line of work never appealed to me," he said. "Until now."

"Don't be mean. Come inside and have some coffee. I've got three or four of Christine's cookies left, too. Just enough to get you through until dinner."

She fixed the dog with a stern look and said, "Enough!" The dog's barking turned to a soft, intermittent growl.

"I'll hold her. She's not trained yet, so that's the only way to guarantee safe passage. Go on in, and I'll finish cleaning up here and join you. The coffee's in the left-hand cupboard next to the sink."

As the screen door closed behind him, Meg remembered the condition of the house. She hadn't vacuumed since she arrived, and the lunch dishes hadn't been washed. She shrugged mentally. Mike didn't seem the type to care and, if he did, tough. She hadn't invited him.

When she pushed off her shoes on the porch and went in, he was looking through her tapes in the living room. "I started the coffee," he said. "Nice range of stuff you have here, and a lot of it. You haven't made the big switch to compact disk, I see."

"Someday," said Meg. "When I marry a rich man."

"They're not expensive," he said. "I'd think an heiress could afford a CD player."

"It's not the player; it's the CDs," she said. "I put most of my records onto tapes, but I can't put my tapes onto CDs."

"Is this all you have?" he asked.

"What? You can't find something you like among these? Yes, that's all. The rest of the cartons there are just books. I use a *lot* of reference books, but I've needed only a few dictionaries on the job I'm doing now, so I've neglected the unpacking."

He went back to the tapes, scanning their hand-printed labels.

"What do you want to hear?" asked Meg. "I can tell you where to look."

"No," he said. "I want to see what you've got. You can tell a lot about a person by seeing what music she likes."

"Well, search to your heart's content. Or I could just tell you what you'd discover. I am brilliant, intriguing, and discerning and have considerably more than my fair share of charm."

"Well, yeah," said Mike. "I knew *that.*"

Meg went into the kitchen to get coffee. Returning, she smiled at the familiar, rhythmic clapping at the beginning of "My Boyfriend's Back." Mike had found the tape she'd labeled "Dancing." She went across the floor to set the mugs on a low table next to the couch, but by that time the Angels had launched into the lyric. "My boyfriend's back, and you're gonna be in trouble. (Hey la-di-la, my boyfriend's back.)" The rhythm of the song made it impossible to walk normally. She took small dancing steps across the floor.

Mike laughed and the instant the coffee was safely on the table, he took her left hand and pulled her into the clear space of the room. Meg didn't protest, because the music filling the room made her want to move, and Mike . . . Mike knew how to dance.

"And he knows that you've been tryin', and he knows that you've been lyin'." Mike's hand held hers firmly as their arms extended and bent again. He released her to let her turn, his hand trailing along her back to find hers again as she completed the spin. They turned sideways, arms up and over each other's heads as they slid apart, one pair of hands sliding down their arms to clasp at the end of the movement. Simple steps, complex steps. Another few bars and the music ended.

They stood laughing in the brief silence of the tape, and then Willie Nelson's "All of Me" began.

"One more," said Mike. "A slow one, just to balance things out." He didn't wait for her to answer.

It had been years since Meg had glided across a floor with someone who knew exactly what he was doing and loved to do it. She let him make the decisions and responded to the subtle clues, moving smoothly in whatever direction he chose. His chin rested lightly against the top of her head.

They both sang the last line loudly with the tape. "You took the part that once was my heart, so why not take all of me?"

"You're good!" said Meg, turning down the volume on the tape player and lifting her coffee. "Really!"

Mike inclined his head. "I am, aren't I?" he said. "Now you understand how I got my high school nickname, 'Dreamboat.' Oh, and you are too."

"Well," said Meg, "thank you. Slow dancing's easy. It's just like baseball."

They took their coffee out to the porch. Meg had found two of the big metal chairs Christine had encouraged her to buy. Christine had been right. They looked perfect and were blissfully comfortable. The dog sat on the grass a few yards away, regarding Mike with suspicion.

"It's amazing," said Mike. "That dog manages to combine a vast number of physical traits in such a way that the result contains not so much as one pleasing element."

"I'm getting used to her," said Meg. "But you're wrong. The space on the top of her head between her ears is exactly the right width."

"I wonder where the heck she came from."

"I'll never know," said Meg. "But she used to belong to somebody."

"What makes you think so?"

"She's socialized, for one thing. Oh, go on, scoff. She may not want to cuddle in *your* lap, but being socialized doesn't mean being robbed of the powers of discrimination. The really telling clue—now listen carefully, a person in your line of work should be interested in the concept of clues—is that she's housebroken. Believe it or not, that isn't an inborn trait."

Mike put his cup down on the porch and rocked back slightly in his chair, clasping his hands behind his head. "What's her name?"

"She doesn't have one. I keep trying things, but they're not right. I had a dog named Tansy when I was a kid. This one doesn't look like her name could be Tansy."

"No, but if you're leaning toward flowers, how about Bladderwort? She does look like her name could be Bladderwort. Or Locoweed. Or Cocklebur. Hey, I've got it. How about Dogbane?"

"Stop!" said Meg, coffee sloshing from her cup. She swiped at her wet shirt. "Look what you made me do. But you reminded me; I want to see Mrs. Ehrlich's garden . . . I mean, your garden. Christine says it's marvelous."

"If it comes up anything like last year, it will be," he said. "Aunt Hannah was quite the horticulturist. There isn't much to see yet. Some hyacinths and a lot of narcissus and tulips. But the lilies won't be out until June, or the roses. Then, begosh and begorra, it'll be worth looking at."

"Which reminds me to ask," she said, "how a Mulcahy can be the nephew of an Ehrlich."

"Mixed marriages," said Mike. "Ever heard of those? Sometimes Lutherans marry Methodists." His voice took on an exaggerated brogue. "And sometimes an Irish lad's eye falls on a bonny German lassie. Me mither was just such a lassie and Aunt Hannah's baby sister. Me father passed his pure Irish name on to me, God bless 'im."

"Thank you for that thrilling explanation. You will now, please, return to your normal, annoying manner of speaking instead of this newly irritating way," said Meg.

"But I was just warming up for a few verses of 'Danny Boy.' I think you're rude."

"Shut up," said Meg. She sighed contentedly. "I love narcissus."

"I must have thirty kinds," said Mike. "Lots of them are ones you've never seen. Stop by anytime. If I'm not there, just walk around."

"Come see the creek," said Meg, getting up. "I want you to understand how right I was to take this place."

The dog followed at a distance while they walked through the meadow and the trees. The sun was going down, and the woods were deep in shadow, but there was enough light left to see by. They stood at the edge of the tumbling water. Mike took Meg's hand and squeezed it.

"Okay," he said. "You were right."

Nighttime was the lonely time. It had been the lonely time for months, but it was worse now. At night, the softness of the air made Meg's skin hurt. The green of meadows and trees, stretching away to the rounded mountains, was invisible. The cement of the kitchen stoop was no longer warm from the sun. The birds were silent.

At night, it often seemed to Meg that she had made a terrible mistake. She had told herself she was going *to* something, but she had merely fled. A door had opened, and she had taken off running, terrified of the one that had closed behind her. What had she seen on the other side of that open door? A house in the country with land and trees and a creek. If she had looked more carefully, she would have seen the isolation, enforced by miles of curving black road. She would have seen the faded yellow of the house turning colorless in the moonlight.

Ten

The sun was setting behind her as Meg turned into her driveway. The post office had been closed, as she'd known it would be, but she'd dropped her stamped parcel in the box with a Priority Mail sticker in front of the building. It was a relief to have one piece of her work finished and sent off, small as the installment was. She'd celebrated by stopping at the drive-in on the outskirts of town for a hamburger and eating it slowly while teenagers sat with their feet on the dashboard in the car next to her. She listened with a pretense of self-absorbed thought while they maligned the local movie theater's recently adopted policy of checking IDs for R-rated movies and parents' conservative views of their planned activities. The conversation was interesting.

"You know what always works for me?" asked a pretty red-headed girl with curls and the face of a Botticelli angel. "I say, 'You don't trust me!' and my dad falls all over himself trying to think of a way out."

"Oh, yeah, that works for me, too," replied the driver. He slapped away a hand reaching over from the backseat toward the onion rings he was holding. "Every time."

As Meg drove home, she tried to come up with the wise response she could use, some years in the future, should she be in a position to need one. She hadn't developed it by the time she turned into her driveway.

A figure arose on her shadowed porch and walked toward the gate. Meg stopped the car and got out, the dog leaping excitedly upon her.

"Mike! How long have you been here?" she asked, bending to pat the dog, who was bouncing on her back legs and scrabbling at Meg's thighs. "Ouch! Off!" Meg raised her knee against the dog's chest, and she dropped to the ground.

"Most of my adult life," said Mike.

"But where's your car?"

"At my house. Last I checked, pedestrian traffic was still legal in this state. I dropped by to see if you wanted to sample the clean night air we enjoy in this rural valley—no, please don't let that animal through with you—and your mangy cur came tearing around the house and crashing against the gate, which I, tidy lad that I am, had neatly shut behind me. She's been hanging around, snarling and giving me dirty looks, ever since. So I've been sprawled on your porch, hoping you hadn't gone to the Berkshires."

Meg unlocked the front door. "She has not been snarling, you big scaredy-cat. Come on in; the dog isn't going to eat you. She wants some food, yes, but she's rapidly getting used to the kind that comes from Purina."

She poured dog food from a sack in the pantry into a shallow pottery bowl and set it on the kitchen floor. "I'm letting the dog in now," she said. "Do you want to climb up on the cabinet? Hide in the attic? Lock yourself in the bathroom?"

"I don't know. Will she tear out huge hunks of my flesh?"

"I doubt it," said Meg. "Let's see."

She opened the kitchen door and grabbed the dog as she raced through. "This is Mike," she said. "Remember? He's the one who wanted to name you Cocklebur. Would you care to respond to that suggestion?"

The dog barked.

"Enough," said Meg firmly. The dog subsided. "Now eat your dinner."

"So," said Mike, seating himself at the kitchen table, "want to go for that walk? There's hardly any traffic, and there's a turnoff down toward John Eppler's that goes back to the foundation of an old stone house. The moon's out. Want to see an abandoned homesite in the moonlight?"

"No," said Meg. "I've got to work. I mean, *got* to." She reached into the cupboard and took out a can of coffee.

"Too many baseball practices. You've been neglecting your professional obligations in the mistaken belief that practice will have some effect on the outcome of our bet."

"We've had two practices. After the second, most of the kids got the concept of which base to head for in the event that contact is made with the ball. They shouldn't have any trouble beating you."

"So you've undoubtedly thought of what it is we're betting."

"I'm working on it," said Meg, spooning coffee into the basket. "But not tonight. Tonight I'm working on using familiar words to decode unfamiliar ones."

"Okay, I'll help. What unfamiliar word do you want to use? How about *victory*? No, never mind, you probably want a word that's unfamiliar to the *students.*"

Meg turned and leaned against the counter, crossing her arms. "So, think of one."

"Like what?"

She shrugged. "I don't care. Ask them what a junction box is."

"Why?" asked Mike. "Are we training electricians?"

"You're missing the point," said Meg. "Okay, how about *ruth.* Tell the kids all about how they shouldn't sit around scratching their heads and whining when they run into *ruth,* not that they'll ever run into it, of course, but pretend they will."

"I can tell them that. I can be quite stern about whining," said Mike. "But if I need to tell them what it means, you'll have to point me to a dictionary."

Meg poured water into the coffeemaker and turned it on. "Yeah, you'll be a big help," she said. "Oh, excuse me, you're being sweet and offering assistance, and I'm giving you a hard time. How *ruthless* of me."

"Ah," said Mike.

"Good night," said Meg.

Opening her eyes in the mornings, Meg would stretch and smile and wonder if the undefined possibilities that seemed to hover in the very air were based on any reality or simply on the contrast daytime provided to night. This morning was sunny and mild, and a breeze blew through the window of her office. It moved the lightweight curtains and carried the bubbling song of a house wren.

"Another one done!" she said, clicking on "Save" and naming her file. It was time for a break. She called Christine and invited herself for coffee.

When she pushed opened the Ruschmans' kitchen door in response to a "Come in," Christine was on the phone but gestured toward the coffeepot and then at a spot across from her at the kitchen table.

"Sit down," she mouthed. Out loud, she said, "About a hundred and fifty thousand." She listened, then continued. "Four boys and two girls. Just like stair steps—two, four, six, eight, ten, and twelve."

Meg poured herself a cup of coffee, refilled Christine's, and sat, watching her friend and openly listening. Christine had pulled her pale hair into a French braid, and the sophisticated look was flattering.

"Let's see. We buy Champion and Adidas and Hanes that I can think of, right off the bat. No. Yes, I guess so. Oh, absolutely. 'Made in America' labels are big at our house."

Meg caught her friend's eye and raised her eyebrows.

"I've got to go," said Christine. "Is that enough to be helpful? Sure. No problem." She hung up.

"What in heaven's name was that?" asked Meg.

"Market research," said Christine.

"Oh, ugh," said Meg. "I hate those calls!"

"Tell me about it," said Christine, sitting down at the table and lifting her cup. "This was something about sweatshirts."

"But what was the 'one hundred and fifty thousand'? And the six kids?"

"That's our mythical income and our mythical children," said Christine.

"Why mythical?" asked Meg.

"I don't buy sweatshirts at a store," said Christine. "I buy sweatshirts at church rummage sales. So the truth wouldn't help the poor researcher at all. And our income, which is considerably less than a hundred and fifty thousand dollars, is nobody's business. And two children isn't very interesting. But *six* . . . now that's interesting. And the poor woman was very friendly and polite, and she has a horrid job. Can you imagine having to call up complete strangers and ask them what kind of sweatshirts they buy?"

"So you just make things up?" Meg was aghast.

Christine smiled and shrugged. "Why not? Do I care how sweatshirt manufacturers make their decisions? I don't think so. But some woman is trying to support her family by getting statistics for them, so . . ."

"Do you always do this?" asked Meg, looking at her friend. It would never have occurred to her to pull the answers to a researcher's questions out of the air.

"No, sometimes I don't have time and just say the kitchen's on fire. But when I have time, I try to be helpful. You want toast? It's homemade bread. Best thing you ever tasted. Five of my six children helped me make it. The two-year-old just played with some dough."

The toast was good. Meg licked a finger and picked up the last of the crumbs. "I think we should start Jane at first base," she said. "Her height's a real advantage. And her arm won't be a problem there. Not that her arm is weak; the problem is she's too strong. From third, she's likely to put the ball into the bleachers. If she overthrows home, at least there's a backstop."

"I don't want to talk about baseball," said Christine. "I want to talk about something interesting, like the possible dangers of two-timing Mike by having breakfast with Jack."

"I should never have told you about that breakfast," said Meg.

Christine swung a crossed leg under the table and kicked Meg. "I'm voting for Mike. Dan, on the other hand, is all for Jack. Dan thinks Jack went through hell with Stephanie and deserves a really nice girl for a change. He's chosen you to be the really nice girl."

"What does Dan know about me?" asked Meg. "We sure haven't spent a lot of time together, and I thought you guys weren't talking much."

"We talk," said Christine. "Conversations about other people are easy. You are a subject of great fascination. I would look askance at you, except that Dan's interest seems merely friendly. We have a wager."

"Good grief," said Meg. "What happens when you both lose?"

"Aw, come on! You can't be dumb enough to break *both* their hearts."

"I am not," said Meg, "breaking anyone's heart. Including my own." She was annoyed and wondered why. Probably because she knew how unrealistic Christine's joking assumptions were. "I'd think you had better things to worry about."

Christine swallowed hard and blinked.

"Gosh, I'm sorry," said Meg, realizing her clumsiness. "I meant generally. I didn't mean . . ."

"No," said Christine weakly. "It's not your fault."

"Come on, Christine. You don't really think Dan's carrying on with someone, do you?"

"No. Yes. I don't know." She got up and brought the coffeepot to the table, then stood holding it for a moment. Meg watched her in silence.

"I must think something," Christine went on after a moment. "My house is spotless. I'm deeply into the 'when you can't clean up the mess inside you, clean up the mess outside' syndrome."

"It is noticeably sparkling," said Meg. "I didn't realize that wasn't normal for you."

"Not like this, it isn't. The only activity that gives me real pleasure these days is pouring boiling water over clean dishes."

She put the coffeepot back and sat down. "If he's not feeling guilty about something, then I've lost my mind. Talk about the classic symptoms. The other night I woke up, and he was standing by the bedroom window, just looking out, not moving. I asked why he was awake, and he kind of started and then he said that Teddy had been having a bad dream."

Meg was dubious. This hardly sounded suspicious. "So you sleep more soundly than he does. Teddy *does* have bad dreams, doesn't he? All kids do."

Christine shook her head. "Teddy has bad dreams sometimes. And yes, I sleep more soundly than Dan does. But Harding was down at the foot of the bed. When Teddy has a bad dream, he can't go back to sleep unless Harding's in bed with him, which is, believe me, just fine with Harding. The only way to keep him out of Teddy's bed is to shut his door. So that means Teddy's door was shut, which Dan would never do to a child who might call out again. And Harding wasn't in there."

She traced the top of her coffee cup with her forefinger. "Oh, blast! I'm just going to say it. I have to talk to someone; I just have to! I was looking for my sunglasses the other day while

Dan was taking a nap. And I'd looked everywhere, so I tried his truck because we'd been downtown together."

She stretched out a leg to jam her hand down into her jeans pocket. She withdrew a crumpled piece of paper and pushed it across the table. "This was in the glove compartment."

Meg smoothed the creases and looked at the paper. It was the purchaser's receipt for a money order. It was made out to a Leslie McAlester, and it was in the amount of fifteen thousand dollars. She looked up at Christine.

"No, there's no Leslie McAlester in town. Dan is not doing work for anyone named Leslie McAlester. Or any other McAlester. And that's a money order. If Dan was buying materials or refunding what he'd charged for a roof that blew off because he forgot to nail it down, he'd use a company check, not a money order. If, for some mysterious business reason, he used a money order, he'd fill in the blank line after 'For.' It would say, 'Italian floor tiles' or 'Refund,' or *something*. This line is just blank. If he used company money for this, how are we going to get by? That would be the entire profit on the job he's been working on for three months."

"You've got to talk to him."

Christine looked past Meg's head, out the window next to the table. Her blue eyes were dull. "There isn't a single finch anywhere near the bird feeder," she said. "I need to get some thistle."

"Christine . . ."

"Somebody called this morning, really early. He talked in the hallway. Then, while the kids and I were eating breakfast, he went into the living room to make a call. There's a phone right here."

"And you think it wasn't just a regular business call?"

"At seven-thirty? Maybe. But why go off to the living room?"

"For quiet?"

"Or for privacy."

The question, thought Meg, was, did Christine really want

to know? Surely she would have thought of how to find out, if she did.

Christine reached for the phone and pushed "redial." She listened and hung up.

"It was the weather," she said. "He called the weather."

"Well, then," said Meg, lifting her cup in a congratulatory gesture. "See, you *have* lost your mind. Isn't that a relief?"

Christine took the plates to the sink. She held them above her head and dropped them. China crashed against cast iron and broke to smithereens.

"He never calls the weather. He listens to the radio, which is free. That was a second call. *He* thought about redial, too."

Meg sat by the edge of the creek, her arms around her knees. The water flashed in the sunlight. A cardinal sounded nearby, and a darting redness caught her eye. The creek made its noises, but Meg was not soothed. Fifteen thousand dollars!

She had spent most of the morning working, with varying degrees of success, and finished a unit of lessons. Needing something more active, she'd carried the abandoned boxes down from the attic and gone through them. None contained anything nice enough to have belonged to her great-aunt. They must have been left behind on purpose, filled, as they were, with the kinds of things that seem worth saving just long enough for one to find a carton and become rubbish the moment the lid is taped shut.

These lids weren't taped shut, though they once had been. It appeared that the tenant who'd left them had opened them to see if there was anything worth hauling to a new home. Meg reached the same conclusion that person had. There wasn't. There was an engagement calendar from seven years before, costume jewelry with broken clasps, half-used spools of thread, old letters, empty cologne bottles . . . There was no point in going through it all. There was nothing that could conceivably be of any value, though at least Meg could tell from the addresses on the few letters with envelopes that the boxes had belonged to Angie Morrison and that she had lived in several different places prior to taking up residence in Harrison, Pennsylvania. It wasn't surprising she'd abandoned the boxes. Meg didn't hesitate to dump the contents into large garbage bags and set them out by the toolshed, where they could stay until she'd gathered enough trash for a trip to the dump.

Someday soon, she'd have to take similar steps with the contents of the heavy built-in drawers at the back of the pantry. She had tugged them out while unpacking, seeking a place for tablecloths, and discovered a sizable collection of junk—rusty screws, dented ice-cube trays, a coiled clothesline, an electric frying pan with one of its legs missing. She'd pushed everything back in and stored the tablecloths on the shelves in the back bedroom closet. Worse than dealing with the drawers, she'd have to wash and repaint the shelves. That would be a major job. They rose to within eighteen inches of the ceiling, and Meg didn't even want to think about the depth of the dust and grime on the ones too high for her to see. She grimaced, thinking about it. Anything could be up there.

The dog was lying not far away, having returned from chasing something through the trees. She was wearing a collar. It had a ring for a leash to be snapped onto. It did not, however, have a rabies tag. The dog had submitted to a bath the day before, standing patiently in the creek and looking aggrieved. She smelled good.

Meg slapped her thigh encouragingly. The dog came closer and sat. Meg reached out and stroked her, moving down her sides and legs. The dog didn't move.

"Good girl," said Meg.

The dog nudged her hand, and Meg resumed petting her. "We're going to go see this person called a vet," she said. "I don't know if you've ever seen this kind of person, but you have to go because it's against the law for you not to have a rabies shot. I don't do things that are against the law, and it wouldn't be right for you to ask me to. I am trusting you to be nice in the waiting room. I know you like other dogs. Or put up with them at least. That is, if we can extrapolate from Harding. But you can't go growling at elderly gentlemen with their cats. Understand?"

The dog wagged her tail.

"Good," said Meg.

Christine hadn't been home when Meg called, but Mike had recommended a veterinary clinic outside of town. "I've never filed a malpractice suit against any of them," he said.

The waiting room at the clinic attested to its popularity. Unsure of her dog's sociability, Meg found a seat separated from other pets and looked around. A woman across the room, holding a puppy on her lap, seemed familiar. As Meg caught her eye, she nodded, smiled, and got up to move closer.

"You're Meg Kessinger, my son's coach, aren't you?" said the woman, glancing at Meg's dog. "What a . . . an interesting dog." She sat down and placed the puppy on the floor, where it nuzzled against and pawed at Meg's dog. The older dog, to Meg's relief, responded tolerantly.

"*That's* where I know you from," said Meg. "You're Brian's mother?"

The woman nodded. "Cheryl Warren," she said. "I'm so glad you decided to coach. I wasn't going to let Brian play this year, but when I heard there was a new coach . . ."

Meg frowned slightly to indicate confusion.

"Brian was on Michael Mulcahy's team last year," said Cheryl. "It was not a happy situation."

She lifted the puppy back onto her lap and Meg reached over to pet it. It was a fat, wiggling cocker spaniel the color of honey.

"Never again," said Cheryl.

"Why?" asked Meg. "Isn't Mike a good coach?"

"Oh, I shouldn't say anything," said Cheryl. "I'm sure Mike

is a wonderful coach for skilled players. But Brian's just a little boy, and it was hard on him, not being so skilled, to work with a coach who only really cares about winning."

Brian had seemed a decent player to Meg. "You mean he didn't play enough?" she asked.

"Hardly," said Cheryl, trying to keep the squirming puppy on her lap. "He spent more time on the bench than a Supreme Court justice. I washed his uniform more from habit than necessity."

The receptionist leaned over her desk. "Warren," she said.

Cheryl got up, holding the puppy, and looked down at Meg. "I'd guess your policies are a little more equitable," she said, smiling pleasantly before she followed the receptionist down the hall.

Ten minutes later, Meg followed the same receptionist to a small room where a young woman in a white jacket appeared, after a few minutes, and began a brisk but thorough exam. She pronounced the dog—temporarily named "Dog Kessinger" in the files—healthy, drew blood for a heartworm test, and gave the needed shots.

"If there's any problem with the blood test, we'll call before noon tomorrow. So, if you don't hear anything, start those tablets in the afternoon. One a month."

The vet scratched behind the dog's ears. "You're going to neuter her, aren't you?"

"Are you suggesting," asked Meg in an affronted tone, "that this dog is not prime breeding stock?"

The vet laughed. "Well . . ."

"I know," said Meg. "Soon. I promise."

The dog rode back from town on the front seat, her nose out the window, the wind flattening her tattered ears. When Meg stopped in her driveway and opened the door, the dog scrambled over her lap and leaped to the ground.

"My word, but you need to learn some manners," said Meg. "We'd better start doing serious work."

No time like the present, she told herself. First sessions should be brief anyway, so it wouldn't take much time away from work. She needed something much longer than the leash. The clothesline was, she thought, in the middle one of the pantry drawers. She went inside and yanked on the wide-set pulls, coaxing the drawer open. It took her a moment to locate the clothesline, which was partially hidden under a hideous plastic place mat.

Strange, she thought, gathering the line. I didn't see that ugly thing before. Of course, she hadn't looked carefully at everything in the drawer. It must have been under other debris.

She sat back on her heels. Undoubtedly it had been. But why was it now on top?

Outside, the dog searched for creatures to chase while Meg sat on the pantry floor and wondered who had been in her house. And why.

"No, I'm fine," Meg said into the telephone. Jack had called to tell her a very bad joke.

"This horse walks into a bar, and the bartender says, 'Why the long face?' "

"Yeah . . ."

"That's the joke. He says to the horse, 'Why the *long face?*' "

Meg had laughed. "All right, I get it. It's only barely worth getting."

"I think it's hysterical," said Jack. "My nephew called up to tell me. It's his favorite joke. Just one more. Say 'Knock, knock.' "

"Knock, knock," said Meg.

"Who's there?"

Meg hesitated, then groaned. "So I'm the perfect victim for . . . how old's Jeffrey?"

"Nine."

"A nine-year-old's jokes. But please!"

"You sound kind of distracted," said Jack.

Her edginess had stayed with her through the evening. She considered telling him about the clothesline, about the switched drawers in her bedroom, about her disquiet. But she didn't know him well enough. Or, rather, he didn't know her. It would all sound so ridiculous, like the overreactions of an easily spooked female. It *was* ridiculous. She was afraid it was also true.

"Is anything wrong?" he asked.

"No, I'm fine."

"Well, shut your windows tonight. It's supposed to rain something fierce. If it does and keeps it up tomorrow, let's do something. I'm working outside these days. Can't do it in the rain. So come see my studio. Ooh and aah over my paintings. That is, the ones that haven't been snatched up by wise collectors. I'll make you some lunch."

"You have a studio?"

"Not much of one—just a few rooms on the edge of town. Come see."

"I should work," said Meg, only because she really should and knew it. Her next deadline was fast approaching, and she had badly neglected her income-generating tasks.

"Work tonight," said Jack. "You're having lunch with me tomorrow. I'll look for you around noon. If it's raining."

"All right," said Meg. "If it's raining. Tell me how to get there." She hoped it did rain. Hard.

At bedtime, she went to the door and whistled. The dog came, now, to her whistle.

"Come in, Rowdy," said Meg, patting her leg and trying out the name. It didn't sound right. The dog hadn't been disruptive since Meg's first nights in the house. Besides, it sounded like a cowboy's name. "Come in, girl. You're sleeping inside from now on."

Then, with the dog at her side, she went through the house and closed all the windows. She locked them as well.

It wasn't rain she was worried about.

Eleven

When Meg awoke, the roof was dripping onto the honeysuckle bush outside the window, and the sky promised more of the same. The gloomy weather held two benefits: she could get some paying work done instead of being obsessed with finishing the fence, and she could obey the summons to have lunch with Jack.

The house was cold, and dampness made it feel frigid. She set the thermostat on the dining room wall, praying—as she had each time she'd needed heat—that the furnace wouldn't explode. Then she started coffee and took a bath.

By the time she emerged from the tub, warmed and rosy, the house was losing its iciness. The dog barked to be let out. When she came back in, a few minutes later, she tracked mud across the kitchen floor.

"You're going to have to learn to wipe your little feet," said Meg, shutting the dog in the kitchen and going to find a ragged towel. When she returned, the dog let Meg clean off her paws and rub her wet coat dry.

"What do you think I should wear today?" Meg asked, settling herself at the kitchen table with coffee and a bowl of cereal. "No, not this robe, though I'm glad you think I look stunning in it. How about a long skirt? It's cold out. What do you *mean,* long skirts make me look short? Yes, yes, I do want honesty. I apologize. So what do you suggest?"

She ate cereal and thought. "You're right. Jeans and a long white shirt and a pretty, short vest. Let me think about the pink socks. You have an extraordinary sense of style for a dog. Though perhaps not ravishing, I'll be darn cute. And just artsy enough."

She spent the next several hours working well. She wrote better when she was in a good mood, and she was in quite a good mood. Outside the office window, the rain fell in a steady mist and the violets that had come up, generous in the yard, were a haze of purple.

As noon approached, she got out of her robe and into her clothes, brushed her short thick hair until it shone, and drove to town. When she found the address Jack had given her, there was a parking place nearby.

The building itself was set well behind the stores that fronted the street. It was a high one-story building, perhaps a converted stable. Jack yelled "Come in" to her knock at the door, and she opened it with curiosity. His studio did not look at all as she had imagined it would. The floors were a rich dark wood that seemed to glow. The main room had minimal furniture; no one would mistake it for a home, but there were comfortable places to sit and a mission-style table. The walls were snowy-white, and paintings and photographs hung on every inch of wall between the windows and covered the back wall of the room. The photographs were black-and-white shots of woods and meadows. The paintings were in many styles, some completely abstract, others impressionistic.

If the day had been sunny, light would have poured through the windows on the other three walls—windows that had not been an original part of the structure, at least not if it had actually been a stable. They were large and plentiful, covered against the gloominess of the day with wide shades of some burlaplike fabric, dyed lilac and blue and moss-green. The center of the room was empty, but, pushed to one side and standing on a heavy drop cloth, was an easel with an unfinished painting and a table covered with tubes of paint and brushes.

The painting was a portrait of a dark-haired woman. She wore cutoffs, revealing strong legs, one crossed in front of the other, and a T-shirt with the sleeves rolled up. She was laughing and leaning on a bat. Meg was startled and immensely gratified.

"I'm back here!" shouted Jack. "Come on through!"

She walked down a hallway past a small bathroom and into a room that held a refrigerator, oven, sink, and a tiny table.

"Hey, kid," said Jack, looking up from the lettuce he was tearing. "I was glad to wake up to rain."

"So was I," said Meg truthfully. "But I'm confused. When I asked if you had a studio, I believe you suggested it was unimpressive. Ha! And something smells good."

"Rolls heating up," said Jack. "We're having chicken salad." He smiled at her. "I'm glad you're impressed." He moved his head to indicate the table. "Get some plates out; it'll speed things up."

Having declared her shortage of time, Meg thought it better not to admit that she wasn't at all in a hurry. She opened a cupboard and took down two blue-speckled enameled plates. "I like the painting you're working on. I didn't know you'd actually used your camera that day."

Jack laughed happily. "It's nice, isn't it? I'm pleased. I didn't think I could really *get* you, even with a good photo to work from. But I have, haven't I?"

"It's amazing," said Meg.

She opened a drawer to take out silverware, and Jack reached around her to pick up a serving spoon. His arm brushed against her. She concentrated on not impaling herself with a fork.

"Let's dish up out in the kitchen but eat at the table in the other room," he said. "It's a tad crowded back here."

108

After the chicken salad, he served cheesecake with lightly sugared raspberries.

"Raspberries? At the end of April?" asked Meg wonderingly. "Gosh, this is good. But how many long-distance calls did you have to deny yourself in order to buy raspberries in April?"

Jack looked at her, his eyebrows drawn together in confusion. "Oh," he said after a moment. "I get it. No, babe, it's not *spending* money I have a problem with; it's *wasting* it. There's a big difference. Fresh raspberries could not be considered a waste of money."

As they ate, the rain passed on, and Jack got up to raise the shades.

"It's clearing up," he said, "and everything is sparkling."

"Are you going to paint this afternoon?" Meg asked.

"Can't dance," he said. "Too wet to plow. Want to stick around and watch a master at work? You could grin at me and I could try to get that subtle dimple right."

"I think you already got it," she said. "And I've got work of my own."

She had been aware it was taking a great deal of thought to guide the food to her mouth but knew it would seem foolish, bizarre, to sit motionless with an untouched plate in front of her, seeing only the curve of his hand on the table. He wore one ring—thick, twisted wires of gold and silver.

"Have you ever been married?" she asked.

He didn't answer immediately. "No," he said, at last. "Almost . . . but no. You?"

She shook her head slightly. "No. It sounds like something went wrong. Did something go wrong?"

"Things go wrong a lot," he said. He sat back in his chair, looking levelly at her. "Forgive me for seeming to avoid the question. It was all quite recent, and it's a little hard to talk about."

"Oh," said Meg. "I'm sorry."

He waved a hand. "Forget it. It hardly ranks as a tragedy. Just a case of being about as wrong about someone as it's possible to be."

"Mmm . . ." said Meg. "That can happen."

"Constancy," he said softly, looking across the room. "It seems so basic." He moved his shoulders and turned his gaze to her. "You aren't much into games, are you?" he said. "I mean, except for real ones, like baseball."

"No, I'm not," she answered looking down at her hands, clasped on the table. "I hate them. I'm no good at them; perhaps that's why."

"Keep being no good at them," he said quietly, and his eyes, when Meg looked up, were contented-looking and very blue.

Meg stood in the library and looked around. She hadn't been ready to drive home and try to fix her mind on work. She had needed to walk, fast and purposefully, and to think. What did he see in her? Jim had been impressed with her competence, her good nature, her calm. But he had known her. Jack didn't know her; he couldn't. Not yet, anyway. But there was . . . affection in him. Or there seemed to be.

If he really did feel that way, why didn't he indicate it a little more clearly? Because he knew how easy it was to be wrong about someone? Because he was still emotionally tied up with someone else? Whatever the reason, it was just as well he didn't, she thought, sighing. She was skittish, too. Maybe that's why the dog had taken to her. Maybe she had recognized a kindred spirit.

The library was large for a small town, with high ceilings and row after row of white-painted shelves. It was quiet except for an occasional burst of childish laughter from behind a closed door with a "Story Hour in Session" sign.

She wandered through the stacks. She loved libraries, loved just being in them. This one was particularly welcoming; there were clusters of easy chairs here and there in open spaces in front of the stacks. It would have been nice to spend the rest of the day curled up in one of them with a novel. It would be nice to lose herself in someone else's life for a while.

Instead, she supplied the necessary documentation to receive a library card, checked out an Angela Thirkell, so she could see what it was Christine liked so much, and the only comprehensive guide to gardening that was on the shelves, and drove home. She passed John Eppler, driving to town, and he honked and waved at her out his open window.

She worked all afternoon and into the evening, pushing everything out of her mind except the word lists. She completed a rhyming phrase match and wrote a set of short poems. She took a break mid-afternoon to call her parents.

"Thanks for the letter last week, Mom," she said. "It was my first mail! I went out to the mailbox, not actually expecting anything since there had never *been* anything, and there it was. It sounds like you're busy."

"As always," said her mother. "You know your dad. But you're the one who must be busy, dear. How's the house? I've been waiting to find out. We haven't heard a word since you called to say you'd made it there. You can't be too busy to write once in a while to your own parents."

"Yeah, actually, I am," said Meg. "That's why I'm calling. I *am* calling, you notice."

"At unnecessary expense," said her father, breaking into the conversation. "Not that we're not happy to hear from you. But what's wrong with the U.S. mail?"

"Gosh, Dad, you sound just like Jack," said Meg. "I've met this guy here who writes letters. I thought letter-writers were a dying breed, that you and Mom were the last ones still kicking, but I guess not. And he has the same reasons you do."

"Now, Margaret," said her mother. "Don't get involved with a stingy man."

"Ha! Look who's talking!"

"Your father is not stingy! He's just careful. Like I am. We're just careful. And you would be more so, if you'd spent your early years poor like we did. Your friend didn't grow up in the Depression, did he?"

"Heavens, Jeanie!" said Meg's father. "What would Meg want with a tottering old man?"

"No, Mom," said Meg. "He didn't grow up in the Depression. I swear. He's in his mid-thirties. And he's not stingy; he's just careful, like you. He's puzzled about why 'Thou shalt not waste money' was left out of the Ten Commandments. Figures it was a printer's error."

"Well, then, he sounds lovely," said her mother. "Now tell us about Louise's house. I was there only once, and I barely remember it."

Meg spent a happy twenty minutes describing the house, the fence, the yard, the dog, her baseball team, and the neighbors.

"This Mike fellow sounds all right to me," said her father. "And it seems you've made quite the impression."

"I wouldn't say that," Meg replied. But when she had hung up and returned to work, she wondered again at her change in fortune. Three years as one of several girlfriends, and now seemingly pursued by two men. It was a pleasant, if disconcerting, change.

The dog lay contentedly on the rug behind her until seven-thirty and then got up, stretched, and nudged Meg's elbow with a cold nose.

"Okay," said Meg. "I'm getting hungry, too. But let's take a walk first and eat fashionably late."

The dog's ears pricked at *walk*.

"You're a smart one, aren't you?" said Meg. "Or was there somebody else who used to say that, and you've just remembered what it means?"

She switched off the screen and got up and they went out into the cool evening. "Want to go say hey to Harding?" asked

Meg. "That'll stretch our legs and make him blissfully happy, all at once. And I can see if Christine has a pot big enough for pasta for when they come to dinner tomorrow."

"Rarrph," said the dog.

"The field's still wet," said Meg. "So we have to go by the road, which means you need your leash."

The dog reared up on her hind legs while Meg snapped on the leash. They walked facing oncoming traffic and moved to the edge of the ditch whenever a car approached. Few cars approached. Meg felt lucky to live on a largely untraveled road. The air was soft and fragrant and, even when she thought about Jack, her mind was easy. No clutching feelings in her stomach. This, she told herself, was a good sign. She wasn't falling for him, after all.

The downstairs front of the Ruschman house was dark but lights were on upstairs.

"Kiddies are doing their homework," said Meg. "Let's go around to the kitchen door."

Harding met them on their way up the long driveway, barking with delight and rearing to crash his chest against the smaller dog.

"You two run off and play," said Meg, unsnapping the lead. "But stay away from the road."

The dogs ran off into the field and Meg remembered, too late, that there would be muddy paws to clean again when she got home. She walked on the smooth concrete of the drive around to the back of the house, her gym shoes silent. The kitchen door was open; only the screen door was closed, and she could hear Dan's and Christine's voices. Meg started to call out, to keep from startling them with a sudden rap at the door, but just then Christine spoke again, and the savagery in her voice stilled Meg's own.

"I won't live with a man who lies to me," Christine said. "I tell you, I won't!"

"I'm not lying to you," said Dan. His voice held no anger. Neither was it light. It sounded, to Meg, as if he was close to tears.

"Well, you might as well be," said Christine. "You're not telling me anything. Something's going on, something that involves money I don't know anything about. I don't know where it came from, don't know who it went to, or why. Something that involves secrets, Dan, secrets you're keeping from me. From *me!* For God's sake! What's the story?"

Meg started to creep away, backing up. She bumped into Dan's truck and froze, frightened unreasonably by the unexpected barrier.

"I *will* tell you the story, Christine," he said, "as soon as I know how it ends."

Now it was Christine's voice that trembled, and no longer with anger. "Just tell me one thing, Dan," she said. "And tell me now. Will I be in the story at the end?"

"Oh, God, I hope so," said Dan. He paused. "You don't think . . . ? Christie! You don't think . . . ?"

Meg slid sideways along the truck and hurried down the driveway. Nearing the road, she whistled for the dog, spoke firmly to Harding to discourage his company, and started home, feeling awkward and guilty.

When the phone rang, Meg lay *The Brandons* upside down on the bed next to her so she wouldn't lose her place and answered. It better be Sara, she thought. If I have to leave Pomfret Madrigal to talk to somebody, it better be Sara.

No one replied to her hello. She waited a second and tried again. "Hello?"

Silence. And then there was a click and the line went dead.

"Same to you," said Meg and picked up her book. She had read a paragraph without understanding a word of it before she realized how disconcerted she was.

"Don't be a dip," she said out loud. Why should she get jittery over a simple disconnection? Not everyone who dialed a wrong number was polite enough to apologize.

Lavinia was waiting, with her endearing absentmindedness and entertaining life. Christine had been right about Angela Thirkell novels, at least in this case. But Meg could not make her way back into the diverting fictional world she had been occupying before the phone rang, and Mrs. Brandon had to wait for half an hour while Meg walked through the house and checked the doors and windows and ate a bowl of cereal and managed, finally, to shake off the feeling that someone had been trying to find out if she was home.

*T*welve

*B*etween the driveway and the kitchen window, Meg had put a bird feeder, driving the post solidly into the ground. It was more for her pleasure than, at this time of year, the birds' survival. The birdhouse from Jack stood farther away. It had gone up too late, it seemed, to be used this spring. Meg grinned, thinking of Seymour and his feathered bride and how they'd had to make do with a cruder home. Maybe next year . . .

She stood gazing out the window at the feeder while cutting strawberries onto the top of her cereal. A tufted titmouse, several chickadees, and a goldfinch shared the perches, flickering on and off until Christine drove up, scattering them. She jumped out of the station wagon and bounded inside, letting the screen door slam behind her.

"Isn't it a gorgeous day?" she said. "Hey, pooch!"

The dog, who had not risen from where she was lying on her side under the kitchen table, thumped her tail twice on the floor. Having learned the sound of Christine's engine, she no longer broke into a paroxysm of barking at her approach.

"Yes . . ." Meg looked curiously at her friend. "It is."

"Here," said Christine, ignoring the unasked question. "I've brought sticky buns. I made them this morning. They're the best things you ever tasted."

"You need to work on that false-modesty thing you've got going," said Meg. "When you're good at something, just admit it."

"Let's play," said Christine, sitting down at the table and stretching luxuriously. "Let's oh, I don't know, go shopping. Or have a picnic. Or go put our feet in the creek."

"You must have forgotten that I'm entertaining tonight," said Meg. "The Ruschmen are coming to dinner, and I need to impress them. Mrs. Ruschman is the *snottiest* old bat. So, I've got to make the pâté for the Beef Wellington and whip up a few soufflés. And before I can start on that, I have to finish one last worksheet and find an envelope to put this batch of work in. And before I go into town to mail it, I really want to paint the *last three pickets*. And after all that, I have to start on the stuff for the next deadline, which I will never, ever get done on time because we have nine hundred and sixty-four baseball practices scheduled. I am *behind*."

"Speaking of behinds . . ." said Christine. "The PTA president, who is one major ass, roped me into making brownies for some do. I'd forgotten. I guess I couldn't play much either."

"Wrong kind of ass," said Meg. "If someone is an ass, she's a donkey. A fool. A stupid or silly person."

"You're right," said Christine. "I forgot I was speaking to a wordsmith. Talking with you, the term that should have come to mind is 'butthead.' "

"I'm glad we got that cleared up," said Meg. "There was what I think was an indigo bunting here earlier. I can't believe it. Chicago's got birds, but if you try to encourage them with a feeder you spend most of your time looking at pigeons."

"Mmm," said Christine dreamily.

Meg glanced at her. "And I'm probably wrong, but I'd swear there was a flutter-winged dimwit out there last week."

"Mmm," said Christine again.

"You're not listening," said Meg. "What's with you?"

Christine started. "What?"

"I was talking about birds," said Meg. "Beautiful birds. Amazing varieties of birds, to go along with all the green and the clean smells and the late-April breezes." She gestured toward the window. "It's a miracle."

"No," said Christine. "It's Pennsylvania. Now eat a sweet roll with me before I go put on a fetching gingham apron and you get on with your piddling concerns."

She left a half hour later, reminding Meg never, ever to slam the oven door on a soufflé.

The fence was neat and sturdy and, best of all, finished.

"You've increased your property value at least fifty bucks," said Mike, gripping a picket and shaking it gently. "You did a nice job. But it makes the paint on the house look even worse than it did before."

"Shut up," said Meg. She had been on her way back from a walk to the creek when she saw his car turn into the driveway.

"I just got through a half hour ago," she said. "Haven't even cleaned up yet." A closed can of paint, with a brush resting on top of it, still sat on the grass. "What are you doing away from the office?"

"Longing to see you," he replied. "Actually, I'm on my way down to Doylestown to take a deposition. Want to come? It's a beautiful town."

"I should have known you were doing something that required you to look like a lawyer," said Meg. "You've got on a tie. I can't go, but thanks. A woman's work is never done. I have to mail stuff and grocery shop and teach doggies how to do as they're told."

Jane and Harding were coming over when Jane got home from school, to start Harding's obedience lessons. When Meg mentioned the need to work with her own dog, Christine had jumped on the subject and begged her to work with Jane and

Harding too, to save Christine from driving them to town for lessons. Meg was happy to acquiesce. She hated to see a dog that hadn't been civilized, and working with Jane would be fun.

"Have you decided what we're betting?" asked Mike.

"How about painting my house?" suggested Meg. "If I win, you paint it; if you win—ha, ha, ha, fat chance—I paint it."

"You missed your calling when you didn't go to law school," said Mike. "Keep thinking. How about hitting the Main Street Cafe with me tonight? Or someplace else, if you're getting tired of homemade pie."

"Can't tonight," said Meg, a little surprised at a feeling of regret. The idea of sitting across the table from him for an hour was appealing. "But soon."

She waved as he drove away, then picked up the paint can and brush and headed for the toolshed. She had taken the lawn mower out a few days earlier to see if it functioned and knew there were shelves where she could store paint—at least until it got cold again. She dropped the paintbrush near the kitchen door so she could take it in and clean it.

The shed was shaded by a huge maple tree. There were gaps between some of the planks, and it needed a fresh coat of paint even more badly than the house. She unhooked the door and stepped into the spiderwebbed dimness. The shelves had been constructed by, or for, a taller person; the space underneath held a huge, heavy lawn roller. There was an old shovel but no trowel, rake, or spade. Meg would have to buy those herself.

She stretched for the bottom shelf but couldn't quite tip the paint can onto it. She looked around for something to stand on. Not the mower; it had wheels. Next to the lawn roller, pushed back against the wall, was an old wooden milk crate with a wadded-up tarpaulin inside.

I'm a dolt, she thought. If I'd bothered to look out here before painting, I could have kept paint off the grass.

She pulled the crate out and upended it, stood on the bottom, and slid the paint can onto the shelf. When she picked up the crate to right it, the tarpaulin fell out. Scooping it up to stuff it back in the crate, she heard a clatter. She looked down at the concrete floor of the shed. Something was lying by her right foot. She picked it up and looked to see what it was, then tucked it into her shirt pocket and put the crate back in place.

Someone, it seemed, had once used the tarpaulin and then gathered it up for storage without realizing that a tape cassette had fallen onto it. That was the only logical explanation. After all, why would anyone deliberately hide a tape cassette in a toolshed?

At the grocery store, Meg selected salad greens and bought what she needed for spaghetti. She'd have to use two pots to cook it, but she'd done that before. What for dessert? Ice cream was easy but not practical, given her freezer. Mike was wrong. It did freeze ice, if she gave it long enough, but ice cream would be mush by dinnertime. So, she'd pick up something at the bakery.

She turned up an aisle and saw Jack setting a quart jar of honey into his cart. She was glad she'd changed into a clean shirt and cutoffs, which flattered her, before driving to town, even though the day was really too chilly for such attire.

"I thought it was only the mothers of large families who bought that size," she said, stopping beside him.

"Oh, I'll use it, eventually," he said, looking happy to see her. He pulled her gently away from her cart and pushed her up to the shelf. "There," he said, pointing to the tiny print on the stickers below the honey jars. "And there. See?"

"Ah," said Meg. "Unit cost. A man after Ben Franklin's heart. But why don't you get your honey from Mr. Eppler?"

"John Eppler is a heck of a beekeeper and a rigidly upstanding pillar of the community," he replied. "But he thought I should have gotten Hannah Ehrlich's lawn mowed more often and blamed me for the rosebush that didn't make it through the winter two years ago. He didn't like it that she left me an extremely nice oil landscape . . . Anyway, he's not someone I deliberately run into."

Meg looked at him sternly. "And was the rosebush your fault?"

"I don't think so. Fact of life, you know, like so many things. But John and Hannah went way back—she left him her IBM stock, if that gives you an idea of what good friends they were—and the only way to have satisfied him would have been to show up at her house at nine in the morning and not leave until six."

"Christine says you did a lot."

"Not enough." His eyes were serious. "She was a wonderful woman—tough, funny, good-hearted. You think there's always going to be time; you can finish this or that later . . . No, I didn't do enough. And I should have realized how forgetful she was getting. I should have . . . Oh, what's the point?"

He sighed, shook himself slightly, and smiled at Meg. "Taking a break from the computer to stock the pantry? Good idea."

"Somebody's got to do it. You have the day off again?"

"Dan didn't need me today," he said. "He's off somewhere doing something. I've got to kill some time while a tile floor sets before I grout it, so . . . Want to go get coffee?"

Meg was tempted. "I'd love to," she said regretfully. "But I've got a ton to do."

"How about dinner?" he said. "I need to check the attic anyway after yesterday's rain; I could stop by and do that, and then *you* could cook something for a change."

"Can't tonight," said Meg, hating to pass it up. "I've got plans tonight. Tomorrow?"

Jack frowned. "Got an evening job tomorrow. But I need to see what's going on with your roof before any leak there might be has dried up completely and—"

"Hey," said Meg. "I'm not ancient. I can climb the attic stairs."

"What?" Jack seemed taken aback.

"Keep up with me," said Meg. "I checked the attic yesterday when I got home. The floor was dry."

"Great," he said. "Because leaks are bad enough, but the wet wood they leave behind can lead to all kinds of problems. Unless you're fond of carpenter ants and falling plaster. How's your heating system? Do you even know what you've got?"

"It's one of those mammoth things that look like giant octopi. Gravity, forced-air. Old. I haven't been down there since the day I moved in. The system works. I've turned it on a few times, and it works . . . sluggishly, but it works."

Jack whistled. "They don't even make *parts* for those things anymore. I'll take a look at it. How about if I stop by on Monday, about five-thirty?"

"Harding, come!" said Jane. The big dog didn't budge. He was staring fixedly at a squirrel that was pretending to ignore him from a safe distance. " 'Come,' I said. Come!"

"First rule, Jane," said Meg. "Don't repeat it. He heard you. The darling fellow isn't deaf; he just doesn't realize that what you say matters. He has to learn to come the first time you tell him, as soon as you tell him. By the time you've shouted four or five times, he's already run out in front of the truck or caught the rabbit you don't want him to massacre. Here, I'll show you."

She took the leash and walked around the yard with Harding for a few moments. Then she stopped and waited for him to become interested in the squirrel again.

"Harding, come!" she said.

The dog stood, statue-like. Meg hauled the leash in rapidly, hand over hand. When he arrived, surprised, at her side, she praised him effusively. She handed the leash to Jane.

"You try it," she said. "Be quick about making him obey. He has to associate the spoken command with the action of arriving next to you. Say it once. Use his name first. Oh, and while you're training him, don't *ever* give him a command you can't make him obey."

They worked for a while. Eventually, Harding got the idea.

"It's not that he's dumb, Jane," said Meg. "He's just not used to having to do what he's told. You're going to see to it that he *gets* used to it. Pretty soon we'll put him on a long rope, and you'll wait until he actually starts chasing a squirrel before you call him."

"What'll happen?" asked Jane.

"Let's see how prophetic I am," said Meg. "My guess is, he'll keep going. But if you've timed your command right, dug your feet in, and called him just before he reaches the end of the rope, he'll find out real fast what happens when he ignores you. He'll hit the end of the rope and get jerked right off his great big feet."

"I couldn't!" said Jane, aghast. "It would hurt him!"

"Not really," said Meg. "And how much does getting run over by a truck hurt? I'm not talking about being mean to him. It would be a rotten way to *introduce* him to the idea of coming when he's called. You won't be correcting him—which is a nicer way of saying 'knocking him for a loop'—before he's had a chance to learn the command and deliberately disobey it. You do want him to live a long, long time, don't you?"

Jane put her arms around the Lab and hugged him. He responded by knocking her down and licking her face.

"Oh, yes!" she said. "Mom says he's a doofus and he is. But he's got the most important thing a dog can have. He's got *loyalty.*"

Meg thought about it. It was the most important trait a dog could have, and Harding did have it. He spent a good deal of time at or near Meg's house, coercing his beloved into wrestling matches and trips to the creek. But when it got close to three o'clock, he took off for home.

"You're right," said Meg. "The best dogs are the loyal ones."

"The best people, too," said Jane, looking up from her sprawled position on the ground.

"Hmm . . ." said Meg. She sat down beside the girl. "Maybe . . . But with people, don't you want honest and friendly and, I don't know, *good* even more than loyal? I mean, loyal's great, but . . ." She searched for an example. "What if a friend of yours were doing something she really shouldn't do, maybe something illegal or dangerous. Or, say, Teddy was. Anyway, whoever it was, the person asked you to be loyal and not tell. What would you do?"

Jane thought a moment. "I don't know about my friend," she said. "I guess it depends how awful it was. But I'd never tell on Teddy. I mean, I might tell Mom or Dad if it was dangerous, but I'd never, ever tell anyone else. That would be worse than what he'd done."

Meg gazed at her. The child's mouth was set firmly. She looked a lot like Christine at the moment.

"I guess you come by it naturally," she said. "Your mom's surely the loyal type."

"Yes, she is," said Jane, nodding. "But Dad *really* is. He says you have to be loyal to your family. Always and no matter what."

That's funny, thought Meg. She would have thought loyalty involved communicating. Or was he one of the do-as-I-say-not-as-I-do types? She quelled her resentment of the man. It wasn't right to judge him. She had no idea what was going on with him. And Christine, it seemed, was happy. Perhaps they had talked long into the night, and everything was, after all, just fine.

At dinner, Meg was reminded of how little she knew Dan. He praised the food and participated with interest in the conversation. Meg understood why, besides his physical attractiveness, Christine was so in love with her husband. It didn't hurt that he, like Christine, loved her kitchen.

"You wouldn't believe the times I've had to pull old hand-made cabinets out to replace them with golden oak," he said. "And nobody wants these plain glass doors anymore. It's all little individual panes but usually, of course, not individual panes at all—just wood strips over glass to make the doors look like individual panes."

"What do you do?" asked Meg. "I mean, when somebody's decided to rip out great old stuff and modernize?"

"I do it," he said, shrugging. "People want what they want. It would be harder to legislate taste than morality, and you know what they say about *that.*"

"Isn't there a market for the old stuff? The mantels and banisters and all the things you rip out? In Chicago, there are places that specialize in selling that."

He shrugged. "Around here? I doubt it. Mind if I see the rest of the house?"

"Feel free," Meg said. "Just don't look at it with a contractor's eye. Don't sit at the dinner table and tell me about the sixty-five thousand dollars I need to spend to keep it from falling down. Please."

He was gone for quite a while and when Meg looked inquiringly at him on his return, he shook his head, raised his eyes as to the heavens, and sighed dramatically.

"I appreciate your silence," said Meg.

"You ought to," he replied. "It's taking its toll on me. But, someday, we have to talk."

"Someday," said Meg.

When it was time for dessert, she brought in a platter of éclairs from the kitchen.

"Zowee!" said Teddy. "Éclairs! From the bakery!"

"The one thing my perfect wife doesn't make," said Dan. He winked at Christine. "She makes only the things she can make better than anyone else. Granted, that's a lot of things, but not éclairs. Nobody can make better éclairs than the bakery."

"They make good muffins, too," said Meg. "Jack brought some over one day."

"Grab the lad," said Dan.

"Dan has a strong interest in such an occurrence," said Christine.

"Which would be?" asked Meg.

Christine looked at Dan, who grinned. "It has to do with who mows the lawn for the month of July."

Meg put her elbows on the table and clasped her hands under her chin. She looked back and forth from Dan to Christine. "Oh, please! My future will be decided by *July?*"

"Actually," said Dan, "I just like the guy. He's decent and he works hard and he deserves to be happy."

"I take it, he hasn't been?" asked Meg, assuming a casualness she did not feel.

"He doesn't talk much," said Dan. "He hardly talks at all. But I think he's had his share of disappointment. His relationships, the few there have been since he moved here a number of years ago, have been both casual and brief, except for one. That one was serious. It ended recently and, I think, badly."

"The lovely Stephanie," said Christine.

"The legend-in-her-own-time Stephanie," said Meg.

"Maybe he's gay," said Jane.

Dan, Christine, and Meg all stared at her. Teddy helped himself to another éclair.

"Maybe he's what?" asked Christine.

"You know, Mother," said Jane, disgusted with her parent's thickheadedness. "Gay. Maybe he's gay."

"No, Jane," said Dan. "I don't think so."

After dinner, Dan took the children home. "They've both still got homework," he said to Christine. "And I've got to finish an estimate. So if you want to stay and yak, why don't you? I'll get them in bed by nine, I swear."

When they had left, Christine began to clear the table.

"Don't," said Meg, taking plates out of Christine's hands. "I'll do this in the morning."

The two women went into the living room with the rest of the dinner's large bottle of wine. Christine poured some into their glasses and lifted hers. "To a lovely new friendship that has not yet proven to be a terrible mistake." She took a swallow. "You can drink, you know," she said. "I wasn't toasting *you.*"

"But what was that?" asked Meg. "Do your friendships often turn out to be terrible mistakes?"

Christine waved a hand. "Sakes alive, child, of course not. I was making fun of Dan, but since he wasn't here to hear it, there wasn't much point. I had to explain to him about women and friendships. No, he knows pretty much about women and a reasonable amount about friendships. I mean, I had to explain about women's friendships."

"What about them?"

Christine pushed off her shoes and put her feet on the coffee table. "*You* know. Like how we hadn't been in the same room three minutes before it seemed we'd known each other most of our lives? Like how that sometimes happens?"

"Oh," said Meg, nodding. "*That.* I always figured it was because women have never had enough time. So it became a survival skill—figuring out who you thought you could be friends with really fast."

Christine raised her glass. "There you go."

"Or else women are just crazy."

Christine raised her glass again. "Could be." She gestured out the window at the fence, invisible in the darkness. "He thinks you did a nice job," she said. "The fence does look terrific. Now you can get that puppy you said you wanted."

"Ha, ha," said Meg. She glanced over at the dog, who was dozing in front of an easy chair. "Destiny had another plan. But the work wasn't wasted. Mike says I've increased the property value by fifty bucks."

"Ah," said Christine. "I'm seeing a lovely vision . . . Dan behind a huge power mower."

"Let me borrow your glasses," said Meg. "I need to give you *the look.*"

"You're just afraid I'll jinx things by daring to speak of them."

"Yeah," said Meg, "that's it." Actually, in a way, it was. She liked it that both Christine and Dan assumed two men would fight for her attention. She just knew it wasn't true. Especially of Jack. She hated to confess her insecurity about him, as if saying "I just don't know what he could see in me" would make Christine take a good, hard look and realize she was right. Instead she said, "I'm glad Dan approves. Your daughter was a big help."

She pushed the shoe off one foot with the toes of the other and curled her shoeless foot under her on the couch. "Which reminds me, you were right that she's angry about Mrs. Ehrlich. Jane thinks she was neglected."

"She wasn't," said Christine. "Well, maybe she was, but people tried. Dan went over every day to check on her. Jack was there at least as often and really *worked*. John Eppler played whist with her and brought tomatoes and asparagus. I visited, and so did Jane, and Mike came when he could."

Christine sighed and leaned back at her end of the couch. "Jane just isn't making much progress in getting over it. She knows Hannah was worried and upset before she died, and that makes it worse for her."

"But you don't know what that was about, right?"

Christine swirled wine in her glass and watched it. "Not a clue. I asked, of course; it was so obvious that something was wrong. But she'd sigh in that way she had and shake her head. 'I'm just tired,' she'd say. 'It's nothing.' She wouldn't tell me anything."

"I wonder," said Meg. "I wonder what got her so upset."

"Me too," said Christine. "But we'll never know."

Thirteen

*G*o! Have a good time! I'm not a nincompoop," said Meg. "I'm perfectly capable of helping Jane deal with equations that involve two variables."

Christine hesitated in the doorway. "They *have* to be in bed by eight-thirty. They have to be asleep by nine. The school bus comes early."

"I know where you store the bats," said Meg. "Any trouble, a couple quick whacks on the back of the head . . . they're asleep. Go!"

She was looking forward to the evening, glad that the Bensons were so happy with their addition that they'd insisted on taking their contractor out to the fanciest restaurant in the area. Christine and Dan needed time together; Meg didn't mind abandoning vocabulary exercises for an evening. Now, if they would just *leave*.

Christine looked different in a knee-length, black crepe dress and high heels, her blond hair swept up, delicate silver earrings emphasizing the slenderness of her neck. "You don't look like my mother," Teddy had said a bit resentfully. "You look like a *lady*."

"We're *going,*" said Dan, tugging his wife out the door. "We'll be back before midnight."

Jane bent over a worksheet at the kitchen table and pushed her hair behind her ears. "It doesn't make sense," she said, reading from the page. " 'One number is five less than the other. Together the two numbers total fifty-three. What are the two numbers?' Well, what *are* the two numbers?"

Meg pulled out a chair next to Jane and sat down. "Choose two letters, any letters."

"*Any* letters? Not x and y?" Her interest was piqued.

"Heck, there's more to life than x and y," said Meg. "How about t and j? Teddy is five less than you. Or h and p. Or whatever."

It didn't take much to intrigue Jane, who tended to make the most out of whatever fun there was to be had. As they worked, she changed her variables' letters for each problem.

"Sometimes," said Meg, "you really have more information than you think you have. You think you don't know enough, but all you have to do is put what you do know together."

Teddy was working on a social studies report. "We have to tell about neighbors," he said. "It's baby work. The only hard part is, it's supposed to be neat."

He wrote slowly and painstakingly for ten minutes, then looked up at Meg. "Could I tell about a neighbor I *used* to have?" he asked. "We're supposed to say what's good about neighbors and we have to put in details. If I tell about Mrs. Ehrlich, I can think of lots of details."

"Sure," said Meg. "You probably learned a lot about neighbors from Mrs. Ehrlich."

"How do you spell *narcissus?*" he asked a few minutes later.

Meg told him. "Are you writing about her flowers?"

"Sort of," he said. "Not really. I'm telling about neighbors helping each other. Mrs. Ehrlich was happy because Jack drove a long way to get narcissus she wanted and dug holes for them, and she said she could think all winter about how pretty they'd be. And then she told me the story about the handsome man who fell in love with his own face in the water."

"That's probably why Mike couldn't plant them for her," said Jane. "He was too busy looking at himself in some water."

"By George, that's what they were," said Teddy. "Isn't that a funny name for flowers? By George?"

"She had ones called Sir Winston Churchill," said Jane. "She used to talk to them. 'Are you thirsty, Sir Winston?' she'd say. 'Are you getting along with King Alfred?' That's another kind of flower, King Alfred."

"I know him well," said Meg. "You gave me six bunches of that fellow and I bought six more a few days later. I don't know Sir Winston."

Jane disappeared and returned with a small catalog. She turned the glossy pages slowly. "Here it is," she said, pointing to a lovely photograph of creamy-white double narcissus with yellow at the center. "Jack used to tease her about being in love with Sir Winston Churchill. 'Make him leave his cigar outside if you let him in the house,' he said. She had to tell me why he said that."

Teddy finished his report and put it neatly into his backpack. "What's her name?" he asked, reaching out to pat Meg's dog as she trotted by with Harding in loving pursuit.

"She doesn't have one yet," said Meg. "Well . . . she's had about fourteen, but none of them has stuck. I'm still thinking."

"Before she was your dog," said Teddy, "I had a name for her. Danger Dog. Maybe that's not a good name anymore."

"How about Rag?" said Jane. "Or," she giggled, "Hag? Or Gag? Those would be good names."

"Or Wag," said Teddy, getting into it. "Or Bag."

"Or Bag Lady," said Meg.

The children looked confused.

"Never mind," said Meg.

"Do I *have* to take a bath?" asked Teddy. "I'm not dirty."

"Your mom said yes, you have to," Meg replied. "Do you want some help?"

Teddy looked at her in horror. "I'm *seven*," he said. "I know how to take a *bath.*"

He wandered off and, eventually, Meg heard running water.

Jane glanced at Meg. "Teddy thinks you're a good neighbor, too," she said tactfully. "He didn't mean to be rude. He just knows more about Mrs. Ehrlich."

"It wasn't at all rude," said Meg, suddenly aware of the difficulties Jane would face in her life from being too worried about other people's feelings. "Really, it wasn't."

Jane sighed, relieved. "He misses her, like I do. She used to read to him and tell him stories."

"I gathered that," said Meg. "Like about Narcissus."

A meow at the door signaled Charlie's return home for the evening, and Meg got up to let him in. As he curled around her ankles, Meg's dog came into the kitchen and spotted him. She let out a short, eager bark and rushed at the cat. Meg lifted him into the air, but Harding was even faster. Coming seemingly from nowhere, he inserted himself between Charlie and the dog. He let out one deep bark. Meg's dog looked at him in disbelief.

"See," said Jane smugly. "I told you he was loyal."

Meg was surprised. Harding had never before stood up to her dog. "He is, indeed," she said. "How stupid of me. I didn't even think about the fact that Charlie and my dog don't know each other."

"I did," said Jane. "But I wasn't worried."

Meg could hear the phone ringing as she put the key in the lock of the kitchen door. She wrestled with it, pushed the door open, and raced through the house into the living room, the dog at her heels.

"Where have you *been?*" a familiar voice asked. "I was getting worried."

"Oh, Sara, Sara," Meg replied, sinking onto the couch next to the lamp she'd learned to leave on while she was out at night. "Get over it. I live in bucolic splendor now, not in the land of muggers and street gangs. The down side is, when you're out late at night, it's probably to visit the neighbors. I was baby-sitting Christine's children. She's been such a sweetie, I was glad for a chance to return a favor. But, to make my point about rural life crystal-clear, her kids don't know what a bag lady is."

"How's doggie?" asked Sara. "Still hanging around?"

"She's moved in," said Meg, "and made herself at home." She peered at the floor. "As a matter of fact, I think she's got her own tiny shoes with gridded soles that she puts on just so she can leave little clumps of mud here and there when it's rained. When are you coming to see me?"

"Soon. Soon. I swear!"

They talked for nearly an hour, and Meg was yawning ferociously by the time she hung up. She brushed her teeth, pushing the door to the attic closed as she went down the hall, and crawled into bed. Half asleep, she remembered she hadn't locked the kitchen door. She groaned and got up.

The dog jumped up as she left the room. "I'm not *going* anywhere!" said Meg irritably. "Can't you just *park* it?"

She turned on the kitchen light and went to the door. Before she got there, the light flickered. It flickered again as she turned the bolt. She looked at the ceiling. The light flickered again and went out. She sighed. She'd change the bulb in the morning.

The sheets felt delicious against her bare legs as she slid into bed. She closed her eyes and enjoyed the feeling for the couple of minutes it took her to fall asleep.

Barking and a weight on her back brought her to startled wakefulness. The short-legged dog had somehow managed to leap onto the bed. Meg rolled over, dislodging the dog, and sat up.

"Good grief!" she said. "What? Did someone toss an empty cigarette pack out of a car window and did that make a dangerous noise?"

The dog barked frantically.

"What?" said Meg, this time with no sarcasm in her voice. She reached out a hand. "What?"

The dog took Meg's wrist in her teeth and closed her mouth. It hurt.

"Ouch!" said Meg, shocked. She got up, and the dog jumped from the bed, raced from the room, and stood on her hind legs at the foot of the attic stairs, scratching frantically at the door.

Meg felt her heart thundering in her chest. If someone was in the attic, she didn't want to go up. She stood irresolutely outside the door. There was no way to lock it, no way to protect herself if a stranger was, indeed, hiding up there. She pulled the door open, and then she smelled it too.

She ran for the kitchen door, leaping off the stoop to the car. She swung open the hatchback, yanked out the fire extinguisher, tore back into the house, and took the stairs two at a time. At the top she saw the blaze.

Crackling flames had spread over a section of floor and were reaching toward the rafters, which had not yet caught. She pulled the ring pin of the extinguisher and aimed for the base of the flames, sweeping back and forth until foam had blanketed the area. She sank down cross-legged, breathing hard and shaking.

The dog whined and licked at her face. Meg pulled her onto her lap and rested her cheek against the dog's head. "Thank you, thank you," she said. "Oh, thank you."

Fourteen

The electrician stood next to the kitchen table and adjusted the tool belt around his waist. He was a big, boyish-looking man in loose-fitting jeans and an old T-shirt. "You are one lucky lady, Ms. Kessinger," he said. "The wires in one of the junction boxes were loose. Another few minutes, you wouldn't have been able to put it out without a pumper truck. This far out from town? We'd be looking at ashes."

"One of the junction boxes," said Meg. "Where the wiring for this room comes together."

He nodded, and his eyes brightened. "There you go," he said, pleased that she knew what he was talking about. "It's old work. The stuff in here's all working off the same box, which is right up above there." He pointed at the ceiling light. "With the wires loose the way they were—vibrations from trucks going by, from just about anything, will eventually do it—the electricity's going to arc. Spark touches something off . . . well, it's a major problem."

"The electricity arcs?" asked Meg.

"Like in the movies, when Dr. Frankenstein's making his

monster. All that electricity sparking between the monster and the machines?"

"Okay," said Meg. "Gotcha."

"Like that, but not so dramatic. Your wires had come loose and the current tried to jump over the gap. It arced. The spark set off a fire."

"Just like that?" asked Meg.

He nodded. "Just like that."

"This sort of thing happens often? Just accidentally like this?"

"Not real often," he said. "But too often. You shoulda got this place inspected. A house this old . . . Heck, there's no sap left in wood this old. It's *dry*. And your junction boxes are all uncovered. That's crazy." He stopped, embarrassed at his bluntness. "I mean, well, you've only been in the place awhile . . . The previous owner shoulda known."

"I knew," said Meg, feeling stupid and careless. "A friend of mine told me. I need some coffee. You want some? I made it the old-fashioned way, on the stove. I figured the electricity in here wasn't going to work and didn't want to find out."

"I would," he said. "Black, if you have it."

Smart and funny, thought Meg. What else did a person need in an electrician?

"The only way I could get to you this morning was to skip breakfast," he continued. He pulled a chair away from the table and sat, crossing one foot over his knee and leaning back. He dropped a hand to scratch the top of the dog's head, a gesture the dog did not appear to resent. "But Dan said it was an emergency, so here I am."

Meg poured two cups of coffee and sat down across from him. "I'm grateful," she said. "Can you make it so I have power back in the kitchen and cover the boxes? I mean, like, now? And then, as soon as you can schedule it, can you rewire the whole darn place?"

"Sure," he said, "if you can wait a few weeks for the rewiring part."

"You tell me," she said.

"Yeah, you can," he said. "I'll check the connections in the other boxes before I put plates on 'em. Even if something did happen, a cover would contain it."

Meg nodded. "Deal, Mr. Halversen," she said. "Rewire the whole place. I want conduit up the wazoo. I want you buying those . . . those little red plastic things that fit over the ends of the wires—"

"Redheads. And it's Lyle, not Mr. Halversen."

"Redheads by the truckload, Lyle. And it's Meg."

"Okay." He nodded slowly. "I'll give you a bid."

She didn't care if she had to finish paying him with the last dime in her savings account, and she probably would. The night had passed slowly, and before she'd finally fallen asleep where she sat on the couch, she'd had plenty of time to think. Afraid to try to turn on any lights, she'd curled up in the dark with a blanket around her shoulders and concentrated on taking long, slow, deep breaths. Eventually, she'd stopped trembling, and then had sat very still and thought about the house—the line of its low roof against the sky, the way sunlight came through the kitchen windows in the morning, the smell of the basement.

The house was the first thing she'd ever really cared about owning. Things you care about, she told herself, you take care *of*.

When Lyle was finished, he drove off in a shiny black Jeep. Meg walked out with him and watched gravel spit back from his tires as he pulled out onto the road.

Early in the morning, she had walked over to the Ruschmans' and caught Dan before he left. He'd called the electrician for her, and Christine had been shocked and sympathetic.

"Just live *here*," she said, "until you've rewired the place. You're going to, aren't you?"

"Rewire? Yes," said Meg. "I'm going to."

"Then just stay with us until it's done. Dan, don't you think she should just stay here?"

Dan grinned. "She's welcome to stay here, but it's completely unnecessary, unless she's got the heebie-jeebies. Lyle will put it right." He looked at Meg, his smile fading. "I should have looked up there. Wiring isn't my area; I never do it. But I know enough to spot uncovered junction boxes. And if I'd spent some time checking them, I would have noticed wires coming loose."

"Good grief, Dan," she replied, "it's not your fault. I begged you *not* to be the expert. I didn't hire you to inspect the place." She looked at Christine. "Is he Catholic?"

"You'd think," said Christine. "No, but it's hard to tell him from the real thing."

Meg didn't have the heebie-jeebies. She was just sleepy, which made it hard to concentrate on the worksheet she needed to finish. Adding to her physical weariness was guilt about her carelessness and false economy. Still, she thought, having herself to blame was better than the apprehension that had crept into her mind as she was drifting toward sleep in the deep stillness of the very early morning and kept her awake for another hour—the ugly thought that the fire had not been an accident. Bad as it was to have been so irresponsible as to nearly destroy her own home, it was better than having to wonder if the fire had been connected to the other odd occurrences in the house.

She yawned and tried to concentrate on the computer screen. As soon as Lyle had checked and covered the junction box for her office, she'd started on a list of words, but she'd only half finished by the time he left.

She got up, took a bath, and wrestled with three more words. Then she sat and stared at the last two, *serene* and *prostrate*. She had room on the page for four lines of copy. It had to be light verse; that was the format she was using for this worksheet. She was stuck. She was sleepy, disheveled, and stuck. Maybe if she got dressed and brushed her hair, she'd feel more energetic.

The dog stretched and yawned near her feet. Meg glanced down.

"Thank you," she said, and began to type.

> My dog is quite the calmest dog that one has ever
> seen.
> He never gets excited; he is peaceful and ———.
> A burglar came last night and took the silver, cash,
> and more,
> And stepped right over Rover, lying ——— on the
> floor.

The dog got up and pushed her nose against Meg's hand.

"What? You don't like it? I made the dog a *boy*," said Meg. "It couldn't be about you, anyway; the word list doesn't include *insufferable* and *odious*."

The dog whined.

"Gosh, I'm *kidding*," said Meg. "Could I be anything but kidding, Hero Dog? Hey, want to go for a ride? There's a nursery on the other side of town, and I think this warm weather's going to hold. Want to put in some flowers?"

She pushed back her chair and got up. The dog ran toward the front door.

"Yeah, well, wait a minute. It may seem silly to you, but I make it a rule not to leave the house in my underpants."

If she would be carrying flats of flowers, she should wear old clothes. Her work shirt from a few days ago hung from a hook in the closet; as she pulled it on, she felt an object in the pocket. She'd forgotten about the tape.

She stood staring at it. It hadn't been long ago that she had sat on the pantry floor wondering why someone would have come into her house. The obvious answer—to look for something—had made no sense to her. What could such a person have wanted to find? But here was something she had found, something that might have been deliberately hidden.

Curiosity underlaid with uneasiness took her into the living room, where she slipped the cassette into the player and waited. Nothing happened. The spools turned, but no sound came out. She fast-forwarded a bit and turned up the volume. Nothing.

The dog leaped against the door. "All *right*," said Meg, relieved that there was nothing on the tape. "Just a minute."

She had pulled on a pair of jeans and her sneakers and was standing in the bathroom brushing her hair when a voice from the living room startled her. It was a woman's voice, husky and sultry. She was suggesting, in graphic terms, certain cooperative behaviors.

Meg went into the living room and turned down the volume on the tape player.

"Good heavens!" she said. She backed up and sat on the couch, staring at the machine. Why would anyone record *this*?

There was silence on the tape except for breathing, some sounds of pleasure, and what sounded like bedsprings creaking. Then the woman spoke again, calling out. "If you've got anything cold to drink, bring me some."

"I think this is the appropriate time to ask for an ashtray," said Meg dryly.

The tape rustled. "The stuff I'm taking back is going to net a pretty penny," the husky voice said.

Someone spoke from a distance. He—it must be a he, given the woman's earlier suggestions—was too far away for his words to be clear.

"She surely left you a lot." It was the woman's voice. "You did wait until she'd died to take it, didn't you?"

The other voice spoke again. The comment, whatever it was, was short and angry.

"Oh, for heaven's sake!" The woman was annoyed. "I was kidding! Don't be so damn touchy!"

The bedsprings creaked again; there were more rustling noises. Then footsteps moved away. The rest of the tape contained indeterminable noises and more conversation, but whatever was being said was being said in another room. Then there were sounds, laughter, footsteps, and the faint noise of a door closing.

Meg let the dog out, alone, and sat cross-legged on the couch, paging through a magazine, listening to nothing. She ejected the cassette and looked at it, groaning at the length of tape left. But there might be something else and, if so, she wanted to know what it was.

She took the cassette into the kitchen and put it in her portable machine. While the silent tape ran on, she emptied the dish drainer, washed the window above the sink, and swept the floor.

The phone rang, and she hit "pause," then went into the living room to take the call.

It was Christine. "I'm going to John Eppler's to get some honey," she said. "Will you give me coffee if I come by on the way home?"

"Gosh, let me think . . . Is it my turn?"

"I'll be there in, oh, half an hour or forty-five minutes. Spend the time straightening up, would you?"

"Ha!" said Meg. "I already did." She grinned and hung up, thinking about how Christine was going to get something a lot more interesting than coffee. Coffee. She'd have to make more. Knowing Christine, what remained in the pot would hardly suffice. She went back to the kitchen to turn on the water in the sink and get the coffee out of the cupboard and reached over to the tape player to push "pause" as she went by. The spools did not resume turning, so she pushed "pause" again, this time more firmly. The tape began to play, but, as she expected, nothing but silence came from the speakers.

She measured coffee into a fresh filter, poured in water, and started the machine. Then she sat back down at the table and gazed at the tape player, wondering how much more blank— most likely blank, she reminded herself—tape it had to run through. Something didn't look right.

"Oh, shit!" she said. The dog looked up. "I mean, heavens to Betsy! What did I do?" No wonder the tape hadn't resumed the first time she pushed "pause"; it hadn't been "pause" she had pushed. It had been "record." She had ruined the last several minutes of tape, erased whatever existed.

She pushed "stop," wondering what, if anything, she'd missed. "The Watergate investigators could probably tell us," she said to the dog. "But I don't have access to their equipment."

There was nothing she could do about it now. She pushed "play" and listened to twenty more minutes of blank tape as the coffeemaker gently rumbled and blurted. How good were the chances that the tape's silence would have been interrupted by useful conversation during the exact few minutes she'd erased? Small. Really small.

So, there was almost certainly nothing else on the tape. That was regrettable, since her level of curiosity was high, but it would be fun to play the beginning of the recording for Christine. And Christine might have some ideas about the questions that arose in Meg's mind.

It appeared that Angie Morrison had recorded herself engaged in what most people considered a very private experience and then hidden the tape. Why? And who was the man who had inherited so much? And from whom? It couldn't be Meg's great-aunt; all she'd owned was this house and four thousand books. From whom, then? Mrs. Ehrlich?

She rewound the tape and found the husky voice again. "You did wait until she'd died to take it, didn't you?" What did that mean?

The dog barked in the front yard, and Meg looked out the window to see the mailman slow and stop at her box. She ran out the door and through the gate, shouting to keep him from pulling away.

"Morning, Ms. Kessinger," he said. "Not much today. You got something for me?"

"Just a question," said Meg. "I haven't been getting the previous person's mail at all. Did she give you a change of address?"

The mailman shook his head. "No. She just had us hold it, like for vacation. Said she didn't have a new place yet."

"Okay," said Meg. "I thought, if something got delivered here by mistake, I should send it on. In Chicago, things keep coming to the previous resident, sometimes for years."

"Well, you gotta expect that in a place like Chicago," said the mailman. "Out here, we usually know when things change. 'Less it's addressed to 'Resident,' we'll just hold it downtown."

Christine's car edged around the mailman on the shoulder and pulled into the driveway. Meg walked alongside it until her friend had stopped.

"I've got, let's see . . ." Christine looked into her backseat. "Clover honey; raspberry, creamed honey; and beeswax candles." She selected a jar. "Got anything to make toast out of? And I want to see the smoking ruins."

"You can see them, although they're unimpressive," said Meg. "But don't chew too loudly because I have something just the opposite, something extremely impressive, for you to listen to . . ." She stopped, swallowing hard at a sudden thought.

"Listen to what?"

"A poem about a dog," said Meg, her face warm.

The taped conversation, confusing as it was, involved secrets and what seemed to be substantial and ill-gotten gains. What if the woman's voice belonged, not to Angie, but to Leslie McAlester? If it did, was her partner Dan?

"This is heavenly," said Meg, spreading more of the creamed honey on a toasted bagel. The tape kept edging into her mind. It was hard to keep pushing it out. She concentrated on the honey.

"Tell me about it," replied Christine. "The man is a genius. He grows the raspberries and mixes them in. My kids would live on it if I didn't think a bit of protein now and again was necessary."

"He seems to dislike Mike," said Meg. "It's hard to imagine anyone actually disliking Mike, unless he won a case against him."

"He disapproves of him," said Christine. "He disapproved of Hannah's will and thought Mike should have made it more precise."

Meg's interest in the tape receded behind her surprise. "But he didn't 'make it' at all," she said. "And what you quoted about the linens was pretty precise."

"Let me rephrase. John thought Mike should have persuaded her to be more precise about the descriptions of things. Any, as he put it, 'reputable attorney' would have pointed out how vague it was. But nobody had any trouble figuring out what stuff she was talking about. There were no squabbles at all, so far as I know."

"But why did Mr. Eppler care?" Meg had trouble thinking of the man as "John." Maybe after living down the road from him for a few years she could manage it as easily as Christine did. "Didn't he get what he expected?"

"Who knows what he expected?" said Christine. She got up and took an apple out of the refrigerator. "Can I eat this?"

"Well, I won't have any dinner, but go ahead. It won't be cold."

"Oh, great," said Christine. "If God had meant people to eat apples that weren't cold, he wouldn't have put all these refrigerators down here." She washed the apple at the sink and dried it on her jeans. "John inherited a sizable chunk of IBM stock," she said. "Seems pretty precise to me. I doubt it was his own inheritance he was miffed about."

"Then what?"

Christine, who was chewing, held up one hand to indicate a need for time.

"This is *good,*" she said, swallowing. "I don't know. He

seemed to think Mike's getting the house was a case of coals to Newcastle. But the will was clear on that point, so I imagine John was just looking for something to quarrel about. Who knows? He surely couldn't stand Angie. Maybe that was it—he just extrapolated to Mike since she worked for him."

Meg tried not to show how intense her curiosity about Angie was. "What's she like? All Mr. Eppler would say directly is she drives too fast."

"I hardly know her," said Christine. "So all I know is what anybody who so much as glanced at her would know. An absolute knockout. Not at all classy, but whoa!"

"What people of *your* generation call 'a red-hot mama'?"

"Gosh, Meg, you're just so funny," said Christine dryly. "It's no wonder John doesn't think much of her. He didn't get to be the president of the Chamber of Commerce, on the board of directors at the savings and loan, and the chairman of Saint Paul's building committee by approving of people like Angie. She reels men in. They walk around looking dazed. It's all quite deliberate. The few times I saw her, like at the Fourth of July picnic in town last year, she flirted with every man in sight. Including Dan. Especially Dan. It drove her nuts that there was a man in town who didn't have his tongue hanging out. And her taste! Well, I can't criticize her taste in men too much, I guess, but her taste in general, though expensive, is pretty flashy. Her car, for example, is purple."

Meg's stomach knotted at the mention of Angie's flirtation with Dan. She tried to think of something, anything, to say.

"Purple?"

Christine leaned sideways to toss her apple core across the room into the wastebasket. "Purple. T-top. Spoiler. A Firehawk, and she knew how to drive it. She needed all eight cylinders."

"Well," said Meg, "to each her own. Why did a woman like that live in a place like this?" Her house—it felt already so much like her house—just didn't go with a purple sports car.

Christine laughed. "Because she spent all her money on her *car.*"

"Where do you think she went?"

"I don't know. I don't care," said Christine. "Ask Mike; he's the one she worked for." She carried her cup to the sink. "I've got to go get some things done before baseball practice. Can you come for supper after? Fast, easy. Bacon-lettuce-and-tomato sandwiches?"

Meg had forgotten about practice, which was scheduled for when Jack was supposed to come over. She'd have to call him and change their plan. When was she going to get her work done? In Chicago, it hadn't been a problem to work at home. There wasn't anything else to do at home.

"Sure," she said. "I'd like to."

Jack wasn't at his house or at his studio, so Meg left messages at both places. She spent the rest of the afternoon resisting the breeze through the windows in her office. As she started out the door with her bat in her hand, the phone rang.

"Standing me up, I hear," said Jack. "What did I say? Or have you decided you don't care if your furnace blows you to king-dom come?"

"If I thought it would," said Meg, "I'd skip baseball practice. The furnace is just slow, not dangerous."

"And you'd know, right?" He laughed at her.

"I asked Dan," said Meg. "I had a fire in the attic. It started in one of those junction boxes you warned me to cover. Scary, yikes, and all that. So I got paranoid and—"

"You had a *fire?*"

"Uh-huh. I put it out and got an electrician and things are fine now, but it made me nervous, so Dan checked the furnace."

"You're okay?"

"I'm *fine.*"

146

"Well, can I still come by? You make better coffee than I do. How about Wednesday morning? About six?"

"You're kidding."

"Yeah. You're probably a real witch at six."

"I am never a real witch," said Meg. "But, just to be on the safe side . . ."

"Around eight?"

"Great."

Christine hit fly balls to half the team while Meg worked with half on the fine points of base running.

"Try it again, Suzanne. A double again; you're being waved on to second. This time, try to hit the *inside* of first base with your *right* foot."

The girl looked down at her feet, then back at Meg and nodded. She stepped to the plate and picked up a bat.

"Okay. Swing! Go!" Meg clicked the stopwatch and observed the speedy child with approval as she tore down the baseline, fists clenched, arms pumping. She hit the inside of the bag and made an efficient turn.

"Yeah!" shouted Meg. "See how much faster that is?"

She timed the rest of her group, then waved them over to her and chose a tall, cheerful boy with dark hair that had been curly the week before and was now cut so short he looked like an army recruit. "Spence! What do you do when you're on second with first base open and the batter hits a grounder to the left-field side?"

The boy recited the answer. "Wait until I see the ball in the air toward first before taking off for third. Never run into a tag."

"Good," said Meg. "Now, let's say you're on third. There's a fly ball. What do you do?"

He hesitated, unable to deal with the generality of the question. "Infield or outfield? he asked. "Is the infield fly rule in effect? How many outs are there?"

Meg smiled. "Good answer," she said. "Let's get specific."

She took the team through the possibilities, reminding them of why they would have base coaches.

The players rotated. When Meg and Christine had gone through the same routines again, Meg called the children in.

"First game, Saturday, at three. I want you here *no later* than two-thirty for warm-ups and so we know who's here. Anybody not going to make it?"

There were no raised hands.

"Good. Let's pass out uniforms."

"Finish your book report, Teddy," said Christine. "Ask Jane about the spelling. Meg and I are going to get supper ready."

"Guests are not normally expected to work," said Meg, taking a tomato out of boiling water and peeling it. "At least you could assign me something simple, like setting the table."

"Fine," said Christine. "Set the table. It does make more sense for me to do the really complicated stuff, like making toast. We'll eat here in the kitchen."

"How many places?" asked Meg, taking a stack of plates out of the cupboard. "Will Dan be here?"

"No," said Christine. "He's catching up on stuff at the office, so he'll just eat there."

"Does he have one of those nifty black lunch boxes with the curved top for the thermos? You know, the kind all the big strong men carry in one hand, with their hard hat in the other?"

"No. He throws a bagel in a sack," said Christine. "But when he's working at the office, he uses the kitchen there."

"That must be some office."

"Not really. It's just a few rooms, but it's comfy," said Christine. "Sometimes he has to spend a lot of time there."

She dropped bacon onto a paper-towel-covered plate and looked around. "*Glass* glasses? Are you nuts? For you and me, fine. But give the kids those big plastic ones. I've spent enough long hours on my hands and knees getting tiny glass shards off the floor."

Meg went back to the cupboard, reflecting. Christine was so . . . well, *serene*. Was it better to mention the change in her mood, or to ignore it?

"You and Dan, uh, seem to be getting along," she said at last.

Christine jumped back from spitting bacon grease. "Uh-huh," she said. "Things are going to be fine. I'm sorry I was so moody and dramatic."

"Don't be. It was totally reasonable. So, everything's straightened out?" Who was Leslie McAlester? Had Christine found out? Why was she so closemouthed all of a sudden?

"Pretty much," said Christine. She was not going to provide details. "So how are things with all your boyfriends?" she asked. "The attention still making you jumpy?"

It took Meg a moment to catch up with the adjustment in topics. She moved a fork closer to its plate and put one hand on her hip. "Just what makes you think I'm jumpy?"

"Come on!" said Christine. "Mike likes you. Jack likes you. Both of them are adorable. There are at least forty women in town who would trade places with you in the blink of an eye. And you're pussyfooting around like maybe they're both fortune hunters or something. You don't have a fortune I don't know about, do you?"

"Oh, please!" said Meg. "I wish."

"So are you, despite your assurances otherwise, still getting over Jim?"

Yes, thought Meg. I guess I am. "What's wrong with a little hesitation? It's not like I've run screaming from the opportunity to get to know either of them. I just stop short of clutching at their ankles, which seems entirely reasonable."

"You stop a lot short," said Christine. "I think maybe either Mike or Jack would have a better chance if he were less attractive."

Meg thought about that. "I think maybe you're right," she said.

The dog ran ahead of Meg down the path toward the creek. The moon was out and Meg rarely needed to switch on her flashlight. She sat with her back against a tree near the edge of the water, listening to its gentle sounds. The dog rustled through the undergrowth. Meg pulled her sweater closer around her shoulders and hugged her knees.

Was Angie Morrison the woman on the tape? If not, who was? And whom was she talking to? Why had she made a recording and then hidden the tape? Had someone been searching Meg's house for it?

She stared at her denim-covered knees, the voice on the tape coming back to her. "You did wait until she'd died to take it?" Until who had died? Was it, indeed, Hannah Ehrlich? And *had* the man waited until she'd died?

As hard as she tried to keep her mind off Dan Ruschman, it kept returning. How had he acquired fifteen thousand dollars? And what had he told Christine to make her believe that "things are going to be fine"? It couldn't be Dan on the tape. If it was Dan, then it was likely that he was the person who'd gone through the medicine cabinet, checked the bottoms of the dresser drawers, rifled through the built-in section of the pantry, invaded her home. It couldn't be Dan.

Meg looked up. The moon, huge and bright, was in the section of sky visible above the creek. Something moved among the trees to her left, and the dog bolted across the path.

There was something else banging at a door she'd shut and locked in her mind. She gritted her teeth and opened the door. Jane and Christine both had said Mrs. Ehrlich was worried about something before she died. Had she suspected that she was being robbed?

Meg herself was worried about something. Did any of this

have anything to do with her and, if so, what? Just how closely was she connected to all the questions she couldn't answer?

She closed her eyes and tightened her mouth, shaking her head. The only way to get any answers at all was to find Angie Morrison. She could explain—perhaps not everything, but probably enough. Would she? Could Meg make her, somehow? Maybe. If she could find her.

Fifteen

*J*ack honked as he turned into the driveway. He parked by the kitchen door, and Meg watched through the window above the sink as he got out of his truck and walked around the front end. The dog stood between him and the door, barking. He crouched and stretched out a hand, talking softly. Meg could hear the encouraging sound of his voice but not the words. The dog moved warily toward him and took something from his hand.

Meg opened the screen door. "The way to a dog's heart is through the offering of succulent morsels. You're a quick study."

"Olive branches are hard to come by around here. Luckily, bacon isn't."

He put his arm around her, squeezing her shoulder quickly, and then went into the house. "Hey, the kitchen looks great!"

"Thanks," said Meg, happy that he liked it. "It might even encourage me to learn to cook." She turned on the water to fill the coffeepot carafe.

"Heck," said Jack, coming up behind her and putting his hands on her shoulders. He rested his chin on the top of her head. "Stick with me, kid. You won't need to learn. Division of labor, specialization . . . it's what makes the world go round."

I could lean back, thought Meg. Just a little, very subtly. But her heart was thudding painfully, and she did not.

Water spilled over the top of the carafe. She had to move to turn off the faucet. Jack pulled out a chair and sat down at the table. "How's the water pressure in the bathroom?"

"Fine," said Meg. "If I had a real shower, I might find it lacking, but I've got one of those hoses from the faucet up to a sprinkler, all surrounded by a quaint little suspended shower-curtain thing. I've resorted to baths. Now stop being Mr. Fix-It and relax. Do you want something to eat?"

"Already ate," he said. "Whilst slugabeds were still in dreamland."

"Oh, yes," said Meg. "The bacon."

"I would have been happy to bring you some, too," he said, grinning at her.

"Right. That's what I need. Fried fat for breakfast. I can just imagine what I'd look like if you *did* do the cooking."

"What?" said Jack, looking at her in confusion. "You *diet?*"

"Should," said Meg. "Don't."

"You're nuts." Jack shook his head slowly. "Completely nuts. You look perfect. Healthy. Strong. Great." He smiled. "Yes, I must say, great."

She leaned against the sink and gazed at him. His arms were crossed on his chest, his legs stretched out in front of him. His head was slightly tilted, and he was smiling cheerfully, his eyes alight with good humor.

"Thank you," she said.

She arrived at the diamond on Saturday well before the time for her own team's game. She wanted to observe the umpire, get a sense of what he considered the strike zone, and see how well other teams played. Mike Mulcahy stood in one dugout, his arms resting on top of the chain-link fence that protected the team from errant throws and zinging foul balls. Meg sat in the first row of the bleachers behind his team and eavesdropped unashamedly. She knew from the general chatter that the game was in the fourth inning.

Mike's team took the field, the first baseman throwing grounders to the infield, the outfielders tossing another ball to each other. This was made somewhat difficult by the fact that the center fielder had sat down, cross-legged, on the ground and appeared to be selecting the perfect blade of grass to stretch between his hands to make a whistle.

"Hey! Peterson!" yelled Mike, motioning the center fielder in. He turned to a small boy standing on the bench, bouncing lightly against the fence behind him.

"Go on out to center field," he said to the boy, who jumped off the bench, grabbed his mitt eagerly, and jogged across the infield.

The boy referred to as "Peterson" trudged toward the bench. "You taking me out, Coach?" he asked. He seemed surprised and, Meg thought, a bit truculent.

"Yeah," said Mike. His voice was neutral. "I would never have made you play if I'd realized you were so tired."

The boy started to speak, seemed to think better of it, and sat down, watching his replacement hurl the ball, with a great swooping, inefficient throw, toward the right fielder.

Mike's team was triumphant, bringing Cheryl Warren's comments back to Meg's mind. She wished she had paid better attention to how many innings various players spent on the bench. She had noticed that Peterson remained there, watching the game in moody silence.

After clapping his players on the back and gathering up the team's equipment, Mike found her on the sidelines writing the starting lineup into her score book.

"I noticed you scouting your opposition," he said, grabbing her around the neck, yanking off her baseball cap, and rumpling her hair hard enough to hurt. "Decided on our bet yet?"

"I was thinking," said Meg, squirming out of his grip, "of something really appropriate, like a brand-new, still in its original box, official-league baseball."

"You mean something really cheap," said Mike, punching at her shoulder and jumping back, feinting another blow.

"Boy, do I hate overly confident men," said Meg. "Stick around, big guy. You'll be laughing out of the other side of your face."

"I'll stick around and watch your game, if you'll buy me dinner afterward," he said.

"Ha! With the coaching tips you'll be picking up for free? Dream on! Anybody who drives the car you drive does not need dinner bought for him by a struggling freelance writer."

"All right, then. We'll go Dutch. I've always wanted to go to dinner with a really sweaty girl. Especially one who's been properly humbled."

Go Dutch, thought Meg and was aware of what felt like a skipped heartbeat. Maybe Jack would show up to watch the game. Maybe . . . But she needed to talk to Mike.

"All right," she said. "Keep score for us, at least until some parent who's got a clue arrives." She waved the score book at him. "And *do not* give any hits that aren't hits. I want real batting averages to work with, not those phony 'Well, he's only eleven; who could have expected him to keep a fly ball in his mitt?' statistics. Give me accurate records."

"Yes'm," said Mike. "Want I should keep all the bats in a nice neat row for you, too?"

"Shut up," said Meg.

"You know," said Mike, "they make things besides hamburgers here. You could, maybe, take a more adventurous approach to dining out. If you're watching your pennies, you could have passed your baseball cap. I'm a soft touch. Besides, I always feel sorry for a loser."

Meg's team had, indeed, lost, but she was pleased with how

they'd played. "Nah," she said. "You find a good thing, you stick with it. At least until it gets boring."

"Good things don't have to get boring," he said.

Meg felt a small tremor of nervousness. She shrugged. "Maybe not."

"Heard you had a fire," he said. He looked up from his dinner. "That could have been bad."

"Could have been. Wasn't," she said. "Thanks to the dog you get such pleasure out of maligning."

"I told you to get the place inspected."

"Don't lecture me, please?" said Meg. "I know it's my own fault. If I'd done what you told me to do or Jack told me to do, it would never have happened. But it's all right now. The place has *been* inspected. Dan Ruschman went over it with the proverbial fine-tooth comb. And Lyle Halversen has checked the wiring. I don't want to get into it again." She smiled at him, trying to counteract her defensiveness. "Please?"

"You seeing a lot of Jack?" he asked, squeezing a lemon wedge into his iced tea. A seed shot across the table.

"Not really," she said. "Why?"

Mike stirred his tea. He clinked his spoon against the rim of the glass and set it down. "It's not my place to give you advice about your personal life . . ."

No, thought Meg, it's not. But she merely looked at him inquiringly, wondering what was on his mind.

He started to say something, paused, started again. "Let's just say he must have skipped school the day they taught the kiddies about Copernicus. Or else he figures the man had it all wrong. We live in a Jack-centric universe. Hadn't you noticed?"

"Actually, I hadn't," said Meg, unable to keep a note of coldness from her voice. "You want to elaborate?" She doubted that she wanted to hear what he might say.

He looked at her seriously, then smiled suddenly. "Nope. On to new topics. How's work going? Having any fun?"

"Tons," she said, more than willing to change the subject.

"Though I'm not getting it done fast enough. This is my favorite of all assignments—vocabulary worksheets, I mean."

"I don't remember ever having worksheets for that," said Mike. He, too, seemed determined to ignore the disagreement. "Spelling, math, grammar, yeah. Vocabulary? I don't think so."

"That's because kids used to read," said Meg, putting down her hamburger and leaning across the table. "Then maybe they'd talk about the story. Now they read, too, of course, but not a whole heck of a lot."

"Is this heading toward a diatribe about TV?" asked Mike. "You can save your breath; I'm in agreement."

"Actually, no," said Meg. "Though there may be a connection. Even *in* school, kids don't read. They don't have time. Let's say the selection is 'The Three Little Pigs.' First they do a prereading exercise on sibling relationships. Then they read the story. Then they write a diary entry for each of the swine brothers, make a diorama out of popsicle sticks showing the inside of the oldest brother's house, do a vocabulary worksheet, draw their favorite character, perform a role-playing exercise in which they explore methods of resolving conflict without using a pot of boiling water, do a cross-cultural activity comparing houses around the world, choose music for the soundtrack of a movie made from the story, and take a two-page test." She sat back in the booth. "And now they're done. They could read another story, but, unfortunately, the semester's over."

"Why?" he asked, impaling a cherry tomato. He seemed genuinely curious. "Why do they do all that?"

Meg sighed. "I wish I knew. What I do know is that, in 1927, a typical vocabulary test for grade-school children included *depredation, avarice, artless,* and *sportive.* High schoolers got *sudorific* and *casuistry.* Now they need a worksheet in order to deal with *ambition.* Maybe Johnny can't read because he hardly ever *does.*"

"You're being sportive," he said.

Meg grinned. "I wish."

She ate for a few moments in silence, took a swallow of iced tea, and asked, "You still without a secretary?"

"Unfortunately," he said. "But I'm interviewing next week. Why? You decided you want the job?"

"Work for you?" said Meg. "In a pig's eye. Why didn't you start looking as soon as Angie said she was leaving?"

"Laziness," he said. "It was hard for me to believe that somebody who did as little work as Angie would make much of a difference."

"Not a workaholic, huh?" asked Meg.

"No, she missed that label with plenty of room to spare. She was smart. The girl was no dummy. But she was totally bored by law."

Then why, wondered Meg, did she keep the job as long as she did?

"Where did she go?" she asked, sliding casually into the question uppermost in her mind. "When she left for her more exciting life?"

Mike lifted his shoulders. "I don't know. She didn't say. It was a 'So long; it's been good to know ya' kind of thing. We weren't close."

"But didn't you have to get an address, like to send her 1099 or whatever?"

He frowned slightly. "She was planning a long vacation. A little-deserved one, I'd say, if I were the harsh sort. She said she'd let me know where she settled. Why?"

Meg, ignoring his question, picked up the menu and looked again at the dessert choices. "Where do her parents live?"

"I haven't the faintest idea where her parents live. One of the few things I know about her is that she isn't on speaking terms with her parents."

He caught the waitress's eye and raised a hand. "I made her fill out one of those 'who to call in the event of an emergency' things. You know who she put down? Me! Like that's going to be a big help if I walk in from lunch and she's in a diabetic coma."

"She has diabetes?"

"Not that I know of," said Mike. "Just an example."

He looked up at the waitress as she approached the table. "Coffee, please." He glanced at Meg. "Do you drink coffee?"

She nodded, then realized what he was doing and rolled her eyes. "Very funny," she said.

"Two," he told the waitress. "Thanks."

He relaxed against the back of the booth and placed his hands flat on the table. "What's this all about, anyway? Do you need to get in touch with Angie? Did she steal the bathroom sink or something?"

"No. Not that there was anything left in the house that was worth stealing. She left a bracelet at the back of a drawer, and I would think she'd want it."

"Believe me," he said, "she has plenty."

At eight-thirty, the phone rang and Meg reached over from the couch to the end table to reach the receiver. It was Christine.

"So?" she asked. "How was supper? And don't you consider that fraternizing with the enemy?"

"It's undercover work," said Meg. "I'm very good at it."

"Can you come over? Dan's out and the kids are in bed. There's nothing on TV, and I finished my book, and I want to talk to you anyway."

Meg didn't want to talk; she wanted to think. "I've been gone absolutely all afternoon and evening. I just got home twenty minutes ago. I hate to leave the dog."

"Bring her along. What's one more?"

"And I'm sleepy."

"At eight-thirty? Don't be ridiculous. I'll see you in ten minutes." She was starting, thought Meg, to sound like Jack.

Harding came charging down the driveway, nearly getting himself run over as Meg pulled up.

"Did you know I brought your pal?" she asked, as he stood on his hind legs and stuck his massive head through the open window. His tail waved so frantically that his whole body moved.

"Get off, you moose," she said, pushing the door open.

Christine was scrubbing the sink and singing "Just a Closer Walk with Thee." She motioned to the table. "Sit, girl, and describe your evening," she said, pouring coffee.

"Do you think I drink too much coffee?" asked Meg.

"Of course not. You don't drink any more than I do, the exact right amount. Now, *tell* me!"

Meg rolled her eyes. "He's nice; he's a good coach; I paid for my own dinner."

"And how are things with Jack?"

"He's nice; he's a good painter; he made me chicken salad."

"Please," said Christine. "Don't bore me with so many details."

"It's funny," said Meg. "Jack is incredibly interesting. Everything about him is interesting. So why is Mike the one I feel comfortable with?"

"Because Jack's so interesting."

"Maybe," said Meg. She took a small, chewy cookie from a plate Christine pushed toward her and bit into it. "Can I have milk? These need milk, not coffee."

"Heathen," said Christine, gesturing toward the refrigerator. "Help yourself."

Meg found a glass and poured milk. When she sat back down, Christine was watching her, her lower lip caught in her teeth and a look of amused curiosity on her face. "And what is it that's so interesting about Jack? His talent? The way his blue jeans fit? His ability to find beauty in the world and create it where it isn't usually found? His sober dependability?"

"Say 'Knock, knock,' " said Meg.

"Oh, no," said Christine, shaking her head firmly. "Teddy got me with that last week. I asked you a question."

"I know. I was trying to answer it, but you wouldn't cooperate. His sober dependability? He's dependable, yes. But sober? The man tells the *silliest* jokes."

Christine swallowed slowly and set down her cup. "You," she said, "have made an impact."

"Meaning?"

"Jack has been the premier sobersides for as long as I've known him," said Christine. "Smart, capable, helpful, but . . . silly?" She shook her head. "You're bringing out another side of him, his *joie de vivre.* I salute you."

Meg laughed. "Oh, *right,*" she said. "I always bring out the best in the men I know."

"Don't sell yourself short," said her friend. "People are different when they're happy. You make him happy. So, with all these intriguing traits of Jack's, why are you having a social life with Mike?"

"Social life?" asked Meg. "A few dinners at the Main Street Cafe is a social life? Be that as it may, maybe it's because I like him." And, she thought, he can dance.

"Or maybe," said Christine, "you're really the type who's bowled over by success. You like envisioning yourself at cocktail parties with lots of lawyers and their well-dressed spouses."

"Definitely," said Meg. "That's always been a fantasy of mine." She took another cookie. "How did he get so successful? How many big cases can a mainly rural county have? Do you do nothing all day but bake?"

"No," said Christine. "I also make all my own soap from leftover bits of fat and occasionally slaughter a pig."

"A true Renaissance woman," said Meg.

Christine nodded. "Except for spinning. I make a point of not spinning."

"Whereas I," said Meg, "toil not, *neither* do I spin."

"Yes, Lily, we've noticed. However, Mike does. Toil, that is. I don't really know how he got so successful. He'd been in some large firm in Philadelphia, but when he arrived here last spring, he started pretty much from scratch. Nobody was too impressed; he was young and unknown and devoid of the trappings. His secretary drove a better car than he did."

"His car is expensive," said Meg.

"Now," said Christine. "Sedate, classy, American-made, new. The perfect, successful lawyer's car for a conservative, rural environment."

She lifted her hair from her neck and twisted it on top of her head, sticking a pencil through to hold it in a knot. "If a contractor drives an expensive car, everybody assumes he's a rip-off artist. If a lawyer doesn't, everybody assumes he's incompetent. I guess Mike figured that out. By the end of the summer he had acquired the all-important trappings, and everybody who'd dismissed him started thinking he was some real hotshot after all. See, you're just like everyone else."

"But of course," said Meg. "I've secretly pined for a hotshot lawyer most of my life. Any hotshot lawyer."

"Don't be too hasty," said Christine. "There's more to life than cocktail parties. Which one's the better kisser?"

"Christine! How old are you? Fourteen? Look, if I have anything interesting to tell, I'll tell it."

Christine set down her cup, looking embarrassed. "I . . . that's what I wanted to talk with you about," she said. "You haven't told anybody about the money-order receipt I showed you, have you?"

"Of course not," said Meg.

"I knew you wouldn't; that's why I hesitated to mention it. I just . . . well, you know, I shouldn't have said anything about it to anybody besides Dan himself. It was indiscreet of me, and I was feeling guilty about—"

"About telling tales out of school," said Meg. "Don't. Really. I'm just glad it's cleared up."

Come on, Christine, she thought. The subject has been broached. *Tell me how it got cleared up.* Oh, please, I need to know!

"Thanks, Meg," said Christine.

Something tightened in Meg's chest. She pushed back from the table enough to cross her legs. "So," she said, making her voice casual. "What was all that about?"

Christine stood up and carried her cup to the coffeepot. Her cup, Meg had noticed, had been half-full. "Oh, nothing important," she said. "And, like you said, it's cleared up now. You ready for coffee?"

"No, thanks," said Meg. Come on, she said to herself. Just tell her. Tell her about the tape. Tell her it scares you. Yeah. And then what? What if the old, desperately unhappy look comes back and she asks you to destroy it? What are you going to do?

She pretended not to have noticed Christine's tacit refusal to answer her question. "So," she said lightly. "Who's Leslie McAlester?"

Christine finished pouring coffee. "A woman Dan had some dealings with." She walked back to the table, turned her chair and straddled it, resting her arms on the back. Her eyes met Meg's. "Please drop it," they said.

Meg crossed her arms. "That's it?"

Christine's mouth tightened and she nodded. "That's it," she said.

"Why aren't you asleep?" asked Sara, yawning. "*I'm* nearly asleep and it's an hour earlier here."

"Don't say that," said Meg. She was lying on her bed with the telephone balanced on her stomach. "It makes me think you're getting old. And if you are, I am, and I'm not ready. I just wanted to talk to somebody I know really well."

"Lonely? Coming face-to-face with the truth of the 'old friends are the best' maxim?"

"I guess," said Meg. "I'd miss you no matter what, but things have just gotten sort of . . . strange here. It makes me homesick."

"Not for Jim, I hope."

Meg laughed. "No, not for Jim. Even the fantasies are fading—you know, the ones where he drives up, bleary-eyed from twelve straight hours on the road, to tell me how he had to lose me to realize the depth of his adoration. They've been replaced by ones in which he drives up, bleary-eyed, to find me entertaining a handsome gent on the front porch. I'm sympathetic but dismissive. As he drives away, I can see his shoulders shaking with sobs."

"How *are* the handsome gents?"

"Okay, I guess. But even that's strange."

Meg hesitated. Sara was, perhaps, too loyal to admit there was any cause for Meg's feelings. "But," she continued, "I think it's weird to have two extremely eligible men fluttering around my flame, which tends to be the flickering kind."

Sara was staunch. "You are insane," she said. "You're smart and funny and competent and cute. Why *wouldn't* two men be interested? Why wouldn't sixty? You just wrapped yourself up with Old Wandering Eye too long and you've forgotten."

"I like your opinions," said Meg. "They're so sound." She was right; Sara was too loyal—unable or unwilling to admit what Meg knew—that she wasn't someone men sought after. "I *do* miss you."

"Hey! Let's meet in New York! I'm going this weekend for my cousin's wedding, so I've already got a hotel room. Drive up!"

This sounded wonderful. "Aren't you going to be all tied up doing stuff?"

"Some. The rehearsal dinner's on Friday night and you know it'll drag on, but if you got there at eleven or so, we'd have until three or our eyes closed of their own accord and the whole next day until the ceremony at six. You could come to that or not."

"Your cousin Deedee?"

"Yeah."

"Not."

Sara laughed. "My plane leaves kind of early on Sunday. I

wish I'd thought of having you come up. I'd have taken the last flight out. But it's not that far, is it? It's worth it. Oh, come!"

Sara was right; it wasn't that far. It was definitely worth it. Sara! New York! A chance really to *talk* to somebody about everything that was worrying her. A hotel with a decent shower. She could get a full day's work in on Friday, have Christine keep the dog, get back Saturday night . . . "Okay. Yes, it sounds wonderful. Tell me what hotel and where it is."

They worked out the details. Meg turned on her side and propped herself on an elbow. "Listen, when you get to O'Hare, do me a favor."

"Sure. What?"

"Pay attention to the sax player near the garage elevators at the airport and hum the tune for me when I see you."

"You *are* homesick," said Sara. "Do *not* dream about Jim."

Meg did not dream about Jim. She dreamed about trying to listen to a saxophone solo that was drowned out by the loud barking of a dog.

"Tell your dog to be quiet," said the saxophone player.

"Is that my dog?" asked Meg.

She sat up in bed. "Be *quiet!*" she said.

Sixteen

The weather held for several days, but Meg's mood deteriorated. She was immensely glad she'd made plans to see Sara, for her loneliness, which had begun to fade as she progressed in making a niche for herself, had returned redoubled. It was difficult to worry alone. What she wanted, she could not have; what she wanted was for Christine to help her stop worrying about what was going on, and Christine had refused to do that.

She saved the file she had just created of a group of words, similar enough in length to support a crossword puzzle, and sighed, feeling itchy and depressed. She'd reached for the phone more times than she could count but, except for one call, asking Christine to take care of the dog while she was in New York, which Christine readily agreed to do, she couldn't make herself dial all seven digits. When Christine called, as she did, Meg invented excuses. Deadlines. Cracked plaster. More deadlines. She felt guilty, despite the factual truth of what she said. She *was* busy, but that wasn't the reason her routine had changed. She wanted to explain, but how would that conversation go? "So you won't tell me who Leslie McAlester is.

Just tell me this. Is her voice deep and husky?" She could follow up with, "And were Dan's dealings with her legal?" Maybe they were. But if they were, why couldn't Christine tell her about them?

"Why do I care?" she asked the dog. "Maybe Dan stole a lot of stuff from Mrs. Ehrlich and gave all his ill-gotten gains to a woman he was having an affair with. Is this any of my business? I mean, no one's been in my house *lately*."

The dog regarded her silently.

"You're darn right, it isn't. Christine knows what's going on; Dan told *her*. And she's happy, which means that, if he's the man on the tape, he's obviously decided to dump Ms. Sultry. Christine doesn't care, so *why should I?*"

She had to get out, out into the cool, bright morning. She picked up the phone. Mike himself answered.

"I see you still have no secretary," she said. "I need advice of the botanical rather than jurisprudential sort. Is the weather going to stay wonderful? What's the last frost date around here? And what's the nursery on the far side of town like? Any good?"

"I'm fine, thanks," he said. "And you?"

"Hankering for flowers. So answer the questions, Counselor."

"We haven't discussed my fee."

"How about . . . a little bank in the shape of the Statue of Liberty? I'm going to New York on Friday; I could pick it up. Oh, never mind, I forgot. You're a lawyer. How about a great big huge bank in the shape of the Statue of Liberty?"

"How about a milk shake? If you're going to the local nursery, you'll be coming right by here. Unless you want exotic stuff, it's fine. Aunt Hannah had to range far afield to find her fanciest stuff. But it's got the basics. Stop by. We can go get a milk shake, and I'll give you my meteorological predictions and hold forth on the subject of frost dates."

"At ten-thirty in the morning?" asked Meg. "Besides, I'm bringing my faithful canine companion."

"No sweat. We'll go to the drive-in. They make a mean milk shake."

She drove into town and parked outside a small white clapboard building with a lettered sign hanging from a cross-arm post. "Michael Mulcahy—Attorney at Law," it said.

The front office, which was unoccupied, was thickly carpeted and held a huge, gleaming mahogany desk. A bell had jangled as she opened the door, and Mike stuck his head out of an office down a short hall.

"Come on through to my private waiting room," he said, gesturing down the hallway past his office. "I'm on the phone. I'll just be a second."

She glanced in his office as she went by. He was sitting in a high-backed swivel chair, his feet on an antique desk with curved legs. The surface of the desk was covered by stacks of papers and files, which had spread to the tops of wooden filing cabinets and glass-fronted bookcases. The floor was covered with a beautiful old Oriental rug. The "trappings," as Christine had put it, were much in evidence.

Mike smiled at her and lifted one finger.

Meg dropped onto a burgundy sofa in a pleasant room at the back of the building. There was a tree visible outside the window, with impatiens planted thickly around the trunk. There were bookcases in this room, too, though they were neither as old nor as pretty as the ones in Mike's office. She sat gazing at the bookshelves and listening to what she could hear of Mike's conversation, which wasn't much.

He appeared in the doorway, jacketless and, as usual, tieless. "Let's go. Your animal may be chewing through the seat belts. She got a name yet?"

"I tried 'Stella' for a few days. I liked yelling 'STEL-LA' in a real deep voice. But it wasn't right." She nodded at his office as they passed. "Impressive," she said. "But I might point out that it's hard to see the grain in cherry when it's completely covered by file folders."

Mike put a hand between her shoulder blades and shoved. "Keep walking. If you're not offering to come in and spend three or four days filing, I see no reason for you to mention the situation."

At the drive-in, they sat in the front seats, leaning against the doors and drinking milk shakes while Mike answered Meg's questions. The dog lay on the backseat and ate a hamburger Mike had bought for her.

"A conservative wouldn't plant anything tender for another week or so," he said. "But, heck, where's the joy in life without some risks? I put impatiens out behind the office four days ago. I wouldn't try, oh, torenia yet."

"Well, you know the local climate better than I do, but it's so warm!"

He shrugged. "So, try it. Like I said, live dangerously. If you get charged with cruelty to flora, however, we never had this conversation."

Meg dropped him back at his office and went to the nursery, where she spent a happy hour wandering among the seedlings. When she drove home, it was with the seat next to her full of primroses.

"Look at these!" she told the dog, who had refrained from jumping into the front and crushing them. "If you could see colors, you'd be stunned. This one is almost purple."

She had dug a bed near the front porch the day before, so it would take only a half hour to set out the plants. The nursery also had racks of seed packets, and she had bought pole beans and lettuce. A stop at the hardware store had gleaned her a spade, a rake, a hoe, a garden fork, and a trowel, most of which clattered against the hatchback window every time she hit a rough spot in the road.

The earth was soft and dark. When she had carefully tipped the plants out of their plastic pots and loosened the dirt around their roots, she set them in place and pressed the soil down firmly. The dog lay near her on the grass.

"Later, maybe tomorrow, we can put in beans and lettuce," said Meg. "I realize you don't care about such things, but human beings think they're good. What? So do rabbits? But that's why I let you live with me . . . so I won't have to put up a garden fence. Haven't we gone over this? Your job description's pretty clear: Keep strangers out of the house and the garden."

Jane showed up promptly at three-thirty with Harding, and Meg's prophetic abilities were borne out when the girl put the dog on a long rope. He obeyed her commands eagerly and quickly, as long as nothing distracted him. When a robin flew down onto the grass nearby, however, she had to haul the rope in, hand over hand.

"You ready to try to get the message across?" asked Meg.

"I guess . . ." said Jane reluctantly. "I know he has to learn."

"Okay," said Meg. "We'll entice him to do evil. Entrapment, I know, and it wouldn't stand up in court, but we're not going to court. I, for one, think the FBI should be able to get away with it. How moral is morality that's never tested?"

"What's entrapment?" asked Jane.

"A setup," said Meg. "And it'll save us time if we set him up instead of waiting for a brave squirrel."

She whistled for her dog and took a tennis ball out of her pocket. "I've discovered she can chase this for hours. Now, Harding's going to want to chase it, too. Or her. So he'll take off when she does. Don't call him until he's almost played out the rope. Then yell loud and clear. Remember, use his name and the command."

A moment later, Harding found himself on his back in the grass.

"Don't repeat the command," said Meg. "Just tug him in gently and then make a big deal about what a good dog he is for 'obeying' you."

By the time they went inside to get something to drink, Jane was the proud handler of a dog who came when he was called.

"Of course, he still needs to practice a lot," said Meg. "And don't try it off-lead yet. We've got some tricks to use with that, if we need them. Do you want pop or lemonade?"

Jane chose lemonade. "I asked Mom why you call soft drinks 'pop.' She says it's because you're from Chicago. Do people in Chicago really talk differently?"

"Sure," said Meg. "Out here, you all say, 'Oh, look, there's a police officer.' In Chicago, we say, 'Cheese it, Louie! The cops!'"

"Uh-huh," said Jane. "I bet." She hitched herself up onto the cabinet next to the sink. "You really know a lot about dogs. You're almost as smart as Mrs. Ehrlich."

"No," said Meg, sitting down at the table. "I'm sure I'm not. I just like dogs and had them all the time I was growing up. And I read a lot."

"So did she," said Jane.

Meg was uneasy about the ethics of involving Dan's own child in efforts to reduce her nervousness about him. But, after all, she was trying to *reduce* it.

"You said that somebody inherited Mrs. Ehrlich's best silver. I thought you inherited her silver."

"I did. Just not her best silver."

"Well, who got that?"

Jane shrugged. "I don't know. She told me I would, but she must have changed her mind." She looked at Meg challengingly. "People are allowed to change their minds. The silver I did get is very nice."

"Of course," said Meg, aware that Jane would brook no criticism of her late friend. "It's just that, from what you've said about her, it sounds like you were a really special person to her."

"Yes," said Jane. "I was. But she must have had a reason."

She emptied her glass and shook it slightly, clinking the ice cubes. "I didn't even know she had two sets of *good* silver, but I guess she did."

"What do you mean?" asked Meg. "You hadn't ever seen the set you got?"

"Oh, she never used her *good* silver. Or her good china. She hadn't used it for years because she didn't hardly ever have company anymore, not for meals anyway. So she put it all away. Except for one spoon from her *best* silver. She thought it was so pretty she kept it downstairs and took medicine with it. That's how I know what it was like. She showed me the spoon in her bedside table. It was beautiful, with fancy flowers all over the handle. The handle was . . ." She drew curves in the air. ". . . sort of like that, and the spoon part was pointy. Not sharp, but like you could use it for grapefruit."

She sat swinging her legs gently. "It had Tiffany's name on the back—you know, the girl who always throws her bat—so I asked if it used to belong to someone named Tiffany, and she explained. She said someday I'd have it and a lot more just like it and knives and forks and everything, even a special piece to use for serving asparagus. She said I should think about her when I used it. She got it from her husband's grandmother, and she always thought about her when she used it. And then . . ."

Jane twisted sideways and looked out the kitchen window. In a moment, she went on. "And then she laughed, and she said she had put it in her will for me, because I was her good friend, and I was really young, and that meant someone would be thinking about her for a long, long time. But I'll be thinking about her for a long, long time anyway."

"I know you will," said Meg. "I hope the person who got the best silver does, too, whoever that is."

"Well," said Jane bitterly, "it's a little late for them to be thinking about her, isn't it?"

At six o'clock, the Laundromat was nearly empty, and Meg had her choice of washers and dryers. She drove home feeling productive, with the backseat full of clean clothes. As she pulled into the driveway, she saw her dog racing through the meadow, her wide-set legs making her appear to be churning up the ground as she ran. She leaped upon Meg as she got out of the car, alternately barking joyously and whining.

"Yeah," said Meg. "You've bonded, all right. I like you too, pup."

She sat for a moment on the stoop of the kitchen door and let the dog dance around her until the greeting ritual had run its course. It was another beautiful evening. She breathed deeply. The air was cool and sweet, and no thumping bass from passing car radios pulsated through it.

"So it's a little dull and lonely here, compared to Chicago," said Meg. "There are nice things, too, don't you think?"

The dog scratched at the door.

"Oh, all right," said Meg. "Just because I don't feel like eating yet doesn't mean *nobody*'s hungry."

The kitchen was dim, and Meg could hear the hum of the refrigerator, laboring to maintain its minimal cooling. She switched on the light and smiled at her sight of the room, then felt loneliness swell again. Curtains in a flowered pattern of pink and blue and pale green hung at the window, a gift from Christine, who had made them from another of Mrs. Ehrlich's vintage tablecloths. Christine had helped with other things, too. She'd dragged Meg to the First United Methodist rummage sale, where they'd found an old juicer that worked with a lever instead of an electric switch and a set of old, brightly patterned tin canisters. It was, as Christine had said, a wonderful kitchen.

Except for the floor. It was silly to fixate on the kitchen floor when so much else needed to be done. The floor was *fine*. But, thought Meg, this room was the only room so close to perfect, and it could actually *be* perfect if the floor were right. If the wood in the traveled part was in nearly as good condition as the wood under the cabinets . . .

The dog cleaned the last of the food from the bowl on the floor, looked up, and barked.

"All right, I'll do paying work," said Meg. "But that *isn't* the last of the dog food, so don't get all frantic on me. I can spare a half hour to aim a hair dryer at a few tiles and see what's under here. Then I'll do real work. And I'll write every minute tomorrow."

She chose a spot in front of the sink—the spot that would have sustained the most damage. When the dryer had persuaded the adhesive to let go, she carefully pulled up a tile. She looked at the floor, then moved on to the neighboring tiles. Fifteen minutes later, she sat back on her heels and stared at the results in dismay.

The varnish had worn away, that much was clear. What was also clear was that a liquid had soaked into the bare wood, and a large, irregular stain marred the narrow maple boards.

The dog sniffed with curious interest at the floor.

"Good grief," said Meg. "What in heaven's name did she spill?"

She replaced the tiles, which didn't stick as firmly but stayed in place. The stain would have to be bleached out. If it *could* be. With what? Oxalic acid? And allowed to dry thoroughly and then sanded and refinished. Maybe a tiled linoleum floor wasn't such a bad idea.

She tried to work. Outside her office, the darkness was thick and much too quiet. When ideas were coming, when she could get caught up in productive thought, she didn't mind the quiet, didn't even notice it. Tonight, she noticed. She gazed out the window, wishing she could eradicate the fields that lay between her house and Christine's. She took in breath and let it out slowly. It wasn't fields that created the problem, because the distance they imposed was merely physical.

That isn't Dan on the tape, she told herself. It isn't. Even if it is, *so what?* Just forget the stupid thing and get your friend back.

She put her elbows on the desk and rested her forehead on her hands, loneliness spreading its chill to the tips of her fingers.

174

Seventeen

$\mathcal{A}$ great many people were heading, if not to New York City itself, at least in that general direction. Meg watched their cars go by as she sat on the grass twenty feet off the highway. Her own car was motionless on the shoulder, its flashers blinking in the dark.

"No," she said out loud and with great bitterness, "it *doesn't* take long to get to New York. *If your car runs.*"

By the time a highway patrol officer stopped to investigate and helped her arrange a tow, it was nearly ten. By the time a service station attendant had explained the impossibility of dealing with what appeared to be a thrown rod, it was past eleven.

She called the hotel and found Sara in her room. "So there's no way to get there except by cab, and I can barely afford a cab to get back *home,* which is less than a quarter the distance."

"Borrow a car and come in the morning," said Sara, which was, it seemed to Meg, a much better idea than not going at all. "Call me before ten or so and let me know if you can."

Meg didn't crawl into bed until almost one and then fidgeted, frustrated and anxious, for another hour. Whose car could she borrow? How could she pay for a thrown rod? The dial of the clock glowed, the only light in the house except for the bulb she kept burning in the bathroom.

Her eyes opened, but the room was still pitch-black. It wasn't the alarm that had awakened her. It must have been a dream. What had she been dreaming? But the dream was gone. Maybe she'd simply become so dependent on the dog that she was subconsciously insecure in her absence. After Jim, she'd slept badly for weeks while getting used to being alone. She smiled wryly. He'd been replaced by a dog.

She lay very still, concentrating on relaxing, waiting to drift back into sleep, but sleep would not come. She sat up and twitched the covers off her legs, swinging them over the side of the bed.

A noise froze her motion. Houses—and especially old houses—made noises as they responded to gravity, to wind, to . . .

Someone was moving in the house. She sat very still, turning her head slowly, trying to locate the sound. It came closer. Someone was walking through the living room. Not tiptoeing. Walking.

She stared at the hallway, taking shallow breaths and trying to imagine how many steps it would take her to reach the window. Her heart skittered. Unless she pried the nails out of the jamb—hardly a silent activity—the window wouldn't open.

A bobbing glow lit the dark floor in the hallway, moved past her door. The footsteps moved past behind it. Whoever it was didn't care about making noise but didn't want to turn on a light. Why? And then she knew. Because he thought the house was empty. Lights would be noticeable from the road; noises were not.

She eased off the bed, the muscles in her legs taut. The springs sighed. She took one cautious step, another, another. She reached the doorway and looked down the hall. The noise of something being dragged across the floor came from the back bedroom.

She took three quick steps across the hallway and into the living room, needing to cover the distance to the front door before the noise stopped. The noise stopped. The front door was twenty feet away. If she could get outside, she would be safe in the thick darkness. Even if the intruder could see well enough to discern her in her dark blue T-shirt, which she doubted, chances were he couldn't catch her. Few people could.

A feather would glide across a floor without being heard. She tried to move weightlessly, the wood satiny against the soles of her feet. Was there someone behind her, watching her, lifting an arm? She had to keep her balance, couldn't afford to turn even her head. Just move forward, she told herself. Another silent step. One more. Forward . . . The door was ten feet away. She took another step and felt the narrow plank beneath her give slightly even as she heard it creak.

There was the sound of movement behind her. Meg broke for the door, turned the bolt, yanked it open, and slammed into the screen. The outer door flew open as she hit it, and she was outside, leaping down the porch steps and racing across the cold grass.

How far to the fence? She slowed, dropped to the ground and crawled, grateful for the blackness of the night, frustrated by it as well. There it was, just in front of her. She scrambled over, her shirt catching on a picket. She ripped it loose and dropped again to the ground, lying flat and turning her head to look back at the house.

Through the fence, she could see the glow of the flashlight sweeping the yard. What now? The meadow between her house and the Ruschmans' was uneven and profusely scattered with brambles, shrubs, and trees. She could move across it, but barefoot and in the moonless night, only very slowly. If he guessed where she'd gone, if he followed her with the flashlight, her speed wouldn't save her because she wouldn't be able to use it.

Scattered with trees . . . Where were the closest trees outside the yard? Just beyond the fence. There were apple trees there, a small grouping. She peered into the darkness. They should be to her right, if she'd come over the fence where she thought she had.

Crouching, she crept toward where the trees should be. They rose in front of her, their clouds of blossoms barely perceptible. A few more feet and the bark was faintly rough against her palms. She passed the first, went on to the second. Its lowest branch parted from the trunk no more than three feet off the ground. She pulled herself up, gripping the trunk with one hand, feeling for branches above her with the other. She climbed carefully and silently but quickly and, in a few moments, was fifteen feet off the ground. Unless he caught the dark blue of her shirt directly in the beam, she would blend with the trunk and branches.

She felt the outside corners of her eyes tighten, prelude to a sneeze, and clamped one hand across her mouth, fighting the involuntary response. The flashlight glow disappeared into the house. She sneezed, the muffled sound like thunder to her ears. The light did not re-emerge.

She stood, one arm clinging to the trunk, frightened and furious that she had to wait helplessly while the intruder took his time deciding what to steal. After what seemed like hours but she knew could not be more than twenty minutes, the beam reappeared in the yard. It moved steadily toward the road. He was walking in that direction. The light went off. Meg stopped trying to breath silently. If he wanted to find her, he wouldn't have turned it off. Or would he?

She stared at the road, hoping for the light to go on again, to show her where he was. Only blackness met her eyes. There was no sound. Wherever he was, whatever direction he had taken, he was moving noiselessly. She moved uneasily on the branch, lowering herself to a sitting position.

The night air had turned her legs to ice. She pulled her knees up and stretched her T-shirt down to her ankles. Her arms around the trunk began to cramp, and the branch she huddled on became painfully hard. She shifted her weight, bark snagging against the nylon of her underpants.

What was the most logical thing to do? Walk carefully through the meadow to the Ruschmans. If he realized that, and if he wanted to find her, he would be waiting in the meadow. But it didn't make any sense for him to want to find her. He was almost surely far down the road by now. Or up the road.

Stay in the tree, she told herself. It is often the rabbit that thinks it has escaped that ends up in the talons of the hawk. She closed her eyes and counted slowly to five hundred, resting her head against the trunk.

She jerked awake, tightening her arms around the tree. How long had she dozed? The sky seemed lighter. It was lighter; she could make out the fence thirty feet away. She was frozen, could no longer bear her motionless wait. She stretched her left leg down, found the next branch with her toes, and let it take her weight. Slowly, stiffly, she descended.

Both detectives, a young man and a woman in her thirties, were sympathetic but patronizing. They introduced themselves and accepted coffee at the dining room table.

"Even out here," said the woman, "it makes sense to lock your doors at night."

"I thought I had," said Meg.

The detective inclined her head toward the kitchen. "The door hasn't been forced," she said. "You positive you bolted it when you came home?"

Meg sighed. "I'm from *Chicago,*" she said. "In Chicago, Detective Stanley, we lock our doors. But, no, I'm not positive. It's just the kind of thing I *do.*"

"But it was unlocked when you came back in the house this morning."

"That doesn't mean I left it unlocked last night."

"No," agreed the young man. "But when there's no sign of forced entry, it's a logical conclusion. We've had trouble with this kind of thing from time to time. The Stansburys, next house that way . . ." He nodded toward the east. "The one time they left a window unlocked when they went back to the city, their place hosted a party they hadn't authorized. But breaking and entering . . . well, kids around here aren't normally that determined."

"It wasn't kids," said Meg.

Detective Stanley raised an eyebrow and drummed her fingers on the notebook that lay in front of her on the dining room table. "No?"

"There was only one person. No conversation. No, 'Hey, man! Let's get outta here!' No panicked flight. No car. How many kids go off by themselves at three-thirty in the morning, on foot, to try the doors of what may very well be an occupied house?"

"Do you have a theory about who it was?"

"No. Not specifically. How could I?" Maybe Dan Ruschman, who's married to my good friend Christine, she thought. Probably not, but *maybe*. "Not kids looking for a place to make out, have a party, or smoke questionable substances, however. A burglar, I'd guess. One who thought I wasn't home."

"How many people knew you'd be gone?"

"For all I know, everybody in town. For all I know, it was announced at the PTA meeting, or the *Journal* printed it in their 'What's Up Around Town?' column. Besides, I wasn't secretive about it."

"But nothing's gone. You said so yourself."

I lied, thought Meg. Something is definitely gone. The tape that I found in the toolshed and hid in the house has mysteriously vanished. But I'm not telling you about that, because I'd have to tell you things I don't want to tell you, and it wouldn't do any good anyway.

Soon after she'd come in the house, she had managed to

stop shivering. And as soon as she stopped shivering, she realized what had happened. She had walked, slowly and deliberately, to the couch, tugged out the middle cushion, unzipped its upholstered cover, and groped unsuccessfully inside it. The tape was gone.

She had been right. Someone *had* been in her house, who knew how many times? This time, he had been mistaken about her being gone. Perhaps he had not watched as carefully. Perhaps, as before, he'd seen her leave; clearly, he had not seen her return. Lulled by the absence of her car, by the quiet of the night unbroken by a dog's furious barking, he had felt secure.

She had called the police. But, before they arrived, she had wound her way through the possible ramifications of telling them this particular detail. What did she have? Her memory of an unusual voice making some suspicious but inconclusive remarks. The only thing that made it more than merely a perplexing and bizarre recording was her knowledge that Dan Ruschman had, somehow, found a way to get ahold of fifteen thousand dollars his wife didn't know existed and that this was a secret. It was not knowledge she could share.

Still, no one—not Dan, not *anyone*—had the right to invade her home.

"Somebody had been going through my things not long after I moved in and, I think, my first night here," said Meg.

The woman officer lowered her chin and raised one eyebrow. "Going through your things?"

Meg explained, realizing how ridiculous the story sounded.

The younger detective looked at his partner as if requesting permission to speak and then cleared his throat. "It, uh, seemed to you that someone had gone through your medicine cabinet and two drawers in a dresser were switched and a clothesline had been moved? Was anything missing on any of these occasions?"

"No," said Meg. "No, Detective Schultz, nothing that I know of was missing."

He frowned. "Is there any reason for people to think you keep a lot of cash? Jewelry? Small, portable valuables?"

"No."

The woman shifted in her chair. "Because the person who came in last night wasn't after your computer," she said. "Or anything heavy. He, or she, didn't bring a car."

"It wasn't a woman."

"Because?"

Meg couldn't articulate why she was so sure. It seemed insane to say, "Because I wouldn't have been so scared." She shrugged. "Because it just wasn't."

"Lock your doors." Both detectives stood. "We'll file the report," the woman said. "I'm sorry you were startled."

Meg's mouth tightened. Sorry she'd been *startled?* It sounded as if someone had knocked unexpectedly at her door.

"Thank you," said Meg coldly. She had hoped for a team with fingerprint powder and the ability to locate a single dropped hair. She had hoped for far too much.

"No checking for fingerprints? Like on the doorknob after I was so careful not to touch it?"

Detective Stanley closed her notebook and tucked it into her pocket. She smiled suddenly, which made her immensely more appealing. "You'd be surprised how infrequently we look for fingerprints," she said. "I assume there are a number of people who have been in the house with your permission? And, in this case, well . . . you don't know who had legitimate reasons to be here before you moved in. Unless you've scrubbed every surface in the place since then . . . ?"

Meg didn't bother to respond.

"Feel free to call us if you have any more trouble."

"Can I ask you a question?"

"Of course."

"Did the woman who used to live here, Angie Morrison, have a record? Did the police ever deal with her?"

Detective Schultz smiled self-consciously. He had obviously

dealt with her, and not minded. "She tended to ignore the posted speed limits," he said. "She got some warnings, which didn't do any good, and some tickets, which did a little." He shook his head and smiled. "She's somewhat noticeable," he said, then blushed suddenly. "I mean, her car is."

"I want to find her," said Meg. "Do you have any suggestions?"

The woman frowned. "You want to find her?"

"Yes," said Meg, using the story she'd told Mike. "She left a valuable bracelet in a drawer in the bedroom. Really valuable. I need to send it to her. Could you maybe look up one of those tickets she got and get her license plate number and see if she's changed her address with the DMV? Or gotten another ticket somewhere? I'd really appreciate it. So would she."

Detective Stanley nodded. "Sure. I'll check."

The Chopin sonata was as incongruous as the shining sun and the breeze that gently lifted Meg's hair as she sat on the porch. None of the details of the day matched the mood that enveloped her.

"Feel free to call us if you have any more trouble," she mimicked bitterly. The dog got up, stretched, and walked over to her. Meg had phoned Christine, explained her car trouble and asked her to let the dog out. There would be time later to describe her night in the tree. The dog had shown up ten minutes later, leaping on her with gratifying delight.

"I wasn't actually talking to you," said Meg. "But who else is there to talk to?"

The dog's interest was caught by a sound or smell undetectable to human senses. "So, go," said Meg. "Just be sure to come back."

She stood looking out the kitchen window while she tried to eat a sandwich. Maybe it had been a woman in her house after all. Who besides Angie would have been looking for the tape? But that didn't make sense, not if Meg's suspicions that someone had been in the house before then were accurate. Angie wouldn't have come into the house, gone through the medicine cabinet, removed dresser drawers, and searched the pantry. She would have gone directly to the toolshed, days before Meg discovered the tape there, and there would have been no tape for Meg to find. But if not Angie, then who? And why? The tape contained no useful information. What made it worth stealing?

The dog scratched on the door. "Want a sandwich?" asked Meg, opening the door. "I thought I did, but I don't particularly. We'll share."

She put half of her lunch in the dog's bowl. Crouched on the floor, she thought of why the tape had been taken. Only she and the person who made it knew what was on it. Someone else knew only that it existed and feared it contained more information than it did. It was that someone else who had searched so diligently and, eventually, successfully.

The man on the tape had responded angrily to a suggestion that he had not waited for someone's death before helping himself to her property. He was probably angry because the suggestion was true. And the husky-voiced woman was not letting her suspicion of that fact stop her from benefiting from it.

One of two people—the unknown man or the unknown woman—had been in the house. At least, Meg thought, getting to her feet and leaning against the sink, whoever it was had no reason to bother with her or her house again. Luckily, she had hidden the tape in one of the few items of furniture that had been in the house all along. Only Angie herself would suspect that Meg even knew it existed. She let out her breath, aware of the luck involved in having hidden the tape in the couch, of having kept the couch in the first place instead of banishing it, with so many other things, to the Salvation Army store.

The Salvation Army store. The tape explained the break-in there, too. Her intruder had been looking for it before she ever moved in. Other than her uneasy feeling that it might have been her friend's husband who had frightened her in the night, the tape and whatever it suggested had nothing to do with her. Nothing at all.

Forget about it, she told herself, gazing across the driveway into the distance where the low mountains began. It's over. The worst part is the damage that's been done to a friendship, but maybe someday . . . Maybe someday Christine would tell her who Leslie McAlester was, and she'd be someone who dealt in intricately carved finials, not a husky-voiced conspirator, not a criminal of any sort.

"If your car's getting fixed today, I could run you over to Allentown after the game to get it." Christine's offer was a friendly one, but her tone was distant, and her eyes were strangely flat. "Are you coming to the game?"

Meg held the kitchen door open. "Come in," she said.

Christine shook her head. "No, thanks."

"I'm coming to the game since I'm here after all, but the car won't be ready until near the end of the week."

Christine nodded. "I'll be teaching, but if you need a ride, I'll work something out. Let me know." She turned away, walked around her car to the open driver's door, and stood there with her hand on the frame. She looked back at Meg. "Why were the police here?" she asked. "And were you really not going to tell me about it?"

Meg stepped out onto the stoop and let the screen door bump shut behind her. She should have realized that a police car in a neighbor's driveway would cause comment.

"Of course I was going to tell you." As soon as I decided it wasn't your husband in my house, she thought. "I had to call Sara and tell her I wasn't coming and call about the car and check to see if anything was missing and—"

"Why would anything be missing?"

"Somebody was in my house last night. I woke up and somebody was there."

Christine lost her irritated look. "Who?"

"I don't know. I didn't ask. I just ran out the door and climbed a tree. Eventually he left and I came down. The police are sorry I was 'startled.' They say if I lock my door, I won't be startled again."

Christine rested her elbows on the roof of the car and looked stricken. "That's awful. I'm sorry I was pissy. So, *did* he take anything?"

"Not that I know of," lied Meg.

The *Eroica* might help, especially the third movement. Meg inserted the cassette into the player and sat down with her feet on the coffee table. She leaned back and tried to stop moping. She closed her eyes. It was early in the evening, but she was so tired her bones felt heavy.

She'd stayed in the dugout for most of the afternoon's game, trying to remember to call out who was on deck and in the hole in time for them to quit swinging their heels against the fence behind the bench and get their helmets on. She wouldn't have had to go, having arranged for Suzanne's father to help out while she was in New York, but she'd thought it would be good to have something to think about besides odd noises in the night and the feeling of bark against her skin. It had helped, but not much. She knew her team had lost and that the score had been close, but she couldn't remember what it was. She was too tired to remember much of anything.

She would sleep better tonight. The hardware store in town had sent a man out to change the locks on both doors. The dog was at home. Whoever had broken in had no reason to come back.

Think about the music, she told herself. Pay attention to how inevitable each note seems to have been, once you've heard it. Don't think about the husky voice on the stolen tape, or what she said, or what she hinted at. There is nothing to be done about any of that, and it has nothing to do with you anyway.

It was useless. She could not concentrate on the music. What if she hadn't been so clumsy? What if she hadn't erased those few minutes? Could there have been something telling on that section, something that was now gone forever?

She opened her eyes and stared blankly at the opposite wall, a realization forming whole in her mind. The problem was not what she'd erased. The problem was that what replaced it was the sound of a coffeemaker and her own irritated, confused voice. Anyone who listened to the whole tape would know she had too.

The world shifted a few crucial degrees. It may have been true that the tape and what it suggested had only to do with her house, not with her. But it was no longer true. And the safety she'd been trying to convince herself she now enjoyed had fled.

Meg was frightened. She could wait and wonder how threatened the thief would be by realizing she had heard the tape. Or she could try to figure out who that person was.

People are likely to be home in the evening, thought Meg. So Leslie McAlester, whoever she was, might be at home, wherever that was.

She looked at the names on the computer screen, from the national directory on the Internet. There were only two McAlesters with the first name Leslie. She had printed out the longer list of those listed only as *L*.

She pulled the phone toward her. The dog pushed against her leg and whined. "Do you want to go out?" asked Meg. "Or are you just trying to tell me you disapprove? I realize that loyalty is big with you. But if I don't do this, I can't live here anymore."

Her tone was light, but she was sickeningly afraid that she was telling the literal truth. She began to dial, hoping she could pull off the deception she needed. Christine's the one who can lie so well on the phone, she thought, not me.

A woman answered.

"Is this Leslie McAlester?" asked Meg. It was. "Is this the Leslie McAlester connected with the, uh, Ruschman matter?"

She had no trouble believing Leslie McAlester's denial of any knowledge of what Meg might be talking about. This Leslie was at least seventy.

Meg apologized and hung up, then went through the same steps for the other name. Although the second Leslie's voice was that of a more likely candidate, she was mystified by Meg's inquiry. More indicative of true ignorance was the fact that the question seemed to bore her.

Meg started on the *L*'s. She had made four calls before there was a positive response to her first question.

"Yes, speaking," the woman said.

"Is this the Leslie McAlester involved in the Ruschman matter?"

"Excuse me, but who is asking?" replied the woman. Her voice was annoyed.

Meg spoke as coolly as she could. "This is Florence Harding," she said. "Dan Ruschman's attorney. I wondered if I could talk with you about the situation."

Leslie McAlester was brisk. "Why are you bothering me at home?"

Talk more! thought Meg. "I am 'bothering you' at home because I work very long hours," she said, letting irritation tinge her voice. "I'm sorry if it's inconvenient."

The woman sighed. "Oh, never mind," she said. "Ask away, though I really don't see how I could be any help. The situation has been taken care of, and I do not intend to take it any further. However, I don't care if you're Sandra Day O'Connor, neither you nor anyone else can make me do business with a thief, which Mr. Ruschman most certainly is. And tell your client that, if I have to put up with any more of this, I will reconsider my decision to drop the matter."

Meg had heard enough. "Mr. Ruschman did not ask me to

call," she said. "I'm very sorry I bothered you. Thank you for your time. I won't call again."

She hung up and looked across the room at the dog, who was lying in the corner watching her. "Don't look at me like that," she said. "She lives in New York. That's close enough to visit here. It *could* have been her."

But it wasn't. Leslie McAlester was not the woman on the tape. Did that mean Dan was not the man? Not necessarily. He was mixed up in something illegal, that much was clear. Did the illegal something involve Mrs. Ehrlich's estate?

"Oh, Christine," she said, sighing heavily. "Where did Dan get fifteen thousand dollars?"

She sat in bed, reading and rereading the same page of *Dombey and Son*. There was too much conflict in the story; she needed something that would keep her from thinking about conflict. She got up and went into the kitchen, with the dog pattering behind her, let the water run into the sink until it turned cold, then bent her head and drank from the faucet. She pushed the curtains aside and opened the window, breathing in the cold night air and shivering. She closed the window. The curtains fell back into place, and she went to bed. It was hours before she slept.

Eighteen

Most of Mrs. Ehrlich's garden was behind the house, so Meg didn't see it until she'd walked around to the back. Mike was sitting on the ground under a flowering crab reading the Sunday paper.

"Gosh, there's a lot of stuff back here," she said. "Is it all perennials?"

He put down the paper, placing a rock on top of it. Evidently, he kept a rock nearby for just such a purpose. "Until I settle a major personal-injury lawsuit or two and can afford a gardener," he said. "Aunt Hannah would have started a few hundred seeds indoors by now and be getting ready to harden them off, but not me."

Here and there along a stretch of border and in a cluster at one end, spiky foliage grew in thick, circular patterns around tall stems. "The lilies are going to be wonderful," said Meg. "Some of them are already two feet tall."

Mike patted the ground next to him, and she lowered herself and leaned back on her elbows.

"Did you invite yourself over to talk about flowers?" he asked.

"Or do you want to cry on my shoulder about having a burglar? It's a manly shoulder. Perfectly suited."

"I keep forgetting," she replied, "what a small town this is."

"You hid in a *tree?*"

"What would you have done? Tiptoed down the hall, tapped him on the shoulder, and walloped him?"

He shrugged. "Probably. But, see, there's a manly fist attached to a manly arm attached to the aforementioned manly shoulder. I can see why you'd take a different tack."

She looked at him, at the breadth of his shoulders and the muscles revealed by his short-sleeved shirt. The manly part was true. "You'd have hidden in a tree, too," she said. "But you'd probably have fallen out of it."

Mike lay back on the grass, folding his arms under his head. "Yup," he said. "Why don't you go stay at Christine's awhile?"

"Why? What good would awhile do? I figure I can move back to Chicago, or I can get over it. Those are my choices. And I can't move back to Chicago because I just authorized a car repair that used up every last nickel of credit I have."

They both looked up at the sky for a few moments in silence. Mike turned on his side, squinting in the sunlight. "I didn't hear your car," he said. "You walk over?"

"Yeah. Somebody told me pedestrian traffic was legal around here. Thought I'd try it." She pulled a handful of clover and dropped it on his head. "Had to try it, actually." She told him about the thrown rod.

"See that quaint little detached garage?" he asked. "Aunt Hannah's quaint little car is in there. She didn't will it to anybody, so I got it, along with all other unmentioneds. It runs fine. She'd have me drive her into town in it, to keep it from freezing up. She herself hadn't driven in years. Take it."

"Oh, that's all right. I'll get mine back at the end of the week. Thanks, but—"

"But what? It's not like it would put me out, in which case you can bet I wouldn't have offered. I can't drive two."

Well, that was true. He was probably being nice because his team had won its game by the slaughter rule. Or so she'd heard. She nodded. "Thanks." She looked at the narcissus nodding their heads in the garden. "You say you got the unmentioneds. Does that mean you got all your aunt's furniture?"

"Everything except the piano," he said. "She left the piano to my sister, Laura, and it had been moved out. I got most of the stuff, though."

Meg looked at him. "Who'd she leave her silver to?"

"All the little boxes and bowls and trays and candlesticks and napkin rings . . . all that stuff went to Laura. And her dishes and crystal. But aren't you the nosy one."

"Oh, come on! What's more fascinating than inheritances? So Laura got her other set of silverware; I mean, the set she didn't leave to Jane."

"There wasn't another set. She left Jane her silverware—a set of sterling. It's nice. The other flatware was stainless, what she used every day. She didn't mention it, so it just went with the house."

No, thought Meg. If the sterling came from Mr. Ehrlich's grandmother, it was late-nineteenth-century at the latest, and more than nice.

"Could I see your house?" she asked.

"Of course," he said, getting up and reaching for her hand to pull her up beside him. "I *think* I raked the living room recently."

He went into the house, holding the back door open behind him. They were in the kitchen, which was cool and dim. Meg's eye fell on a toaster on the countertop. Its cover made it look like a little house. "Jane made this for your aunt," she said, lifting it by the small loop on top.

"It's nice," said Mike. "I should give it back to her . . . but she'd probably think that meant I didn't see any value in it."

"That was Aunt Hannah's room," he said, indicating a room

to the right of the hallway. "That's the bathroom on the left, though you probably could have guessed as much, seeing as how there's a tub in it. My room is this one." He pointed to the right, then turned and gave her an amused look. "Oh, I get it. You're pretending to be interested in the house so you can get invited into my bedroom. You know, when you want something, you should just ask for it."

"Shut up," said Meg.

"When I was a little boy," said Mike, "my mother used to stand me in the corner when I said 'Shut up.' I've come to believe yours was remiss in her duties."

"Ha!" said Meg. "All you had to do was stand in the corner? Sounds exceedingly mild to me." She put out an arm to move past him. "Besides, you're the only person I say it to."

"So it's actually a term of endearment?"

Meg snorted. "Oh, for sure. And here's the dining room. Gosh, it's big."

The huge, round, dining room table was covered with stacks of books and papers. "I tend to work in here and eat in the kitchen," he said.

The living room had a fireplace and lace-covered windows and was large enough to seem spacious despite an abundance of overstuffed chairs. The walls were covered with framed prints and photographs. "It's very Aunt Hannah in here," said Mike. "I haven't changed anything yet, except for the piano. Can you believe there used to be a piano in here, too?"

"I like it," said Meg.

"I haven't changed anything in her room either. Someday, I'll make it into a study, but it still seems too soon."

There was something Meg wanted to do. "Can I see it?" she asked. "It looked like a pretty room, what I glimpsed of it."

Mike shrugged. "Sure."

The bed was mahogany and high, with a lovely candlewick spread. Meg perched on the edge and looked around the room. There was a small bedside table next to her left knee. She reached down and pulled the top drawer open. "Do you mind?" she asked Mike, turning to look blandly at him.

"Go right ahead," he said. "Let me see if I can guess what's in there. A handkerchief. And a Bible. And a copy of *Portals of Prayer*. We Lutherans are heavily into *Portals of Prayer*."

Besides what Mike had accurately predicted would be in the drawer, there was a lovely, rose-gold lady's watch with a black face, a small box of note cards, a ballpoint pen, and a silver spoon in a detailed floral pattern.

"Look at this pretty thing," said Meg, taking out the watch and handing it to Mike. "Do you suppose it still runs?" While he wound it, she turned over the spoon inside the drawer. On the back, it said "Tiffany."

"You paged me?" asked Lyle Halversen. From the sound of his voice, Meg guessed he was calling from his car.

"I just wondered something . . . about the fire I had. Is this a good time to ask?"

"Sure. Nobody on the road but me. What is it?"

"Could it have been set?"

Road noise sounded in Meg's ear. "Did you hear me?"

"Yeah," he said. "I'm just thinking." More road noise. "There wasn't any sign of an accelerant. I'm not a fireman, but I would have noticed that. It was exactly the kind of fire that would result from what I described."

"But you said the wires were loose, like would happen over time. Somebody could loosen them, right? And then put some real old, crackly-dry bits of newspaper nearby? And there wouldn't be any way to tell."

Meg could picture the look on Lyle's boyish, good-natured face. "Hypothetically," she said.

"Well, sure. That *could* have happened." He sounded reluctant.

"But you didn't find any old, melted cigarette lighters up there next to the junction box, I take it." Her voice was amused.

Lyle laughed, relieved. "Just a few, and I figured those were yours."

Meg pressed a bean seed into the ground and covered it with dirt, tapping it down gently. She would put in the poles later, when she'd thinned the sprouts. The early-morning sun lay across her shoulders, and if she knelt long in one spot, felt as if it were burning her calves. When she stood and stretched, though, the coolness of the air reasserted itself.

Of course, she thought, that doesn't mean the fire *was* set. Just that it could have been. She stared fixedly at the old house, unable to abandon what had begun as a queasy uneasiness and grown into near conviction. It would have been so easy.

Meg felt the same way she had when she was a child, lying in a dark room, staring at the bedroom closet door, wondering if there'd really been a noise from in there. Even nine-year-olds knew there was only one way to stop the heart-thumping, and that was to get up, turn on the light, and look in the closet.

She would look in the closet, if she could. But she couldn't find it.

Jane might just have got things confused. Mrs. Ehrlich may not have actually said that the medicine spoon was part of a set. It may simply have been a spoon she had not stored in the attic. Why she would, then, have shown it to Jane and brought up the subject of inheritances, Meg could not guess. But children did often misunderstand what they were told . . .

She rested her hands on her hips and looked around. Leaf shadows moved against the walls of the house, a honeybee lit on a violet at the edge of the turned earth, the meadow stretched away to the woods that held the creek. Many times in the past weeks, she had thought of her great-aunt with awed gratitude.

"How did you know," she asked out loud, "that I needed so much for something to be mine?"

She knelt again to finish the planting. How could anyone ignore this dark, beautiful soil? How had Angie resisted planting rows and rows of growing things? It was mysterious but not one of the questions Meg would ask her when she found her. She wasn't however, going to find her very quickly if Detective Stanley didn't keep her promise.

After waiting all the previous day for a call, Meg had decided the policewoman had forgotten. This morning, impatience had taken over. How long did it take to run a check on license plates? The man who answered the phone at the police station was polite about taking a message.

"Yes, I'll make a note of it," he said. "She'll see it as soon as she comes in."

Meg wanted to remind him that he had a radio he could use, but decided he wouldn't use it for a request as seemingly unimportant as hers.

A black sedan pulled into her driveway, and Meg stood, brushing dirt off her hands. John Eppler got out, holding a sack, and strode toward her, looking as if he were ready to review the troops.

"Brought you some honey," he said. "The light is clover; the dark is basswood. Nice taste, the basswood. Either one'll do you for toast, cereal, biscuits, and burns."

"Burns?" asked Meg, opening the bag and taking out a large jar of thick, amber liquid.

"Natural antibiotic," he said. "A little messy, but the best treatment there is. It should be the natural, raw honey, not that processed stuff from the grocery. You'll heal in no time. No scars either. They use it in China. Not here. I guess the AMA and the big drug companies don't see much profit in bee products."

"Thanks," said Meg. After her recent experience, she didn't like even thinking about burns. "This is really nice of you. I hope I don't need to find out how well it works, except as food. Would you like some iced tea? Or something else?"

"No, I've got to get back. My daughter's coming out this afternoon, and I need to straighten up. She's always after me about the condition of the house."

"Your daughter's visiting? How nice."

"Doesn't come often enough," he said. "At least, not often enough to suit me. But she's a busy girl with her own life. And quite the big-city success."

"Will she bring you more lovely mugs?" asked Meg, teasing him.

"I sure hope not," he said. "There's not an extra inch in that cupboard." He started toward the driveway.

She refrained from suggesting how he might make room.

He waved a hand and got in his car. "Cuts, too," he said through the open window. "Or eye infections. Heals them right up."

The library was about to close when Meg approached the desk with a stack of books.

"Just in time," said the librarian. "Interested in silver, I see."

"Yes," said Meg. "I didn't expect you to have anything, but you did." Several of the volumes had sturdy library bindings, but one, carefully covered in plastic, bore a jacket showing various beautiful old pieces.

The librarian inserted date-due cards, and Meg picked up her books and turned. Mike was behind her in the line.

"Starting a new career?" he asked, nodding at her books.

"I don't actually need a new career," she said. "Yet."

"Wait a second; I'll walk out with you."

When they emerged, Jack was leaning against what was temporarily her car in front of the library, arms crossed on his chest, talking to Jane. The girl was laughing up at him, twirling a lock of hair in her fingers. Mike nodded briefly to Jack, punched Jane gently on the shoulder, and kept walking.

"Good-bye," called Meg.

He lifted one hand and rotated it in the air without turning around.

Meg turned toward her car. "Hey, cutie," she said.

"Are you addressing me?" asked Jack.

"Actually not," said Meg. "But if the shoe fits . . ."

Jack smiled. "Let's all go get ice cream," he said.

"Mom's waiting," said Jane reluctantly. "I need to meet her at the grocery store. I was just at the pet shop." She held up a bag. "Cat brush," she said.

"Lucky Charlie," said Meg.

The sky was darkening and the afternoon's breeze was verging on wind. "I think we're about to get soaked," said Jack. "Let's go someplace where they serve food and have a roof."

Jane waved and hurried down the street as Meg unlocked the passenger door and dropped her books on the seat.

"Jane told me why you're driving Mrs. Ehrlich's car," said Jack. "Sorry your trip got ruined."

"Me too," said Meg. "But that wasn't the worst part of the weekend."

"So I hear," he said. He put a hand on her arm and steered her toward the Main Street Cafe. "Let's have dinner before we have that ice cream."

"No, not there," said Meg. "Do you mind someplace else? I've eaten there a lot lately."

Jack shrugged. "Makes me no never mind," he said. "We can try the Wagon Wheel, if you're a steak-and-potatoes kind of girl."

"Sure," said Meg.

"How did the guy get in?" asked Jack as they walked down the block. "You don't really stay there all by yourself with the doors unlocked, do you?"

"No," said Meg. "I don't. The police think I forgot to lock up."

"And you think?"

"That I probably forgot to lock up." She looked up at him,

grateful for the arm he had put around her shoulders. "It was creepy and it scared me a lot." His hand squeezed her upper arm. "But he didn't know I was there. It's not like he was after *me.*"

"Still . . ." said Jack. "Why don't I put in a security system? The materials don't cost all that much, and there wouldn't be a labor charge."

"Thanks," said Meg. "But I have a security system. A *really* cheap one. It doesn't call the police, but it follows me from room to room and down to the creek."

He laughed. "That's right. The Beast."

Fat drops of rain were pelting down from the sky by the time they crossed the street and went into the restaurant. Cheerful red-and-white-checked tablecloths and the smells of charcoal-broiling greeted them.

"Booth?" asked Jack, and she nodded and slipped into one near the front of the room. It was warm inside after the sudden chill outdoors, and she felt cozy and content. It seemed to have been a long time since she'd felt that way.

"All I need now is the jug of wine and the loaf of bread," said Jack.

Meg grinned at him. "Bet you say that to all the girls."

"Each and every one. Let's see . . . that makes two this year," he said. His eyes darkened for a moment.

A waitress appeared with menus.

"Can I get a steak, medium-rare, with a baked potato and a salad?" asked Meg. "Because, if so, I don't need a menu."

The waitress nodded in a friendly way and looked at Jack.

"A bowl of cement," he said.

"Excuse me?" said the waitress, inclining her head toward him, her pencil poised.

"A bowl of cement," he repeated.

"A bowl of cement," said the waitress, good-naturedly going along with him. "I'm sorry, sir. We don't serve cement."

Jack put his hands on the table as if to rise. "Well, then," he sighed, "I guess I'll have to go eat up the street."

The waitress made a small choking noise. Meg laughed. "Jeffrey," she said.

He nodded and grinned at her. "Jeffrey." He turned to the waitress. "I'll have the same as the lady," he said. "And we'll share a bottle of . . ." He looked at Meg. "Burgundy? Merlot? Chianti in a straw-covered bottle?"

"Burgundy," said Meg. "I'm feeling very basic."

He indicated a choice from a short wine list. When the waitress had pushed her pencil back into her hair and walked away, Jack nudged a foot against Meg's knee under the table. "What's bothering you?" he asked. He reached across the table and tipped her chin up so that she had to meet his gaze. "The break-in?"

"I guess," said Meg. "It was creepy, you know?"

She looked at him, at the kindness in his eyes and the line of his jaw. She thoroughly liked looking at him. Maybe he had some idea of where Angie might have gone. Maybe . . . She opened her mouth, thought better of it, and changed her question to one about his work. Someone had come into her house and taken the tape, and she did not know for a fact that it wasn't Jack. Not for a fact.

Their food arrived, and Meg ate for a few minutes. Jack pushed his steak around on his plate, but otherwise ignored it.

"Aren't you hungry?" she asked. "I'm starving."

"I *was* hungry," he said. "Now I'm just wondering why you're so distracted. And trying like the devil to avoid contradicting my claim that I'm not the pushy, inquisitive type."

"Oh, gosh, I'm sorry," said Meg. "It sure as heck isn't your problem."

"Maybe," he said, picking up his fork. "Maybe not. But you have seemed different lately." He looked at her, started to say something, and stopped.

"What?" asked Meg.

"It's none of my business."

"Go on. What?"

He leaned back in the booth and regarded her steadily. "I thought you and Christine had become friends. It seems I was wrong."

Meg glanced across the room to where the waitress was chatting with another customer. "You weren't wrong," she said. She looked back at Jack. "We're friends. She's great. Why did you think we're not?"

He shrugged. "Oh, I don't know. I had dinner at the Ruschmans' the other night, and Jane was talking about you. It seemed she knew more than Christine. I got the feeling Christine thought so too and wasn't happy about it. Just an impression. Like I said, it's none of my business."

"I've been incredibly busy, that's all," said Meg. "She and I haven't gotten together a lot lately except at baseball games." She pointed with her knife toward his plate. "Eat," she said.

The food was good. Meg felt her tension easing as she listened to stories about the disastrous taste of the woman whose bathroom Jack was renovating. By the time Jack walked her back to the car, she was feeling downright cheerful.

She opened the door. "That was nice," she said. "I knew I needed the food . . . and the wine. I didn't know I needed the conversation. Thanks."

"You're welcome," he said. "Is your car fixable?"

Meg nodded. "Though probably not worth it. It's in Allentown. I'll get it back in a few days."

"Let me drive you over to get it."

Meg hesitated.

"Let me. I'd like to. Just let me know when."

"Okay," she said. "That would be great. It's really nice of you."

He leaned over and kissed her on the forehead, then put his hand on the top of her head and pushed her gently down into the seat. "I like being with you," he said.

*　*　*

The grocery-store parking lot was nearly empty when Meg pulled in and stopped. The dog would be waiting for dinner, but it would take only a moment to pick up eggs and oranges and whatever else that being in the store reminded her she needed. She was standing in front of the coffee filters, near the front of the aisle, when she heard John Eppler's voice. She turned halfway. He was standing at the checkout counter with a stunningly pretty, auburn-haired woman.

Meg couldn't help staring. The woman bore enough resemblance to Mr. Eppler to leave no doubt she was his daughter, but Meg had not expected such elegant sophistication. She had started to move toward them to say hello when Ginny laughed in response to the cashier's comment.

"Not a chance," she said. "There isn't a market in Philadelphia that has produce as fresh as you get right here. Why do you think I come back? To see my dear old dad?"

Meg turned away and busied herself selecting an unwanted item from the bottom shelf. She felt dizzy.

Ginny Eppler followed her father out into the rain, making a comment, most likely about the weather. Meg couldn't hear what she said—just the low, sultry sound of her voice. Her unusual and memorable voice.

Nineteen

$\mathcal{G}$inny Eppler wore a pale silver-gray suit with a white silk blouse, very high black heels, and the merest hint of expensive cologne. Her auburn hair shimmered in the carefully lit store. She looked exactly like the owner of an extremely expensive antique store should look.

"Ginny?" the clerk at the grocery store had asked. "Yes, she does deal in antiques. Not the kind any of us can buy, if Mrs. Lundquist's reports are right."

Meg stood aside to let a woman check out. When the clerk had finished bagging the groceries, she took up where she'd left off.

"Ella's the only one around here who's visited Ginny's store. Said she felt guilty about not buying something from a former Sunday School pupil, but she couldn't afford a *thing.*"

Ella Lundquist was the local symbol of wealth. If she thought a store was high-priced, it was.

"Well, I'd like to ask her about some things I'm looking for," said Meg. "She might be able to steer me in the right direction. She seems friendly."

"Oh, heavens, yes. She's always been friendly," said the cashier. She started pulling another customer's purchases across the scanner, but this time she kept talking. "Takes after her mother that way, but it's her dad that always spoiled her. Pity she can't spend more time with him, the way he dotes on her. You gonna want paper or plastic, hon?"

The elderly man so addressed shrugged. "Whatever Greenpeace wants me to use," he said. "*I don't care.*"

"Then you gotta get yourself one of those nifty net bags like they use in Paris, France," said the cashier. "Meanwhile, you're getting plastic. Anyway, you'd think she lived seven hundred miles away instead of seventy. How long was she here? One day? He said last night that she'd be off again this morning. Well, you look her up when you're in the city. Wakefield Antiques, I think it is. On Walnut, I believe."

Now, having been buzzed into the hushed interior of Wakefield Antiques, Meg was glad she had found her best jersey dress still pristine in its dry cleaner's covering. Her Boy Scout shirt wouldn't have done.

"Could I help you find something in particular?" asked Ginny. Her husky voice was casual and pleasant. "Or would you just like to browse?" Upon letting Meg in, she had risen from a desk in the center of the shop and approached with a friendly smile.

"Actually, you might be able to help," said Meg. "I've been looking for years for a set of sterling flatware similar to the one my ex-husband got from his great-grandmother and that I couldn't get my hands on in the divorce settlement."

One of the library books, *A History of Silversmithing in America,* had given Meg a few phrases to toss around. Precious few, she thought now. She described the design on the medicine spoon as precisely as she could but changed the maker.

"The one I'm looking for is old, mid-to-late eighteen hundreds, sterling . . . The design is floral and almost rococo, with fiddle-shaped handles. It's by Gorham. You wouldn't by any chance know the pattern I mean, would you?"

Ginny Eppler smiled. "No, I don't think so. We have some lovely silver, but the one set of Gorham we have has coffin handles. Why don't you look around and see if there's something similar to what you want?"

"I will," said Meg. Looking around was exactly what she had come to do. She sighed. "I guess it's a wild-goose chase," she said. "But it's such a beautiful old-fashioned pattern. It's hard to find something that's very ornate, but so tasteful." She looked around the shop. "You do have nice things," she said. "Perhaps I'll see something."

She walked slowly around the store, looking carefully at silver boxes displayed on marble-topped mantels, figurines in glass-fronted cabinets, and the sets of sterling flatware. Nothing matched the spoon. It was likely that the silver she was looking for had been sold long ago. She wandered over to a set of Limoges and lifted a plate, turning it carefully in her hands.

"Is this a complete service for twelve?" she asked, glancing with what she hoped was obvious unconcern at the price.

"Yes, it is," said Ginny, moving to Meg's side. "One of the saucers has a small chip on the underside of the rim. Otherwise it's perfect. And there are quite a few serving pieces."

"I see . . ." said Meg thoughtfully.

Ginny regarded her. "I *do* have a beautiful set of sterling flatware that's not on display," she said. "It might be close enough to what you're looking for. Would you like to see it?"

"Sure," said Meg, running one finger around the detailed rim of the plate.

Ginny disappeared through a doorway at the back of the store and returned a few minutes later with a dark wooden box.

"This is a service for twelve," she said. "It's nineteenth-century American, but Tiffany, not Gorham. There are a lot of serving pieces."

She set the box down on the gleaming top of what had once been a built-in sideboard but was now a counter and lifted the lid, revealing the name "Tiffany" on the inside. The silverware, newly polished, glowed, the pieces fitting neatly into their spaces.

"Tiffany doesn't make this pattern anymore," she said. "It's almost impossible to find. Their discontinued patterns almost never come up for auction, at least not in complete sets."

She gestured at the hand-lettered description of the flatware on a small white card in the box. It included a price. "Ninety-six hundred doesn't really reflect its rarity."

Meg smiled calmly. She selected a teaspoon and held it, rubbing her thumb along the floral pattern on the handle. Her eyes moved over the contents of the box. "Oh, how nice," she said. "There are twenty-four teaspoons. That's often a help."

Ginny nodded. "It is, isn't it? But actually, there are twenty-three. One must have gone down a garbage disposal."

No, thought Meg. It's quite unharmed. "I love the shape of the bowl," she said. "You could easily use these spoons to eat grapefruit."

She stared at the ceiling above her bed. Who had inherited Mrs. Ehrlich's china? Had it also been switched for a much less valuable set? What else had been stored in the attic? She sat up and pushed pillows behind her back. Who had access to Mrs. Ehrlich's attic? Besides the Ruschmans. Jack. Mike. John Eppler. And those were just the people Meg knew. Hannah Ehrlich could have had any number of friends in and out of her house. She could have had a cleaning lady. She could have . . .

She groaned and got up. Only a short time ago she had opened her eyes every morning and felt a surge of pleasure. She wanted that feeling back but swam instead in a state of constant foggy confusion.

She pulled on her robe and went into the kitchen to let the dog out and make coffee. The sun, low in the sky, slanted through the window, reflected off the floor, and brightened the creamy white of the smooth old cabinets. Meg wished Christine were sitting across the table from her, drinking coffee and helping her think. She was so tired of being alone. Would she feel so isolated if she hadn't had the weeks of camaraderie?

Was it better to never have something than to have to regret its loss so bitterly? If her thoughts could only produce something sensible, she could try to get it back. Until then . . .

The phone rang. Meg sighed miserably and went into the living room to answer.

"Barbara Stanley," said a woman's voice. "I got your message. Sorry I didn't get back to you sooner. I ran a check on those plates, but there's nothing. Her address still comes up as yours, and there's nothing in the system showing a recent ticket. I'll keep checking and let you know if anything changes."

"Thank you," said Meg. "I appreciate it."

"No problem. Have you had any more trouble?"

"No," said Meg. "I haven't been startled even once since Friday night."

The woman's voice took on mild amusement. "Discovered any more switched dresser drawers?"

"Not a one," said Meg.

I have, she thought, discovered what I believe to be some switched sterling silver flatware. Would that pique your interest a bit more? She was tempted to say it, to change the smugness in the detective's tone.

But, even if she weren't worried about Dan's possible involvement, what was the point in telling the police her suspicions? Where could they go with them? All she had was her memory of an unusual voice and the knowledge of a silver teaspoon that matched a set in an antique store owned by the daughter of the dead woman's neighbor. The tape that might have justified a search warrant to turn up that set was gone.

Mrs. Ehrlich. It turned, inevitably, on her. How conveniently she had died.

"Hmm . . ." said the young man in the shop with the "Dog Grooming" sign, giving Meg a doubtful look. "We can surely make her look better, but . . ."

The dog sat calmly at Meg's left side, looking around. Yips

came from a back room, and there were the sounds of running water and dryers.

"What did you have in mind?" the young man asked.

"Just what you said," said Meg. "Make her look better, less scruffy. The only thing I don't want her to end up with is one of those mustaches that look so fetching on schnauzers and miniature poodles but would just make her look like a wanna-be."

"What *is* she?" he asked.

"Believe it or not," said Meg, "a dog."

Halfway down the sidewalk to her car, she nearly collided with John Eppler, who, although looking straight ahead, seemed not to have seen her.

"Pardon me," he said automatically and then, recognizing her, "Oh! Sorry Ms. Kessinger."

"Meg!" said Meg. "Unless I have to call you Mr. Eppler for the next twenty years." She should just give up and accept the fact that the use of first names did not come easily to the man.

Mike jogged across the street, coming onto the sidewalk behind John Eppler. "Meg," he said. "Morning, Mr. Eppler."

John Eppler turned and regarded Mike, then turned back to Meg. "Be seeing you, young lady," he said and walked away.

"What was that?" asked Meg, looking curiously at Mike. "Hard feelings?"

He grimaced. "Evidently."

Meg gazed at him, but he did not continue.

Fill-in-the-blank sentences, thought Meg. Just do some straightforward, fill-in-the-blank sentences. Easy, fast. No, not fun, but they get the job done. The light verse, the rhyming phrases, the word-play exercises were all more interesting, but they required so much thought. She didn't have the mental stamina.

She tapped out a sentence for *appease*. "A person who is afraid to ask questions cannot_____his curiosity." No, that wouldn't fly. In modern-day educational publishing, "a person" required "his or her." Too clumsy, too bulky. Oh, well, it was a crummy sentence anyway.

Mike would know, or ought to know, what kind of medicine Mrs. Ehrlich had taken, but Meg was afraid to ask him. A jumpy heart. What did a person take for a jumpy heart?

The dog barked once from the front yard, an "Oh, hello" bark, and Meg turned her wrist to glance at her watch. Three-thirty already? She turned off the monitor and got up, yawning. Some physical activity would be good, and it was encouraging to see Jane's determination and Harding's steady progress.

Jane was setting the porch chairs out onto the lawn and watching the smaller dog wriggle adroitly out from under Harding's sprawled form. She called him when Meg emerged from the house, and he got up reluctantly and came to her. She snapped the leash onto his collar and began the exercise.

"Watch," she said. "I think he's getting better."

Meg sat on the porch steps, watching the girl and the big sturdy dog. The child paced around the chairs as Harding struggled to understand that he was supposed to remain near her left leg regardless of which direction she turned. "Harding! Heel!" she said, attempting to complete a figure eight.

"He is indeed getting better," said Meg.

"Well, not about everything," said Jane ruefully. "He got the leftover meat loaf out of the fridge this morning while Mom was at the store. And a carton of sour cream. And we can't find a package of bratwurst we *know* was in there last night or a huge bunch of grapes . . ."

"Forgot the clamp, did she? Your mom?"

Jane came to a stop and the dog looked up at her. She looked sternly back. "Harding! Sit!" He dutifully sat. "Uh-huh," she said. "But she's madder at him than she is at herself."

Something clicked in Meg's mind. "Jane, when Harding ate Mrs. Ehrlich's pills, did he have to go to the vet?"

"No." The child started pacing again, the dog at her side.

"The vet just said to watch him. She said just one of each of the pills probably wouldn't hurt him."

"Do you remember what he ate?"

"I remember the aspirin. She always took a baby aspirin, the little tiny ones that taste like orange candy. That's probably why he thought her pills would be good. And she took alfalfa—lots of it, but *that* doesn't hurt dogs. She said it was for arthritis. Mom was worried about the big pill, the heart pill."

"What was that called, do you know?"

Jane gave two quick tugs on the leash as she turned to the right; Harding adjusted his direction and went with her. "She called it 'my heart pill.'"

"Ah, yes. For her jumpy heart. What did it look like?"

Jane stopped and thought. Harding looked around. "Sit!" said Jane. "Ugly. Brown and green, I think. Kind of big. Why?"

"Oh," said Meg, leaning back on her elbows, "I wondered if dogs will eat just any old pill. It sounds like they will. I guess I'd better keep my medicine up high."

"*Your* dog might not eat it," said Jane. "*Harding* would, but a normal dog probably wouldn't."

"You're calling my dog normal?"

"Just compared to Harding," said Jane. "But she looks *more* normal with her new haircut."

She did. Grooming had emphasized the terrier strain in the dog and given her head a more attractive shape. More attractive, Meg had to admit, not actually attractive.

"You know," said Jane, "if you're worried, you could use one of those reminder boxes, like Mrs. Ehrlich, with all the separate lids that snap shut. I don't think your dog would figure out how to open them." She giggled. "Though she could ask Harding to do it for her."

Jack's house was small and gray, its door a deep purple. Trim at the edge of the roof matched the door, and the path from the driveway was old bricks, laid in a careful pattern. His pickup was parked on the side of the house, but he didn't answer Meg's knock. She was a little early; maybe he was out back. She was turning to go down the porch steps when the door behind her opened.

"Meg," he said. "I was just getting out of the shower."

"I'm sorry," she said. "I'm early. I walked, so I wouldn't have to pick up Mike's car later, and it didn't take as long as I expected. This is so nice of you—driving me all the way to Allentown."

He smiled. "No problem. If you're not put off by being entertained by a man in a bathrobe, come on in."

He stepped back and she went past him, smelling something woodsy that she assumed was his shampoo. His damp hair stressed the clean lines of his face. The doorway was not quite wide enough for her to avoid brushing against the thick terry cloth of his navy-blue robe.

"I like your door," she said.

"Artists can get away with purple," he replied. "Sit down. I'll just be a minute. Want something?"

She thought it better not to answer that question honestly. She shook her head.

He selected a compact disc and put it in the player, and *The Goldberg Variations* began softly as he disappeared into what Meg assumed was the bathroom. Most of the house was one large room, the slate floor near the door giving way to parquet in an intricate design of varying shades, partly covered by a beautiful old rug. A fireplace occupied the wall to her right, octagonal wooden columns framing it and supporting the mantel. The wall above was paneled in the same wood that surrounded the fireplace. One painting hung over the fireplace—dark trees against a golden sky.

Meg sat gingerly on a pale gray leather couch that felt like butter beneath her hands and leafed through a copy of *Gentlemen's Quarterly* she found on a small table. Jack returned in blue jeans and a work shirt, this one with regular buttons.

"You find that outfit in here?" she asked, closing the magazine.

"Yeah. I get all my style tips from the pros." He winked at her.

Meg got up. "I have to admit, *GQ* is not what I expected to find at your house. *Road and Track,* maybe. Or *Handyman.* Even *Architectural Digest . . .*"

"The subscription was a gift," he said. His mouth twisted disparagingly. "It usually goes from the mailbox to the trash."

Ah, thought Meg. Stephanie probably didn't approve of work shirts with fanciful buttons. She looked at the painting over the fireplace. "That's beautiful," she said. "Did you paint it?"

"I wish. No. Hannah Ehrlich left it to me. It puts my own work to shame." He looked at the painting and smiled. "It amazes me to own something so beautiful." He turned his eyes to Meg. "Ready?"

Meg preceded him out of the house and got into the pickup. When they had turned out onto the road to town, she looked over at Jack. "Your house was a surprise."

"What did you expect?" He shifted into third gear and glanced at her.

"I don't know. Something less elegant?"

"A cabin maybe? With plank floors and pelts stretched on the wall?"

Meg laughed. "Maybe."

He moved his shoulders, then sat back and spoke quietly. "I did most of the work on the place while I was . . . involved with a woman, a woman named Stephanie, who cared about, cared a lot about, elegant things. I'm just who I am. Can't do much about it. But I thought we'd be sharing the house, so I made it the way she would like it."

"Did she?"

He nodded. "It was me she didn't like so much. Put a man

who likes to work with his hands in a nice house, he's still a man who likes to work with his hands."

He looked at Meg and smiled, his expression changing from somber to playful. "But I've talked about myself enough. Why don't *you* talk about me for a while?"

"Okay." She glanced at the speedometer. "Do you always drive so slowly?"

"No. On superhighways, I sometimes get up near fifty." He rubbed his jaw. "Tell you the truth, I don't know what everybody's hurry is."

Meg quit trying to resist asking the question she wanted to ask. "Do you enjoy working with Dan?"

He looked at her in surprise. "Of course. He hasn't had a lot for me lately, but anybody'd enjoy working with Dan."

"You don't have different ideas about how to do things?" Silently she added, Or what's ethical and what's not?

He shrugged. "Sometimes. I'm a little fussier sometimes. Less efficient maybe than Dan. It's not a problem. Why?"

"Oh, I just wondered if two competent people doing the same job might not run into . . . I don't know. Problems."

"He's the boss," said Jack. "And he knows his stuff."

Meg looked out the window at the tender green of the fields. "Do you have any idea what the deal is between John Eppler and Mike Mulcahy?"

Jack grinned. "Already getting embroiled in our local intrigues?"

"I guess it's nosy of me," she said, "but Mr. Eppler appears not to be on speaking terms with Mike, and it's mysterious."

"Everything's mysterious with Mike," said Jack. "Like, just what is it everybody sees in him? Help me out here. You spend time with him. Would *you* trust him to represent you?"

Meg was surprised. "I . . . I guess so," she said.

Jack made a small noise. "But you asked about Eppler and him. Who knows? Eppler's been bitter toward Mike for months, and Mike seems to get some pleasure out of goading him. I don't know what it is. Maybe Mike slapped a bee at a town picnic and Eppler saw him."

The phone rang as Meg was eating dinner. She went into the living room and answered, trying to swallow silently. It was Sara.

"How's it going?" she asked. "Still wallowing in the slough of despond?"

"I never was," said Meg. "I was just a little lonely. It didn't help to look forward to seeing you and then not. But I've got my car back. Jack took me to get it."

"Aha!" said Sara. "And?"

"And nothing, unfortunately." Meg sighed. "He is so . . . oh, I don't know. Attractive. And helpful. And the question is, why?"

Sara let out an exasperated groan. "Stop it! You can't do this. Jim's a jerk; he's not typical. Let this guy like you, for heaven's sake."

"Fine," said Meg. "You come visit and meet him and then you tell me I'm his type. When are you coming?"

"As soon as I've got the programming done for this stupid project, which better occur before I retire in thirty years." She hesitated. "Meg?"

"What?"

"I've got some creepy news."

"Which is?"

"I just think it's better to know these things."

"Sara, what *is* it?"

"It was all over the office today. Jim's getting married."

Meg leaned back on the couch and closed her eyes. "Oh," she said. "Anybody I know?"

"Teresa somebody," said Sara. "Nobody at work has met her. Are you all right?"

"Sure," said Meg. "Why not?"

It wasn't him, then, after all. It was her.

Twenty

Out?" yelled Meg, walking toward home plate from her position near third base. "He's *out?* The rule is you have to slide to avoid contact! There wasn't any contact; there wasn't going to *be* any contact!"

The umpire blinked at her. "In my judgment, ma'am," he said with exaggerated politeness, "the ball was imminent, and your runner should have slid."

Meg glared at him. "The ball was *imminent?* Then why didn't it ever *get* there?"

"Sit *down,* Meg," whispered Christine, tugging at her.

Meg yanked her arm free and put her hands on her hips. "Maybe if you'd ever get out from behind the plate, you'd see what was happening in the field, where the plays are going on!"

"This conversation is over," said the umpire, turning his back and adjusting the plate with his foot.

Meg steamed in silence, aware that every player on her bench was watching her, openmouthed. She turned and faced them, noticing that Dan kept his eyes on the score book he was holding.

"Hustle out," she said. "Same positions as last inning. Let's hold 'em."

Nine children moved onto the field. One boy slapped another on the back with his mitt. "Only sissies don't slide," he said. "Sissy!"

Meg reached out and grabbed the back of the boy's shirt. "Sit, Brian," she said. "Now! Tiffany, go in at second."

She sat down and crossed her arms, staring through the chain-link fence of the dugout toward the pitcher's mound.

Christine sat next to her, speaking quietly due to the nearby presence of the players who hadn't taken the field. "Are you all right?"

"Of course I'm all right," snapped Meg. "I'd be better if this league had some decent umpires."

"You're not usually so . . . hot-tempered about a call," said Christine, looking doubtful.

Meg couldn't argue the point. It was true. She glanced at the umpire, wondering if his dark hair and blunt, regular features were to blame, at least in part, for her fury at him.

"It *was* a bad call," she said, "which was the umpire's fault. Patrick would have batted next and scored the runner, or it's real likely, and that would have tied the game, so not being tied now is, in my opinion, his fault too. But maybe, just maybe, it isn't his fault that he looks so much like Jim."

Christine turned on the bench, her eyebrows drawn together. "You didn't hate this umpire last week."

"I didn't hate Jim last week," said Meg.

The dog jumped eagerly into the car and settled down on the backseat. Meg put an overnight bag on the passenger seat in the front.

"Maybe I should call you Barkis," she said, twisting around to look at the dog. "It fits you both in the obvious way and as a literary allusion."

The dog cocked her head, gazing at her owner out of the same eyes that had once seemed so mean.

"Come on, *you* know. As in, 'Barkis is willin'.'" From *David Copperfield*? Heaven knows *you're* willing. It's one of my favorite things about you. None of that, 'Oh, dear, I already made plans for the weekend.'"

Meg turned the keys in the ignition. "Let's go see what there is to see," she said. "It's Saturday. We're footloose. Why not? There's a whole state we know almost nothing about. Mountains, lakes, farms, Amish people in buggies. There isn't another practice until Tuesday. If it weren't for that, we could just keep going until our money ran out. That is, for five days instead of three."

She pulled out onto the road and turned toward town, driving faster than she should. She didn't notice John Eppler wave cheerfully at her from his car as he passed on her left at a more sedate pace. She did notice Christine's house, the driveway empty. She had called Christine and left a message saying she'd be away for a few days.

When she passed Jack's house, he was pulling out of his driveway. He sounded three short blasts on his horn and waved for her to stop. Meg pulled over and rolled down her window, and he left his truck and jogged up to her car.

"Where are you off to?"

Meg lifted her shoulders. "Someplace. I haven't decided."

"I was hoping you'd feel like a movie tonight."

"No. I've got to drive for a while."

"So we'll drive. We'll drive for hours. And my truck, as opposed to this rattletrap, can go anywhere."

"Which means you'd be driving. No, thanks. I'm not criticizing; I wish everyone were as laid back as you, but I want to drive and I want to drive fast."

She put her foot on the clutch and shifted into first gear. "I'll see you in a few days."

"A few *days?*" He put a hand over one of hers on the steering wheel.

Meg nodded. "May I go now?"

He stepped back from the car and held up his hands, palms out. There was surprise in his eyes and something else. Hurt?

She drove away and glanced in the rearview mirror. Jack was standing next to his truck, looking after her. The dog moved on the backseat, catching her eye.

"I can see you watching me," she said, "through the magic of reflected light. Don't you dare give me that reproachful look. I know I was rude, and I already regret it. He can't help it that he's male."

She had been right to question Jack's interest in her. And it was ludicrous to think that Mike's flirtations were anything but a way to pass the time. It didn't matter whether all men were alike, which she wasn't stupid enough to think, or not; she was who she was, and would remain so. She could move anywhere, do anything; what real difference would it make?

She slammed her hand against the steering wheel. That Jim had done nothing she could identify as wrong made her furious. "See, he didn't want to settle down when I was what he'd have to settle *for,*" she told the dog. "Now he's found someone who makes it sound all wonderful and cozy. Why? What makes *her* so great? What was wrong with me?"

The dog, aware that she was being addressed, whined and stood up. She stretched to put her paws on the back of Meg's seat and nudged the side of her neck with a cold nose.

Mike was on the sidewalk in front of his office. "Hey! Lady!" he yelled as she passed. Meg sighed and stopped, waiting for him to stride around her car and bend over.

"I hear you were less than pleased with the officiating today," he said through the open window.

Meg looked angrily at him. "Yeah? Don't the people at the park have anything important to talk about? What? Did somebody think it merited a phone call to you?"

Mike's eyebrows lifted in surprise. "Hardly. The same ump called our game, and the subject of your game came up, that's all."

"Oh, please!" she said. "And you sympathized with him, right? Even though you weren't there and didn't see his stupid call."

Mike's brown eyes went blank. "What's the matter with you?" he asked.

"Good question," said Meg. "Exactly the question I've been asking myself. Excuse me, but I'm blocking the street."

Mike took his hand away from where it had been resting on the open window.

"I'm sorry," said Meg. "Ignore me. There are just some things that I don't want to think about that I have to think about."

She drove away. Near the far end of town, she stopped at a red light and looked around at the small stores, the people chatting on the sidewalk. Saint Paul's Lutheran Church was on her left, neatly tended flower beds in front and around the side. The library was across the intersection on the right.

The library. She pulled into a parking space in front.

The librarian was used to handing out the *Physician's Desk Reference*. "It's pretty technical," she said. "I hope it's helpful."

"Thanks," said Meg. She carried the massive volume to a table and started through the listings for cardiovascular medications. Most of them were tablets. Mrs. Ehrlich had not been taking tablets. Tablets, to the best of Meg's knowledge, were solid colors. That meant Mrs. Ehrlich had been taking capsules. She glanced through the symptoms the various drugs treated. "Jumpy heart" was not among them, but arrhythmia was. Most of the medications prescribed for arrhythmia were tablets.

"Norpace," murmured Meg, her finger stopping on the page. "Capsule." She turned to the color photographs. There were several, of different dosages. Norpace CR was 150 milligrams, was normally taken every twelve hours, and was brown and green.

She got back in the car and turned to look at the dog. "Change in plans," she said. "We're going home."

"Hey, Dave," said Meg, holding the phone in one hand and pulling a notepad closer with the other. "I know you're an internist, not a heart specialist, but I've got a question I hope you can answer."

"Meg!" said her old friend. "Great to hear from you! Sara says you like the house and aren't moving back here. That true?"

"Seems to be," said Meg. "But I miss you guys. Can I rummage around in your brain for a minute, Dr. Clark?"

"Rummage away," said Dave. "But the twins are going to be waking up any second, and Paula's at the store, so make it snappy."

"I want to know what would happen to someone who needed to take Norpace for arrhythmia and didn't."

"Tell me more."

"If an elderly person with a history of severe arrhythmia was taking 150 milligrams of Norpace CR twice a day and didn't take it, what would happen?"

"Didn't take it for how long?"

Meg traced over the word *arrhythmia* on her notepad. "I don't know. A day?"

"Not much. But it's not a good idea to miss doses."

"How long would it take to die from missed doses?"

Dave hesitated. Meg could hear a wail in the background.

"I don't know for sure," he said. "It's not a condition I'd be prescribing for. My guess is, about a week. Maybe more. Depends on how long that particular medication stays in the body."

The wail was joined by another. "Would it be a dramatic death?"

"No," he said. "It would be heart failure."

"Thanks. Go take care of your babies. And kiss them each eleven times for me."

She hung up and sat thinking. If Mrs. Ehrlich had died from missed doses of her medication instead of dying despite taking it, how could she have missed taking an entire week's worth, or maybe two? A person that forgetful would simply not be functioning, and Mrs. Ehrlich had been functioning. How could such a thing happen?

Jane's remarks came back to her. Separate lids that snap open . . . That was how it could happen. Mrs. Ehrlich could have simply forgotten one medication while filling the daily reminder boxes. Then, every day for a week, when she took her medicine, she might have thought she was taking it all.

The phone next to her rang.

"I got your message," said Christine, "and hoped you hadn't left yet. Don't leave. I'm coming over. I'm walking, so you've got ten minutes to get the coffee on. I just had a big fight with Dan, and we need to talk."

"She just said, 'Mr. Ruschman,'" said Meg, "and all I could think was Dan, but she meant Alan! The man Leslie McAlester thinks is a thief is Dan's brother, Alan!"

Christine nodded. "And she's right about him. He *is* a thief, or was, anyway. He stole fifteen thousand dollars while he was working for her, and she found out. He called Dan, and Dan called her, and the upshot was, return the fifteen thousand, and that's the end of it."

Meg rested her elbow on the kitchen table and put her chin in her hand. "And he had to," she said, "because he's Dan. He probably thinks it's his fault that his brother's a thief. How long have you known this?" She really didn't need to ask. Christine had known something since the night Meg had overheard her talking to Dan in the kitchen. This, then, was what she had learned that night.

Christine confirmed Meg's belief. "For weeks. I bullied Dan into telling me. Fifteen thousand was most of what his business had in the bank to pay his salary for the next couple of months, and all of what he had available to pay Jack and the other guys. So now he has to finish everything himself on the jobs they were working on, and I have to borrow money from my sister and teach every chance I get, and we've cashed in the savings bonds we had for college. Dan was scared to tell me because I made such a fuss about the other time—the time Alan needed a thousand. He was going to try to find the money someplace, borrow it, but he couldn't—at least not without my signature on a second mortgage. He thought I'd leave him."

"You didn't."

"Heck, no!" said Christine, smiling. "Over money? Ha! You remember, I told you that Dan had things rough as a kid? He thinks Alan is the reason he's sane today, maybe even just plain alive today. Alan's four years older, and Dan says he took the brunt of things at home. The first time he went to jail, it was for clobbering his father when he went after Dan. The judge thought Alan didn't need to hit him quite so many times. Or with a two-by-four. But the incident got Dan out of the house. So, see, you're not so far off assuming that Dan feels guilty about Alan's situation in life. Of course, he might have helped him anyway."

Meg got up and poured more coffee into the two cups on the table. "Loyalty. Jane says Dan is big on family loyalty."

"Tell me about it," said Christine. "I didn't understand until recently why he was so fierce on the subject. Now, I guess I do. He wouldn't tell me a thing until I swore I wouldn't breathe a word. He thinks Alan will never work again if the story gets out. And he doesn't want people knowing we're so much in debt."

"Gosh," said Meg, replacing the pot and turning to look at her friend. "I wouldn't have told anyone." She sat down and looked steadily at Christine. "I *hated* prying. I didn't know what else to do! At first, I was just uneasy, but after the tape went missing, I got scared. If you'd just told me what was really going on . . . You could have trusted me with what was really going on."

"I *know* it!" said Christine. "I might mention here that *you* could have trusted *me* just a bit earlier, too." Christine had listened with intense interest to Meg's description of finding and playing the tape. "After all, you didn't have a husband making you swear not to tell a soul. When Dan made me promise, I couldn't tell him I'd already talked to you. At least, I didn't think I could. Then it started really getting on my nerves how you changed. You were mysterious and jumpy and busy all the time. But you weren't too busy to keep working with Jane and Harding. I didn't like ranking below a dog, so I figured if I told you what was going on with me, you'd tell me what was going on with you, and we could be friends again."

"I'm sorry," said Meg. "Does it help that it was harder on me than it was on you?"

Christine twisted her mouth, thinking. "Maybe."

"I'm sorry you had to have a fight with Dan about telling me."

"Oh, pooh," said Christine. "It didn't last." She giggled suddenly. "But you actually thought he might be the man on the tape? You really, truly didn't tell me about the tape because you thought Dan might be, not just a lying cheat, but a *crook*? Dan?"

Meg could feel herself blushing. "All right. But I don't know him, Christine. Not really at all. And it fit. You have to admit; it did fit."

"Indeed," said Christine dryly. "It's completely logical. So much so, I'm starting to suspect him myself."

Meg sighed. "You're going to tell him. I just know."

"Bet on it," said Christine, grinning. Her smile faded. "Are you sure the silverware in Ginny's shop is Hannah's?"

"It's hers," said Meg firmly. "Or Jane's, I should say. It's a perfect match for the medicine spoon, and one teaspoon is missing from the set. Besides, what else explains the tape? If I'd had ninety-six hundred dollars, I'd have bought it right then and there. As it was, I did my best imitation of a lady with money and hinted at how I'd be back. At that price, the only thing that keeps it safe is the fact that she's not displaying it."

"Ninety-six hundred dollars is a *bargain?*"

"Seems so. From what I can tell, the price she's charging means she really wants to get rid of it. It's an ornate, discontinued pattern and it's in a fitted case. A fitted Tiffany case. No way it's worth less than twelve thousand, and that would be on the low side. If she puts it out in front, it won't be there long."

"The police could get a search warrant," said Christine.

"How?" asked Meg. "You're a teacher; you're supposed to know about the Fourth Amendment. What probable cause is there? If I had the tape, maybe. Maybe. Without it, how?"

"All right," said Christine. "But Jane could go and look at the silver and then tell the police about her conversation with Hannah."

"Think about that for a minute," said Meg.

Christine did. "Oh. Right. Ginny would never show it to her. Jane would walk into the shop, and the silver would disappear, as if it never existed."

"Yup. And you don't want Jane involved in this, do you? Anybody who would steal from a trusting old lady—because, you see, the only way anyone could have done it would have been to be trusted—is not someone who should know that Jane ever saw that teaspoon."

Christine nodded. "Yes. I mean, no. But how did they have the nerve? Hannah herself wouldn't have been likely to realize what was going on, but she left a *will.*"

"I know." Meg got up and took a shiny white cardboard box out of the cupboard. "Have a doughnut," she said. "If what you told me about her will was typical, it wouldn't reveal what had happened. The details were about where things were, not *what* they were—the will of a woman who was worried about clutter, not theft. Substituting nice things for much more valuable things was virtually foolproof. No one, except Jane, had seen any of her best stuff for years."

Christine got up and paced across the kitchen to look out the window. "So, it was just a matter of time. She was old; she had a heart problem; she was determined not to go to a nursing home. Chances were she'd never move those boxes and trunks out of the attic . . ."

She turned and her eyes were worried. "Just before she died, she was upset. Something was troubling her. Do you think she'd figured it out?"

Meg took a breath and let it out. "Yeah. Did Jane tell you the silver-casket story?"

Christine nodded and thought for a moment, leaning against the counter. "She *hadn't* forgotten it. Far from it. She knew it wasn't the box she remembered."

"So what happened?" asked Meg. "If she thought someone she had believed in was stealing from her, what would she have done? And who was it she suspected?"

"I don't know what she'd have done. She'd have done something, though. The *who* could have been Ginny's lover. Or it may have been more than one person. Someone who had access to Hannah's attic has to have been involved. John Eppler certainly had access. In that case, though, someone else was involved, too."

She lifted her cup and put it down again without drinking. "Wait! Ginny may not know the tape's gone; she probably doesn't know it ever existed. If we could get the police to take this seriously, they could question her, refer to the tape, even quote from it if you remember some quotable remarks—and scare her into telling who it was she was talking to."

"You don't know Ginny Eppler very well," said Meg. "Neither do I, but enough to know she'd have an attorney with her from the moment a cop first asked her a question. And maybe she's the one who made the tape in the first place."

Christine threw Meg a scornful look. "Sure, and was careful

to talk about Hannah's property while her co-conspirator was out of the room."

"Okay, she didn't make the tape," said Meg. "Then it must have been Angie. And she knows exactly who she was taping. So we find her."

"Fine," said Christine through a yawn. "How?"

"I don't know, but people don't just disappear. She left a couple of cartons of junk here, but, unfortunately, that's exactly what it was. Junk. There were some letters, but only a few had envelopes, and those didn't have return addresses. I don't think we can trace her through the brand of thread she buys."

"Well, you figure it out. I'm going to bed." Christine got up and pulled on a sweater. "I've got a thousand things to do tomorrow, not the least of which is to figure out why there's an infestation of fruit flies in Teddy's closet."

"I'll walk you," said Meg, reluctant to have Christine set off alone into the night. "Yeah, I know, you're a big girl. But I've got a bodyguard to walk *me* home."

Meg's dog trotted ahead of them as they crossed the field toward Christine's house.

"The grapes!" said Meg. "The grapes that went missing after your latest memory lapse regarding the refrigerator clamp!"

"What about them?"

"They're in Teddy's closet! I'm so glad the really perplexing mystery's been solved. That'll allow you to apply your mind to the rest of them."

"One of which," said Christine, "is why we're walking across the field instead of taking the road."

"The moon is out; it's light enough to see . . . sort of."

"So? It's still a lot easier to take the road, at least at night."

"Look," said Meg. "I hate to sound dramatic. Heck, I hate to *be* dramatic. But the intruder the other night? The one who got the tape?"

"Yeah?"

"He'd been in my house before. I'm not sure how many

times, but at least three. He's the one who broke into the Salvation Army store." She explained her theory. "And if he's listened to the tape, to the whole thing, he knows I did, too."

Christine stood stock-still in the meadow while Meg told the story. "So, see, it's really a good thing if we don't make up." There was enough moonlight for Meg to see the look on her friend's face.

"I mean," she said quickly, "if nobody *knows* we're friends again. Anybody who's paying any attention to me will have noticed that we've been less than tight for a while. So we better keep it up. If we were friends, you'd know everything on my mind. If I'd heard a strange, tape-recorded conversation, you'd know all about it. If I'd been to an antique store and seen Mrs. Ehrlich's silver, I'd have told you. It's only because we're not friends anymore that you don't know any of that."

Christine's eyes widened. "Do you really think it's . . . dangerous?"

"Come on, let's keep moving. I'm getting cold."

They walked for a few minutes in silence. "Probably not," said Meg. "He'll know the tape didn't tell me anything, really. He doesn't have any reason to think I'm dangerous to him. And, actually, I'm not. Still, he's a real creep."

"Tell me about it! Anyone who'd go sneaking around in somebody else's house . . ."

"He's creepier than that," said Meg. "I think he tried to burn down my house. And, if you recall, I was in it."

Twenty-one

$\mathcal{M}$eg stood looking at Mike's narcissus. No, she reminded herself, not Mike's, Mrs. Ehrlich's. There were pure, pale yellow ones that gave off a heavenly fragrance; snow-white blooms with apricot cups; neat, delicate miniatures and sturdy, tall varieties. They were moving in the faint, warm breeze of a perfect May afternoon.

"How can you still have so many?" she asked. "The Ruschmans' are over with. Your aunt must have planned pretty well to keep them going so long."

"She loved narcissus," he said. "So she put in ones that bloom early, mid-season, and late."

Meg pointed at a sweep of familiar-looking blooms. "There's Sir Winston Churchill," she said. "I recognize him from his photograph."

"If you say so," he said. "I do know it was one of her favorites; I've seen it around for years, but we were never formally introduced."

"So you don't know what that is either?" She indicated a huge cluster of double narcissus combining yellow, gold, and orange at the far end of the border.

Mike followed the sweep of her arm. "Nope," he said. "I might be able to find the charts Aunt Hannah kept. They could be in a drawer I haven't cleaned out. That patch wasn't here last year. It's nice."

Ah, thought Meg, the By George. She walked over and knelt to look more closely, gently pulling a blossom toward her to breathe in the fragrance. "I think she was looking forward to these," said Meg. "You should cut some for her grave."

Mike moved two lawn chairs into the shade and sat down on one. He indicated the other with a jerk of his thumb. "Come," he said. "Sit. Tell me why you were so grouchy the other day."

Meg shook her head. She wanted to eradicate any feeling he might have that she was angry with him, but she wasn't willing to tell him about Jim. "It didn't have anything to do with you," she said. "It was something that happened in Chicago."

He leaned back in his chair, crossed his arms behind his head, and looked at her. "And you're not going to tell me what."

She grinned at him. "When I know you better," she said.

Jane and Harding walked sedately into Meg's yard, the dog close by the child's left leg. Jane stopped in front of the porch where Meg was looking through the gardening book, and Harding stopped too, glancing up at his mistress and then sitting.

"Wow!" said Meg. "You didn't have to say a thing! I'm impressed. Really, I am."

Jane beamed and bent to hug the dog. "Good dog! Good Harding!" she said. She unsnapped the leash from his collar and patted him. "Okay. Go on. Okay."

Harding leaped onto the porch and crouched in front of Meg's dog, front legs extended, his tail waving against the sky and soft, eager whines issuing from his throat. The smaller dog got up, stretched, and walked casually down the steps, Harding at her heels, barking happily.

Jane handed Meg the bulb catalog she was carrying. "I

remembered that you asked for this," she said. "Are you planning your garden?"

Meg groaned and closed her overdue book. "Indeed. The problem is, I want everything, and I want it all right away. I want great, big, huge peonies without waiting twenty years and I want masses of established chrysanthemums and I want . . . But if I put in a lot of spring bulbs this fall, at least April and May *next* year will be pretty. Sit down and rest. Harding is doing really well."

"*I* think," said Jane, sinking onto the chair next to Meg's, "he's developing a reliable moral center."

"He just may be," said Meg.

"There's going to be an obedience contest at the Memorial Day picnic," said Jane. "I thought maybe we'd enter. What do you think? First prize for beginners is a fancy supper at La Petite Maison. For two. If we won, I could give the prize to Mom and Dad for their anniversary."

"Hmm . . ." said Meg. "A fancy evening at the little house. The competition could be stiff."

Jane smiled sheepishly. "I know. We probably wouldn't win, but it doesn't cost anything to enter."

"Then enter," said Meg. "Definitely. Unquestionably. He *is* pretty good, and you've got more than a week to work with him."

"Except the seventh-grade trip is next week," said Jane. "We're going to Washington, D.C., for *three days,* and I'm in charge of the last fund-raising event for it this Saturday. We're having a bake sale and craft fair in the park. So I've got hardly any time at all." She looked at Meg slyly. "And I've got this baseball coach who says she'll bench kids who miss practice."

"You're kidding!" Meg's tone was shocked and sympathetic. "What a witch!"

"Mmm . . .," said Jane. She slid down in her chair and put her feet on the porch rail. "But I had an idea. Would it be cheating if you helped me? I mean, you've already helped me, but if you, like, worked with him extra?"

Meg thought about this. It didn't seem even faintly like cheating. "That's not cheating," she said. "It would be cheating to dress Teddy up in a dog suit and enter *him,* but that's not your plan."

"So, would you do it? Work with Harding some? If he won, the anniversary present could be from you, too. La Petite Maison is so *fancy!* They usually go to the Wagon Wheel."

"Let's not count on his winning," said Meg. Harding was, indeed, making exceptional progress, but he was young and questionably reliable. "But, sure, I'll work with him."

She sat by the creek, watching the play of light on the water while the dog cast about in the underbrush, her tail whipping back and forth.

"Oh, leave them alone, whoever they are," said Meg tiredly.

The dog ignored her and set off through the woods, nose to the ground. Meg rested one elbow on her knee and propped her chin on her hand. She wanted to believe that Hannah Ehrlich had taken her medicine right on schedule and died despite it. She did not believe this. The dead woman had owned an enormous number of valuable objects, and those objects had ended up in the hands of someone who became angry when teased about when he'd acquired them.

So what had happened to the capsules she hadn't taken, and how had she been persuaded not to take them? Would someone who had become convinced of the efficacy of bee venom take other folk-cure advice? How far would John Eppler go to protect his daughter?

Meg got up slowly and trudged back toward the house. Had someone deliberately killed Hannah Ehrlich and, if so, who?

Ginny Eppler stretched out languorously on her camelback sofa and rested her head on the arm. "I've been at an estate sale in

Boston," she said into the phone. "That's where I've been. Why?"

"You should tell me where you're going," said the man on the other end of the line. "Has anyone been looking at the Ehrlich silver?"

"Of course. The caskets sold really well, I told you that."

"Not the caskets," he said, trying to suppress his irritation. "The flatware. The stuff I told you not to show yet."

"Actually, a woman was in a while ago who was *very* interested in it. I'd be surprised if she didn't come back."

"What day?" asked the man.

"I don't know. Last week. Before I left for Boston. It doesn't matter. Fran would have told me if she'd come back to ask about it, so she hasn't yet. But she will."

"You shouldn't have shown it to anyone yet. If she comes back, tell her it's been sold."

Ginny ran her fingers through her glossy hair and frowned. "Sold? Why?"

"Just do it," said the man. He did not want to confide his worry. "Don't show it to anyone."

"Look," said Ginny. "This is ridiculous. Waiting six months made some sense to me, but the china sold the second day I had it out in front. The couple who bought it didn't even blink at the price. The jewelry caskets brought in a lot, and so did the biscuit jars and figurines. Why are you sticking at the flatware? It's not even the best item we got."

"It's the most identifiable. Just do what I say."

"I'm telling you, she was really tempted. She'll be back. And she *wasn't* a cop, wasn't an independent, wasn't anything like that."

"What makes you so sure?" he asked.

"I know serious interest when I see it. And she could afford it. The rubies in her earrings were real. Small and tasteful, but real."

The man took a deep breath. "Describe her. Describe her very carefully," he said.

"Buy these," said Christine. "They're butterscotch brownies, chewy and full of nuts. They have more fat than you should eat in a week, but—"

"I know," said Meg, picking up the package. "They're the best things I ever tasted." She handed Christine the price of the brownies. "I'm going to go stroll around by the crafts. Remember to gaze after me in an irritated way. Maybe you could put your hands on your hips and look huffy."

"No problem," said Christine. "I'll look huffy, you go look at the Ukranian hand-painted, gorgeous blown eggs. The grandfather of one of the kids makes them and he isn't charging enough. Go get one before they're snatched up. I got the best, but there are some almost as nice. Mine's in the car, or I'd show you. Oh, no, I wouldn't. We're barely speaking."

Meg wandered in the direction Christine indicated and found the display. A man was basking in the praise of a small crowd that had gathered to admire the fragile, intricately decorated eggs. She had carefully lifted one from the table when she felt a hand on the back of her neck.

"Hey, babe," said a familiar voice. "I was going to donate a painting I have of a baseball coach. Figured the school would get about a hundred grand, and the seventh graders could go to Jamaica instead of Washington, D.C. But then I thought, the model herself should have it."

Meg turned and smiled. "But she doesn't have a hundred grand."

Jack squeezed her neck gently. "I know," he said. "It's her only flaw. But what would seventh graders learn in Jamaica, anyway? It's probably better to have them trotting up and down Capitol Hill and checking out the Renoirs at the National Gallery. So . . . when can I bring the painting over?"

"Really?" asked Meg. "I can have it? Wow! You can bring it anytime I'm home. How about this afternoon?"

"If this weather holds, I've got to tuck-point a chimney this afternoon," said Jack. "I've been putting it off for weeks because I hate climbing around on roofs. The Corbetts are getting peeved. But I'll call you."

"Great," said Meg.

It was impossible to work. It was impossible for Meg to trick herself into thinking that communicating the difference between *disinterested* and *uninterested,* important as it was, mattered enough for her to spend her time doing it. She turned off the monitor and went into the kitchen to find something to eat, something easy and comforting.

She sat at the table, not tasting the egg-salad sandwich she was eating, and opened the bulb catalog Jane had brought. She leafed though the allium, crocus, iris, and lilies. Her yard would never rival the beauty of Mrs. Ehrlich's garden, but bulbs would be a good way to start. A little elbow grease, some bonemeal, cover them up, and five or six months later . . . beautiful blooms. No spraying, no fussing. Her eyes stopped at a pretty double narcissus with scatterings of gold and orange on pale yellow petals. It looked familiar. "May-flowering," the catalog said. "Pleasantly fragrant." She would definitely order some of that one. It was called Tahiti.

She carried her plate to the sink and set it down, looking at the decorated egg she had put in a glass eggcup on the cabinet. The dog stood up on her back legs and put her front paws on the edge of the sink. She whined.

"Oh, I'm sorry," said Meg. "You want the leftovers?" She took the plate out of the sink and set it on the floor.

"Help yourself," she said. "This is egg you can eat, but stay away from my expensive craft purchase. You may think you want it, but you don't. It bears a resemblance to a real egg, though one from a very unusual chicken, and at one time, that's all it was, and from an ordinary chicken to boot. But it isn't any-more. Got it?"

The dog finished licking the plate and nudged it out of the way to see if anything had fallen off underneath. Nothing had. She lay down on the kitchen floor and put her head on her paws.

Meg backed over to a kitchen chair and sat down, her knees feeling hot and weak.

"That's how," she said. "That's how Mrs. Ehrlich died."

"Hi!" said Jane, recognizing Meg's voice on the phone. "We're leaving on our trip tomorrow! Will you remember to work with Harding? And what should we see in Washington? My teacher left one afternoon free and said she'd take suggestions. Mom says we should walk up the steps of the Washington Monu-ment."

"I'll work with Harding, I promise," said Meg. "Tell your mom she's revealing her age. They stopped letting people walk up the Washington Monument a *long* time ago. See everything. Walk down the Mall, for sure. And go to the Vietnam Memor-ial even though it will make you cry. Oh, and if you get tired of going to bars in the evenings, tell your teacher you should drive around the whole downtown at night. It's wonderful at night. And have fun! Can I talk to your mother?"

"I never get tired of going to bars," said Jane. "Hang on; I'll get her. Oh! And win on Monday night, okay?"

"Without you? Fat chance, but we'll try."

Meg paced around the kitchen until Christine came on the line. "Hannah Ehrlich didn't forget to take her capsules," she said. "She took them."

"What do you mean?" Christine lowered her voice to just above a whisper. "You mean it was just . . . inevitable?"

"The opposite," said Meg. "She died from taking capsules that contained no medicine. They probably contained corn-starch, or sugar, or who knows what, so they'd have some weight. The capsules in the prescription bottle had Norpace in them; the capsules in her daily reminder dispenser didn't."

"Who emptied them? Do you know?"

"No," said Meg. "Not yet."

She drove to John Eppler's house and found him, unusually idle, on the front porch. He folded his newspaper and stood politely until she had seated herself in a cushioned wicker chair.

"Ms. Kessinger," he said. "How are you doing?"

"Mr. Eppler," she said. She had given up on establishing a first-name basis for their relationship. "I'm doing fine except for a burning curiosity about something that seems like none of my business, and may well not be. Why are you so mad at Mike Mulcahy?"

The man looked out across his yard. "You're right. It's none of your business," he said. "But I'll tell you."

"What are we doing here, and why did you insist I walk over?" asked Christine. "Why didn't you just pick me up on your way? Where's Mike?"

"He's at work," said Meg. "I know because I called him to taunt him about only beating Joe Murrell's team by one run last night. So look." She pointed at the narcissus at the end of the border in Mike's backyard.

"Very nice," said Christine.

Meg held out the gardening catalog and pointed to the blooms displayed on page 32. "See any difference?"

Christine peered at the picture, at the garden, back at the picture. "Should I? I don't."

"Neither do I," said Meg. "Because they're the same flower. It's called Tahiti."

"And?"

"And it's supposed to be By George."

"Which means that . . . ?"

"I don't know," said Meg. "But it's peculiar."

Twenty-two

Barbara Stanley's tone was brisk and businesslike. "A car that resembles Angie Morrison's has been found in the city," she said. "But it may not be hers."

"Where?" asked Meg. A break! She'd be happy to have something constructive to do, some streets to walk up and down knocking on doors, asking neighbors—who would surely have noticed someone who looked like Angie—where she lived.

"Behind a deserted factory. Stripped. Must have been stolen, but no report's been filed."

"I think she was going on a long vacation," said Meg. "Maybe she doesn't know yet that it's gone."

"Nice surprise," said the policewoman. "I asked them to let me know when a report does get filed. I'll call you when I hear."

"Thanks," said Meg, trying not to sound as frustrated as she felt. "Did you get anything else? Like, does grand theft auto bring out the fingerprinting team?"

"It depends," said Officer Stanley. "Not early on a Sunday morning. Not unless there's a body in it."

The garbage bags were where she'd left them next to the tool-shed. Meg carried them into the house and dumped them out on the kitchen floor. There might be something she hadn't noticed. After all, when she'd looked through these discarded possessions before, she hadn't been trying to find their owner. She knelt by the heap, sifting, looking and discarding, pushing things away until all that was left in front of her was paper. Postcards were unlikely to help; she ignored them for the time being. She gathered the letters. Three had envelopes; most did not. As she had recalled, none of the three had a return address.

She opened the first envelope. The letter inside was an angry response to a break-up. Near the end, it became more pleading than angry—the type of letter one would keep, at least for a while, to counterbalance moments of insecurity. Still, Angie was unlikely to have recently contacted a man she had, years ago, rejected—cruelly and without cause, if the letter was to be believed—even if Meg could find him.

The other two envelopes were both addressed in the same hand. Meg pulled out the contents. One was a birthday card, one a letter. Angie, it appeared, had a mother. Not, Meg thought, an endearing mother, but at least one who occasionally wrote. A mother was more promising than a thrown-over boyfriend. She sat on the floor, reread the letter, gazed at each envelope. Nothing but Angie's name and address, a cancelled stamp, and . . . a postmark.

Standing at the kitchen window and tilting the envelopes just right, she could make out the faded ink. They had both been mailed from Sinclair, Oklahoma.

Please still live there! thought Meg. Please! And then, when she had gotten a number from Directory Assistance: Please be at home!

Mrs. Morrison was at home but in no hurry to give Meg any information. "Who did you say you are?" she asked, her voice suspicious.

"Meg Kessinger," said Meg. "I live in the house Angie used to live in, in Pennsylvania."

"What house Angie used to live in?"

Meg tried to maintain a cheerful tone. "The house in Harrison, where Angie was for a while. I live in it now. She moved out, and I moved in, but she left something that I want to send to her. Only, like I said, I don't know where she moved."

"What did she leave?" Suspicion was replaced by a glimmer of interest.

Meg gritted her teeth. "Well," she said brightly, "a really lovely bracelet and the pretty little velvet box it's in. It was tucked at the back of a drawer, and she must have missed it while she was packing." The bracelet story was proving quite useful.

"Valuable?"

Why else would it have come in a velvet box? thought Meg. "Gosh, I *think* so! I'm sure she'd want it. If I just had her address, I could send it to her right away. Or even her phone number. Then I could call her, see, and—"

"You better just send it here."

Yeah, right, thought Meg. "Oh! You mean she's there? Great! Could I talk to her?"

"No, she's not here. But she'll show up sometime. When she wants something."

"But where is she, Mrs. Morrison? Where is she now?"

Mrs. Morrison didn't know. Michelle had been bothering her for weeks about it. Michelle thought there was something fishy going on, but that was just plain silly, because Angie was terrible about keeping in touch with the folks at home.

"Who's Michelle?" asked Meg.

"My other daughter," said Angie's mother. "In Tulsa."

Meg had to promise to send the bracelet to Mrs. Morrison if Michelle didn't know where Angie was—which of course, she wouldn't, or why would she have been carrying on about it?—before she got a telephone number.

Michelle wasn't home. Her yawning husband was annoyed, both about being awakened and about the fact that his wife was at the store. She returned Meg's call, collect, a half hour later.

"No, I don't know *where* she is!" said Michelle. She sounded harried but, at least, was not dismissive. "She was supposed to call me from Boston, because . . ." She lowered her voice. "Because I was going to try to get out to Atlantic City this summer." There was the sound of water being turned on. "But she never called. I'm about worried sick, and—*I'm doing it as fast as I can, damn it!*—she was all excited about moving the last time I talked to her. But Boston Information doesn't have a number, and I don't know any of her friends where you are. I was hoping you were one of them, when Wayne told me to call Harrison."

"Sure," said Meg. "I can see why you'd be frustrated. But she's probably just busy. Moving is *such* a hassle. Anyway, I'll see what I can find out, and if I find a number for her or an address or something, I'll let you know, okay? And will you do the same?"

Michelle promised and hung up, and Meg sat looking at the phone for several minutes. Then she picked it up and called Christine.

"At church," said Dan. "Late service. I begged off, but she took Janie to the bus, and then she and Teddy were going to church. You want her to call? It'll be a while."

"The minute she walks in," said Meg. "The minute. Okay?"

Attached to Meg with her dog's sturdy leash, Harding was doing well, really too well, his right shoulder often bumping her thigh. She decided to work on sharp left turns. Running into him a few times would remind him to keep a slight distance and be prepared for shifts in direction. She turned off the path onto the grass and collided with the dog, who stumbled and glanced up at her in surprise. Two right turns were no challenge for him; he did not exhaust the slight play in the leash in the instant it took him to adjust. Another sharp left—he did better at it—and they were back on the path.

Working with Harding was the only thing Meg could think of

to do. She needed to be busy, needed a simple task that would engage her physically but leave her mind free to go over its obsessive and cyclical thoughts.

Christine wouldn't be home until well after noon. Meg had filled the first ten minutes of her impatient wait by calling nurseries. Two had been too busy to answer detailed questions on the phone, but the last had been staffed by a harried man who seemed glad for the relative relaxation provided by a phone call and who responded with enthusiasm to questions about spring bulbs.

"Ah, yes!" he said. "That one's brand-new." He knew all about it and confirmed what she had thought.

She halted abruptly. Harding stopped with her, lowering his haunches to the ground and holding the "sit" position. "Good dog!" said Meg, dropping her left hand to rest on the top of his head. His tail wagged across the ground.

She put her hand, spread out and flat, a few inches in front of his nose. Would he obey the hand signal without the verbal? She moved away. He looked doubtful, began to rise. "No! Sit!" She repeated the hand signal for "stay" and again moved away. This time he held his position, looking interestedly at her. She dropped the leash and jumped up and down, spun in a circle and waved her arms. He'd been through this before and wasn't fooled. He didn't move, except to open his mouth and let his tongue loll from the side.

"Harding! Come!" she said. He moved eagerly to her and sat again, facing her. "Good dog!" She dropped to her knees and hugged him.

"Just a little more practice, you beautiful guy," she said. "You can win Janie that ribbon, can't you?"

Harding heeled perfectly the rest of the way to the creek and twice obeyed the hand signal for "stay." Meg unhooked the lead, and he bounded out into the water, splashing about, his tail wagging vigorously.

She sat on the ground, listening to birds nearby and her own dog barking in the distance, and watched Harding frolic. What was she going to do? She knew, now, not only how Hannah Ehrlich had died and why, but also at whose hands, but she couldn't prove it. The logic that told her what had happened was merely that—logic.

The method was perfect: simple and evidence-free. Mrs. Ehrlich's body could be exhumed and autopsied, but it would reveal nothing. The only drugs it would contain would be those that were prescribed for her. There were no forged prescription blanks. There were no missing drugs. There was no evidence.

Harding emerged from the creek and found an interesting place to dig, both front paws scrabbling wildly at the dirt. Within a moment, a chipmunk's bold descent from a nearby tree distracted him, and he lunged after it. The chipmunk had a change in plans and retreated. Frustrated, the dog circled the tree, then bounded back toward Meg and attempted to sit in her lap.

"Just wet would be one thing," she said, shoving him away, "but you are *muddy.*"

He sat down facing her, his eyes merry.

"Yeah, you're a good dog," she said, holding his head and touching his forehead with her own. She straightened and scratched under his chin. "And at least you're not tracking all that into the kitchen like some dog I could mention."

Her dog, having been abandoned to allow Harding to concentrate on his work, was probably trying to dig her way out of the front yard at this very moment. If so, she would be filthy. With a dog, it was just as well that the kitchen had an easy-to-clean floor. The bare, worn sections of wood that the linoleum covered would have soaked up anything that spilled or got tracked in . . .

Meg's back went rigid, and her hand, clenched into a fist, slammed against the ground. The stains under the neatly tiled floor. Why hadn't she put them together with the stains behind the cabinet? How could she have been so slow?

Harding ran barking up the path. Meg jumped and whirled. Christine was being greeted with wild enthusiasm by the big yellow dog. She pushed past him, not urgently, and hurried toward Meg.

"What?" she asked.

"I'm so glad it's you," said Meg, panting a little. "Gosh, you scared me. I thought you were at church."

"The bus was late, so we were late, so we came home instead. I called right away, like Dan said, but you weren't home. I got scared and changed clothes and came over. If you'd let me *drive* over, I'd have been here sooner. What is it?"

She leaned against a tree, while Meg sank back down on the ground. "They found Angie's car, and then I found Angie's sister. Listen." Meg explained.

Christine slid down the tree and Harding tried to climb onto her lap. "Does that all sound to you like it does to me?"

Meg nodded. "And I should have figured it out days ago. She *is* dead. And she died right here, in my kitchen."

Christine listened, her blue eyes narrowing, as Meg told her about the floor. "He didn't realize that blood had dripped behind the counter. He did know the stain on the floor was a problem, but he didn't have time to get it out. So he covered it up. That's probably one of the reasons he tried to burn down the house. Christine . . ."

The muscles in Meg's legs were jumping under the skin. She made a determined effort to relax. "Christine," she said again, "that means the man who watched my house, who knew when I was gone, who had a way to get in whenever he wanted . . . has already killed two people. Maybe he's been in the house lately. Maybe he's seen my notes about arrhythmia and Norpace capsules. Maybe he's noticed that some of the floor tiles aren't stuck down so tight anymore. Maybe . . ."

Harding stood up, his ears pricked.

The blood had drained from Christine's face, and her voice was gruff and unnatural. "But who is 'he'?"

"Don't say anything." Meg's voice was low and she looked at the creek instead of at her friend. "Somebody's coming. Can you crawl from that side of the tree back behind those bushes ahead of you? *Don't say anything.*"

Out of the corners of her eyes, she saw Christine nod.

"Then do it. Now!"

Meg stood up. "Harding! Come!" she said. The dog, who had started up the path, wheeled and returned, and Meg told him how good he was as she affixed the leash to his collar. She turned and started up the path. She stopped, a look of pleased surprise on her face. Jack, ten yards away, adjusted the knapsack he was carrying over his left shoulder and lifted a hand in greeting.

"Jack! Hey!" she said. "How nice! Did you bring the painting?"

He crossed the last few yards from the trees and hugged her to him.

"I was worried when you weren't at the house," he said softly, pressing her head against his chest. "Your car was there, but you weren't. Yes, I brought the painting, all done up in a plain brown wrapper, though it's not what usually comes in a plain brown wrapper. Unfortunately, I didn't have the requisite knowledge for that particular painting."

The flannel of his shirt was soft and smooth against her face. She rubbed her cheek gently against it and moved her arms to encircle him. With her right hand, she stroked his side.

"Worried?" she said. "Why?"

He released her and stepped back slightly to look down at her. "Because I don't like not knowing if you're okay. Does that make you nervous?"

Meg looked at him. "No," she said. "That doesn't make me nervous."

He pulled her to him again. Meg stretched up her hand to cup the back of his neck. Harding pulled at the leash, trying to get to the bushes, and whined. Meg drew in her breath.

"What?" asked Jack, smoothing her hair with gentle fingers. "Let's walk along the creek, and you can tell me what makes you breathe like that. I brought sandwiches, hoping I'd find you here."

Meg put her hand against his chest and pushed gently. "Jack," she said. "Jack, I . . . I'm afraid I've done something really stupid, something I need to tell you about."

He gazed at her, his eyes soft with concern. "So tell me. There isn't anything you can't tell me."

She turned away from him and looked across the creek at the tangled growth on the far side. Harding danced around her feet, lunging against the leash and barking. Meg thrust her right hand through the loop of the leash, grabbed the leather strap, and yanked him toward her sternly.

"Harding! Quiet! Heel!" Meg's voice was annoyed. The dog moved to her left side and sat grudgingly.

She sighed and turned her head, looking up at Jack and dropping her left hand, spread out and flat, in front of Harding's nose.

"I . . . I was talking about you to . . ." She broke off. "Look, Jack, I don't know how to say this. Just listen for a minute without reacting. Please?" She moved her shoulders nervously. "I shouldn't be so jumpy . . . I should just flat-out confess."

"Meg! What is it? Just tell me. Please!" His eyes were beseeching. "What stupid thing could you possibly have done?"

She moved behind him, putting her left hand against his back and rubbing between his shoulder blades. "I *think* you'll understand. You just *have* to understand."

She stepped to his right side and out in front of him. Turning slowly to face him, she opened her mouth to speak. "I . . ."

She yanked the leash toward her as hard as she could. It caught Jack at the back of his knees and pulled them forward.

He landed heavily on the ground, letting out a whoosh of breath.

Harding, taken by surprise by the unjustified wrench to his neck, looked reproachfully at Meg as she landed on Jack's chest, grabbing for the knapsack and trying to pull it from his shoulder. Christine ran from behind the shrubs, determination if not comprehension in her eyes, and pulled at his arms as he clawed at Meg's face.

"Fuck you," he breathed softly, his eyes furious. He pulled his arms from Christine's grip and closed his hands around Meg's neck. Christine rose, stepped back slightly and drew back her right foot. She kicked the side of his jaw, and his head rocked to one side as he grunted, letting go of Meg and struggling to roll over and rise.

Harding tried to pull away, barking frantically with fear and confusion, but his leash was taut, caught between Jack and Meg. The man kicked out blindly, one foot landing sharply against the big dog's ribs. That was too much for Harding, who sank his teeth into Jack's calf.

Christine unsnapped the leash from Harding's collar, and he pulled away from the thrashing humans. He ran around them crazily, trying to adjust his youthful sense of the order of things and a dog's place in it.

Jack bucked and rose, throwing Meg to the ground, her head by the edge of the water. She bent her knees and kicked up with both legs as he reached down, the knapsack falling from his shoulder. The blow caught him in the stomach, pushing him back, and Meg scrambled to her feet. He made a grab for the knapsack, but Meg took a step and kicked it as hard as she could. It landed in the creek near the opposite bank.

Christine drove into him from behind and he stumbled, then got an arm around her, lifted and threw her down, landing on top of her.

Meg looked around wildly for a weapon. The only rocks by the edge of the creek were small; there were no sturdy branches on the ground nearby. There was, however, a leash. She gathered it and looped it over Jack's head, pulling it tightly around his neck. She lifted, straining, and Christine squirmed out from under him.

Jack grabbed for the leather strap and tried to pull it away from his neck. He maneuvered onto his knees, got one foot under him, and attempted to stand, to allow his greater height to break Meg's hold. He couldn't stand. A small brown creature had dashed from the path and sunk her teeth into his other ankle. She pulled backward with thirty pounds of fury. Jack fell forward onto his chest, his hands still grasping at the leash.

"The knapsack," said Meg. "Look in the knapsack."

Christine splashed into the creek, snatched the knapsack, opened it, and reached inside. She took long strides back through the water. Her eyes were hard and determined, but her voice was light.

"Oh, goodie," she said, taking out an object. "He brought a gun."

Detective Stanley put her hand on top of Jack's head as he slid into the backseat of the squad car and then walked over to Meg.

"We're not going to be able to hold him long on an unregistered, concealed weapons charge," she said.

"I know," said Meg. "And the DA probably won't care that he lied to a lady about having sandwiches in his knapsack, either. I should have let him shoot me."

The policewoman smiled ruefully. "You want to answer the charge that you attacked him—that his, shall we say, 'tussle' with you two was self-defense?"

"If it will help you hold him longer," said Meg. "While we were sharing a tender moment, I couldn't help but wonder why his knapsack contained such a small lunch, and why the sandwiches felt so solid and heavy against the back of my hand."

"Did he, by any chance, make an overt threat?"

"No," said Meg. "But I'd be curious to know why he has a key to the padlock on my cellar doors—a lock I *don't* have a key to but which is, right now, unlocked. Before he came down to the creek, he'd been in the house."

She looked over at the police car and raised her voice. "Did you find my notes? Did you wonder about the floor? And did you *really* think I'd fall for that romantic *crap?*"

She handed the officer a set of keys. "He lost this while he was trying to throttle either me or Christine," she said. "It answers the question I had about how he was able to get into my house anytime he liked. That small key there with the rounded top is the one I've been looking for. When he cut off the old lock and put on a new one, he kept the only key."

She glanced again at the police car. "When you've got him tucked away, see if you can find a bloodhound."

The woman frowned. "What for?"

Meg tipped her head in the direction of the creek. "Well, it wouldn't have to be a bloodhound, but it has to be trained. I'm willing to bet that someone Jack did overtly threaten is buried in those woods."

"Now that the wretched brute can get into and out of the yard," said Mike, "I'm glad she's decided I'm not a sociopath."

It was early evening, and they were sitting on the porch waiting for the search to be over. The subject of Mike's comment lay at their feet. Meg patted her fondly.

"She did a good job of digging her way out from the fenced yard," she said. "I hope the dog the police found is as good at his job as she was at hers."

"Cadaver-trained," said Mike, grimacing. "Everybody's a specialist."

It had taken several hours to locate a dog trained to detect the nitrogen given off by dead bodies, and another hour had been spent waiting for that dog and his handler to arrive. The police had used the time to grid the woods, marking off squares of territory to be searched one at a time.

"Harold Mathieson, the man whose bloodhound we'll use, says it's more efficient to limit the search," Barbara Stanley explained. "But once the dog starts, Mathieson says it won't take but an hour or two. I guessed the wooded area at not much more than an acre. That is, I don't think he would have carried her much farther than that."

Meg hadn't wanted to watch the search going on now in the woods. Neither had Christine, who'd gone home to put ice on her shoulder and let Harding have his choice of what the refrigerator contained.

Mike folded his arms on his chest. "You know, if you'd told me what you were up to, I could have helped. As it was, we each had to snoop alone."

"You were snooping?"

"I had to. You wouldn't tell me anything! You'd been asking about Aunt Hannah's silverware, and then I followed you to the library and saw you check out every volume in the place that would have information about silver."

"You followed me?" Meg stared at him.

"Oh, get huffy!" he said. "Wouldn't you have? So I thought, gee, I wonder what's on her mind? I talked to my sister, asked her about the stuff she got. She'd been a little surprised by the silver boxes and figurines and biscuit jars and what all. They're nice, she says, but nothing really special. Nothing that'll put her kids through college. So I started thinking. I was still just in the floundering-around stage, though."

"What were you floundering through?"

He looked at her and continued, his voice slow and serious. "Aunt Hannah kept a copy of her will at home. Who, besides me, could have seen it, realized the opportunities it provided by the way it was written? Who, besides me, had easy access to her attic?"

He paused, and Meg nodded encouragingly. "Go on."

He reached over and pushed her dark hair away from her face. "I wanted to think it was Jack, but I didn't have much but that to go on. How did you figure it out?"

"Like you said, anybody who'd seen her will was suspect. But that's not an infinite number of people. And whoever it was . . . well, it was someone who'd been watching me, watching the house, knew when I was home and when I wasn't, even though one time—the time he got the tape—he was wrong. That limited it more."

She had told Mike, as they had sat waiting for Mr. Mathieson's bloodhound, about the tape. She'd told him about the indications that someone had been searching her house, about the stains behind the cabinet and on the floor, about visiting Wakefield Antiques, about her conversations with Jane. As she'd talked, he had leaned forward, his eyes revealing that the bits and pieces of the story were taking on, for him, the cohesion they had so gradually acquired for her.

Mathieson, as it turned out, was right about how long it would take his dog. Forty-five minutes after the huge animal began, he found what he was looking for: four feet underground, her grave neatly packed and covered with the twigs and old leaves that nature would have deposited across such a spot. The various officials who needed to deal with the scene came and went, and what remained of Angie Morrison was carried away.

Mike's eyes followed the ambulance as it turned out onto the road. "How did you get to Jack? I would have thought he'd be the last person you'd suspect. You *liked* him. Unbelievable as that was to me, you did."

"Yeah," said Meg. "I did." She crossed her legs and looked at him. "You have some lovely narcissus in your garden," she said. "It's called Tahiti. We looked at it the other day—gold and orange and yellow, a double blossom, pretty. Even so, it's not expensive."

"The flowers at the far end, that you said I should put on Aunt Hannah's grave?"

Meg nodded.

"You said they were called By George. I looked them up on the chart she made, and that is, indeed, what they are."

"No," replied Meg. "That's what they're supposed to be, not what they are. By George is new, so new it isn't in most catalogs. She had to get it from a nursery, but she didn't drive. So she sent Jack. I knew she sent Jack; Teddy told me. She gave him, oh, two hundred dollars for maybe thirty-five bulbs. But when he got there, he discovered that Tahiti costs less than a third as much."

"So he bought the other bulbs? Why?"

Meg sighed. "He hates to waste money," she said. "He had to come back with something, but one narcissus bulb looks a lot like another. Why not spend, oh, maybe sixty dollars and keep the difference? Your aunt wasn't going to live to see the flowers. She'd never know. That's what it came down to. The person who planted those flowers knew she'd never see them bloom."

Twenty-three

Over here!" said Meg. "Leave your stuff and get over here."

The Astros gathered around her in silence, their faces glum.

"How much did we lose by?" asked Meg.

"One run," said Suzanne.

"Uh-huh. Do you know what that means? To play one of the best teams in the league and lose by one run? While we're missing Jane and another seventh grader? It means you all are getting *good,* that's what it means. You played heads-up ball. Your defense was terrific. We've just got to do more at the plate. We can't afford to go up there looking for a walk."

"The ump was calling them so *low,*" said Bobby.

Meg looked at the boy. "Ah," she said. "He was indeed. Could you have hit that last called strike? If you'd swung, could you have hit it?"

"Probably," said Bobby. "But it was a ball."

"You know," said Meg, "I don't care, and neither should you. That's the umpire's job, not yours. If you think you can whack the pitch, do it. That's all a strike is—a pitch you can take a good swing at. Leave the details up to somebody who doesn't have to concentrate on hitting it. If you're looking for the pitch you can hit, you'll swing at everything any ump is going to call a strike. The only time you don't swing is when you get junk."

"Or if the count is three and oh and I haven't touched my hat," said Christine.

"Right," said Meg. "Now the ice-cream-truck man is getting tired of waiting for you, so get on over there and ruin your appetites for dinner. Be here Wednesday at five."

Mike got up from the bleachers and helped Meg and Christine stuff equipment into duffel bags.

"What did you find out?" asked Meg. "When did you get here?"

"Two minutes ago," he said. "It was Angie all right. Skull fracture. It was, uh, not self-inflicted."

Christine crammed a batting helmet into an overstuffed duffel bag. "Did they find the tape?"

"No," said Mike. "The tape seems to have been disposed of. The search warrant for Wakefield Antiques, however, turned up the silverware."

"Which is going to be difficult to prove was your aunt's," said Meg. "It may be rare, but it's hardly the only set ever made."

"Would have been difficult to prove," corrected Mike. "Except that Ginny Eppler decided she didn't like being part of a murder case. That wasn't what she'd bargained for, and it didn't take much, I gather, to get a statement from her. She got involved with Jack when she contracted with him to renovate the really quality stuff he tore out of old houses—things she used mainly for display, like mantels. I guess he just decided to take the logical next step. The DA doesn't think there's much to pin Aunt Hannah's murder on Jack with, but Angie's . . ."

"Is there evidence he did that?" asked Meg.

"Not one conclusive piece, but lots of incriminating indications. He was with her shortly before she died. His right thumb left a nearly perfect print on the buckle of her belt."

"That doesn't necessarily prove he killed her," said Christine.

"No. But it's one piece. And the police will find the clerk who sold him black and white tiles in the middle of April." He smiled ruefully. "The tiles that I thought made the floor look nicer. They'll find his hair in her car. The gun he brought to the creek was reported missing by a Mr. Richard Delaney. Seems Jack's been doing some work for him. Put all that together with the thefts Ginny's statement corroborates . . . It was enough to get him to confess to Angie's murder."

Meg sat down hard on the bleachers. "He confessed?"

"He's in the process," said Mike. He slapped a base against the backstop, raising clouds of dust, and dropped it onto the pile of equipment. "Not much support for first-degree, but the DA was willing to make that charge, and I guess, with the felony theft charges also on the line, Jack opted for the deal."

"His lawyer went for that?" asked Meg.

"It's not a bad deal," said Mike. "He was right to take it." He sat down next to Meg and looked steadily at her. "Second-degree," he said. "The up side being no chance of swaying a jury with his boyish grin."

"Not much of an up side," said Christine bitterly. "It's your aunt's murder I want him charged with. And *that* was premeditated."

Meg shook her head. "No, you don't," she said. "This keeps Jane off the stand with her stories about the forgotten silver casket and the spoon. That would have been hard on her."

"Why did he do it?" said Christine. "Why did he ever start stealing from her? He was so helpful!"

"He probably liked her," said Meg. "Other than being a thief who was willing to murder people when it seemed necessary, he's a pretty nice guy. Whatever his first favor was, it was probably just because he liked her. But doing it gave him a chance to realize how much *stuff* she had, how wealthy she was. So he did more and more for her. The whole thing probably escalated slowly."

"Or maybe," said Mike, "he's not so complex. Maybe he's just evil, and every favor he did for her was motivated by a hope to inherit big time. Then, when he saw her will, he realized she had other plans. So he changed his."

Meg started to object then fell silent. She wanted to believe that something she had seen in Jack had really been there, but did it matter? However bad he was, it was more than bad enough.

"So he's confessed to killing Angie," said Christine, sitting also and looking out at the field. "I wish I were a fly on the wall."

"You don't need to be," said Mike. "Barbara Stanley's off tomorrow. She's coming over to Meg's at eleven o'clock."

Barbara Stanley looked different, wearing apricot-colored wide-legged shorts and a cropped beige shirt. She sat in an easy chair in Meg's living room, slim legs crossed. Christine and Dan were close together at one end of the couch, with Meg at the other end and Mike in a chair next to her.

"I thought," said Meg, "that confessions were, like, secret."

"No," said the detective. "The police aren't under the same constraints as attorneys. See, criminals don't pay *us,* so we have little motivation to help them get away with what they do or to protect their precious reputations."

"Was that a dig?" asked Mike.

She smiled. "Take it however you like."

Meg was glad she wasn't alone. She wanted to know what had happened, but wouldn't have liked hearing about it alone.

"Jack and Angie had been involved," said the detective, "involved enough for her to be ticked off when Ginny came to visit. Seems she planted a tape recorder to find out if Ginny was a threat and got more information than she'd bargained for, but it gave her something to hold over Jack, and she tried to use it when Jack told her he wanted out. She told him she had proof of what he and Ginny were involved in, and they quarreled, and he killed her. Accidentally."

"Was it? Was it accidental, really?" asked Christine.

"Depends on what you mean," said the detective. "Surely one doesn't slam a liquor bottle into someone's head accidentally. But it may be true that he didn't actually mean to kill her when he did it."

"And he couldn't have planned it," said Meg. "If he'd planned it, he would have planned it better."

Barbara Stanley nodded. She rubbed her hands along the arms of her chair, inhaled slowly, and let out her breath. "He says she threw a glass at him and he lost his temper. He was holding a liquor bottle. He swung it . . ."

"He cleaned up," said Meg, "or tried to, and buried her and drove her car away—very fast so it would look like she was driving it—and left it, unlocked and with the keys in it, in a bad section of Philadelphia."

The detective nodded. "Who's telling this story?"

"Sorry," said Meg. "I've just thought about it so much, I can't help it."

"Well, go on. There isn't a lot more to tell."

"He had to find whatever proof Angie was talking about, but he hadn't succeeded by the time I got here. After going through the boxes she'd left and searching the contents and undersides of every drawer—including everything I sent to the Salvation Army—and who knows what else, he finally did find it. And when he listened to it, he knew I'd heard it too. And that made me potentially dangerous."

"That you're guessing on," said Barbara Stanley. "But it's what I'd guess, also. We know from Ginny that he talked to her and she described you. He has to have figured it was just a matter of time before you went after her, and if you succeeded in tying him to Ginny . . . Well, he couldn't risk the scrutiny."

"So why not kill *her?*" asked Meg. "Forgive me for whining, but why kill me? Why not her? She was the only one who could prove anything."

"He's not confessing to any ill intent toward you. Maybe he wouldn't have used the gun he brought."

"Right," said Meg. "We would have just strolled down the creek and when I got hungry, he'd have said, 'Whoops, I must have picked up the wrong knapsack, the one with the gun. Silly me.' Uh-huh. But why didn't he kill Ginny?"

"Again, I'm guessing," said Barbara Stanley, "but she would have been next."

Mike leaned forward in one of the chairs on Meg's porch and put his forearms on his knees. He did not look at her.

"How did you know it wasn't me?" he asked.

The dog was lying next to her chair, and Meg pushed off a shoe to stroke her back with one foot. "I wondered, but it didn't fit. Some things did, enough things to be worrisome. You spent a lot of money on your office—"

"Which I borrowed from Aunt Hannah and am still paying back to her estate, meaning my sister and cousins at this point."

"You knew how your aunt's will was written. John Eppler wouldn't speak to you—"

"Because he's a hardheaded curmudgeon who thinks Saint Paul's should sink a huge amount of money into an addition it doesn't need instead of doing something worthwhile with its resources. Even in Harrison, we need day care and a food pantry and counseling services, and God knows we could use a van to transport people who want to visit their incarcerated sons and sisters and—"

"I know," interrupted Meg. "He's equally eloquent on the subject, though taking the opposite view. You, I hear, are a hotheaded liberal do-gooder who shouldn't even be a Lutheran— you should be a Unitarian—who can't understand that an addition to the church is absolutely necessary and got Mr. Eppler's best friend to side with you in the Board of Stewards' voting so that he had a big fight with her and said things he didn't have time to apologize for before she died. That's what he's most upset about, Mike. He feels terrible about it."

"He should," said Mike, shifting his weight in the chair. "She was upset with him, really upset. She almost left the IBM stock to the county Historical Society. But we talked about it, and there were just too many good years to wipe out with one angry conversation."

Meg leaned toward him and put a hand on his knee. "Tell him that, Mike," she said earnestly. "Really. You have to. Or is your German side keeping your back just as rigid as his? Fight with him during the board meetings, if you want to. But let him forgive himself for fighting with your aunt. He's got enough to face, with his daughter in trouble."

Mike smiled at her, his face relaxing. "My training does not permit me to give in without getting something in return. I'll do what you want, if you admit your best clue was that, unlike what I hear about Harding, I possess a reliable moral center."

Meg sat back and laughed. "Harding's moral center is shaping up just fine. Or at least he sure does hold a 'stay' when he's supposed to, bless his heart . . . and his bulk. The worst thing against you was your willingness to sacrifice the training of young minds and bodies, the noble ethics of coaching youth baseball, to your obsession with victory."

Mike looked at her disbelievingly. "Are you referring to our bet? You're the one who suggested the bet! I'm not obsessed with victory, though I may have become a bit obsessed with the idea of beating *you*."

Meg made a dismissive gesture. "No, I'm not referring to our bet. I'm referring to Brian Warren. Or, rather, Brian Warren's mother. She told me all about your true character . . . how you kept Brian on the bench because you just had to win, win, win. That's a pretty lousy trait in a coach, at least in the kind of coaching we do, and until I watched you with your kids, I wasn't sure."

"You still might not be, except you've had the pleasure of

dealing with Brian yourself. His mother's oblivious. She either doesn't see that her son won't follow basic rules, or she thinks benching a kid for breaking them shows a character flaw in the coach. He nearly drove me crazy, that kid. I couldn't figure out what his problem was."

"Oh, dear," said Meg. "You should have spoken with his mother. I did, and I learned all about it. He has 'oppositional defiant disorder.' Those of us in the know sometimes call it ODD. He has to be handled delicately."

Mike's eyebrows rose. "Oppositional defiant disorder? You mean he's a brat."

"Please!" said Meg. "His mother must know what she's talking about. She read an article in a magazine." She linked her hands behind her head and leaned back. "I guess I don't have the delicate touch that's needed, either, so it appears he's going to spend a large part of another season cooling his heels, and I'll replace you in Cheryl Warren's mind as the coach who cares only about winning."

She looked at Mike. "Actually, I didn't need to see any good qualities in you at all. It made too much sense that it was Jack."

"Why? I mean, before figuring out about the narcissus, which is a pretty fragile thread to hang a suspicion of murder on. Why did it make sense that it was Jack?"

"Well, it was a man, and it wasn't Dan. Mr. Eppler? Possible, but really unlikely. He might have killed your aunt, but there had to be another man involved to explain Ginny, and that was someone who knew your aunt well. Jack had seen the junction boxes in my attic, knew they weren't covered—"

Mike sat forward, surprised and angry. "That was him too?"

"Sure," she said. "I think he was just trying to burn the house down. He didn't have any reason to be worried about me then. Of course, any number of people might have known about the junction boxes. Including you."

She rocked a little in her chair. Could she explain? "It wasn't any one thing; it was a combination. He was . . . tailor-made.

My dream man, except I never felt really comfortable with him. Why? Either I was even more insecure than I thought I was, or he wasn't who he seemed to be."

"You're not insecure. You're one of the least insecure people I've ever met."

"In some ways," said Meg. "But let's not get into that. The point is, Jack was a different man with me than he'd been with Stephanie. Which one was the real Jack? The casual craftsman who wore silly shirts and told dumb jokes? Or the formal, serious, deliberate person Christine knew and who was reflected in the house he lived in? I realized it didn't matter which one was the real Jack. What mattered was that he was so chameleon-like. Did you ever see his paintings?"

Mike shook his head. "He wasn't in the habit of inviting me to lunch."

"They're . . . like nice copies of other people's styles. He could make himself be whatever, whomever, he needed to be. Who *does* that, except someone with an eye to the main chance?"

"How about someone who just wants you to like him?"

"Trying to make a good impression is one thing. Being a phony is another. This controlling man just happened to have an endearing goofy streak? He just happened to have Glenn Gould's original version of *The Goldberg Variations*, which just happens to be Bach, which I just happen to love? Christine was surprised that he could be silly, and the more I thought about it, that side of him, his goofy side, was all easy stuff—sew some buttons on a shirt, disparage a dog, tell some bad jokes. Yours, on the other hand, is deep and real, excessive enough to be truly annoying."

Mike hit the back of her head.

"Ouch! Watch it!" She grabbed his wrist and pushed his hand up to slap his own face.

"You're intrigued by men who have buttons on their shirts?" said Mike. "I didn't know you were so easy to impress."

"Little white buttons shaped like the side view of a rabbit," said Meg. "On a blue work shirt. It's a great look." She regarded Mike soberly for a moment. "Not one you could pull off."

The dog stretched and yawned.

"That animal," said Mike, "needs a name. "You've been calling her a dozen things but mostly 'Girl.' Why not call her . . . what is it? Isn't there a precise term for the female of the species?" He hit his leg with a clenched fist. "Darn! I know there's a word. Whenever I think about you, it's right there on the tip of my tongue . . ."

Meg looked at him, unperturbed. "Besides which, of course, Jack was already handsome—"

"I think the word you mean to use is *passable.*"

". . . already passable. So all he needed to do to get me interested—which he had to do once the dog moved in—was to be the kind of man Dan told him I liked. He needed access to the house. If I liked him, he could get in even while I was there—"

"Which would explain fingerprints in a house he'd never been in before."

She nodded. "And keep him pretty much up-to-date on what I was doing. It all fit. Okay, that's not enough either, but it made me wonder, and then other things started to make sense."

Meg gestured toward the side fence. "I thought maybe I could get him to make me one of those beautiful curved archways . . . have a real garden gate with clematis growing up it. He seemed to have plenty of time. And, when I thought about it, wasn't that odd? Dan, in the same line of work, never has any time, never has any extra money. Jack had the time and the money to live extremely well, paint, do anything he wanted. How?"

"We thought he sold his paintings."

"That's what he wanted people to think. Ask a few painters how much they make selling their work. Not David Hocking. Somebody else. And did you, or anyone else around here, ever get a postcard about a gallery showing? Even Christine, who knew about his fancy art school, couldn't name a gallery that showed his work. And, of course, the missing By George nudged the pieces into a pretty tight fit."

They sat quietly. "Is this going to help Jane or make the whole thing worse?" asked Mike.

"I don't know. I've wondered. Christine's wondered. She thinks it will help, long-term, anyway. She'll have the fabulous silver but that isn't what matters. What matters is that the questions will be answered. Jane's pretty tough when she has to be. And she won't have to absorb it and deal with it alone. Unlike Michelle."

Mike looked questioningly at her.

"Angie's sister, Michelle," said Meg. "She's probably the only person in the whole world who actually cared about Angie. I need to get down to the jewelry store and find a pretty bracelet and a little velvet box. It will make me feel less guilty about lying to her." She explained. "I'll pretend I misunderstood Angie's mother about where to send it."

"Let me pay for it," said Mike. "I knew the woman. She worked for me. It's the least I can do."

"We'll split it," said Meg, glad he understood. A question nagged at her. "Why does Jack dislike you? Does it have to do with Stephanie?"

Mike rubbed the space between his eyes. "Partly. I asked her out. She went. She was suspicious of Jack. He was pretty darn good at hiding his other interests, but he didn't always answer the phone when she thought he'd be at home. She caught him in lies about how he spent his time. She was sure he was involved with someone else, and it irritated her, and I knew it, and I asked her out. It was immature. I was more interested in annoying him than in getting to know her. He was so holier-than-thou with his attentiveness to Aunt Hannah . . . I never liked him."

"And Jack didn't like your dating his girlfriend."

"Heck, she was more than that. They were engaged. He figured he had it made. Stephanie is beautiful and rich and descended from the purest of the Puritan stock. He'd been after her for years."

Meg's eyebrows rose. "And she dumped Jack for you?"

"No. She dumped Jack because she didn't trust him. She and I were not a good combination. But did I detect surprise in your voice? It's not impossible that a woman would dump Jack for me."

"No," said Meg, watching a barn swallow swoop gracefully over the yard and thinking how true his statement was. "It's not impossible."

Mike followed her gaze and let out a long breath. They sat in silence for a few moments. He reached down and scratched the dog behind one ear. "She does need a name," he said. "She deserves one."

"I know," said Meg. "I hoped she'd name herself, by having some trait . . ." She looked at him sternly. "I mean an *important* trait."

"But she does, and I have a suggestion. How about Fido?"

Meg gazed at the dog. "Fido," she repeated. She glanced at Mike. "You've been using familiar words to understand unfamiliar ones."

He smiled. "I'm amazingly coachable. *Fiduciary* being a word we legal experts use a lot. For you common folk, *fidelity* works as a reference point."

"Faithfulness," said Meg. "She has it all right."

"And it's an important trait."

"Yes," said Meg.

The dog got up slowly, stretching fore and aft. She put her front paws on Meg's lap and looked at her with bright and eager eyes.

"Unless," said Mike, "you think it's too masculine and the other dogs would tease her."

"The ones who've studied Latin grammar? They wouldn't dare."

Mike reached for her hand and swung it gently between their chairs. "I've given up on your thinking of a bet," he said. "So I've thought of one. It involves something I'd like to get when my team ends the season ranked, oh, at least three places above yours. It's something that fits your requirements. It really matters."

Meg's heart did not clatter against her ribs. It merely shifted and then beat steadily with—how odd it felt—an abundant gladness. "And you're going to get this . . . how?" she asked.

"By out-coaching you," said Mike. "If necessary, with my eyes closed and wearing a straitjacket. It'll be a snap."

"Shut up," said Meg.